holefield
to Fleet
stories.
hip, his
rldwide
is now
cluding
tective
tective

to the

...han Scholefield writes good, punchy tales with credible characters' – *Guardian*

'A professional storyteller of the first order' – *Irish Times*

'Scholefield's colourful, keen prose and well-fleshed characterisations deftly immerse readers' – *Publishers Weekly*

'Scholefield writes with an assured, dry wit' – *Evening Standard*

'Crime writing at its best' – *Publishers Weekly*

'A storyteller of the spellbinding kind' – *Liverpool Echo*

Born and educated in South Africa, Alan Scholefield began as a journalist there before moving to Fleet Street, and from there to Spain to write short stories. Giving up journalism for full-time authorship, his first novel A View of Vultures became a worldwide success and, later, Venom became a film. He is now the author of more than twenty novels, but also a highly-praised police series featuring Detective Superintendent George Macrae and Detective Sergeant Leopold Silver.

He is now settled in Hampshire, and is married to the novelist Anthea Goddard.

Burn Out

Alan Scholefield

HEADLINE

First published in 1994
by HEADLINE BOOK PUBLISHING

First published in paperback in 1995
by HEADLINE BOOK PUBLISHING

10 9 8 7 6 5 4 3 2 1

ISBN 0 7472 4610 6

Printed and bound in Great Britain by
Cox & Wyman Ltd, Reading, Berks

HEADLINE BOOK PUBLISHING
A division of Hodder Headline PLC
338 Euston Road
London NW1 3BH

This ae night, this ae night,
Every night and alle,
Fire and sleet and candle-lighte,
And Christ receive thy saule.
A Lyke Wake Dirge

My thanks for his help go to Dr Robin Ilbert, Senior Medical Officer, Winchester Prison. Any mistakes are my own.

1

He was alone when he first saw her.

He was standing on a stretch of grass below the castle ruins, with the river on his right and the tennis courts to his left.

Was he certain, they had asked?

Yes.

And how had he got there?

He couldn't remember. Walked, he supposed. His car was parked in the square so he must have walked.

How? Down Castle Street and along the river?

Probably.

He hadn't followed her from the square, had he?

No.

He was sure about that?

Well . . . pretty sure . . .

They asked because earlier he said he'd been confused, wasn't that correct?

Yes.

If he was confused then he might have, mightn't he?

What?

Followed her from the square.

Maybe. But he didn't think so. Anyway what bloody difference did it make?

They'd decide about that. Okay?

Okay.

So why had he gone there in the first place then? Because of the tennis courts?

He supposed so.

He supposed a lot, didn't he?

He said he supposed because he couldn't remember. Didn't they get it? He couldn't bloody well remember!

Right . . . okay . . . no need to get excited. To get back to the tennis courts . . . there were often girls on the courts weren't there?

Of course. And men too. And children.

Was that why?

Why what?

Did he go because there were children?

Why would they say that?

Couldn't he guess?

Jesus . . . they didn't mean . . . Listen, he'd never touch a child. Never!

Why had he said that about the children then?

Because . . . well, because children often played on tennis courts. He had when he was a kid . . . He hadn't meant anything by it.

Well, why say it then?

It's just that they'd said about him being confused . . . and going there because women played—

Not women. They hadn't said women. Girls. That's what they'd said. When you're seventeen you're a girl not a woman. Okay?

2

Yeah. Okay.

Well, if he hadn't gone there looking for girls what had *he gone there for? Was he going to play?*

No.

Not really dressed for it, was he?

No.

Okay then . . . Listen . . . They wanted him to think before he answered. Take his time. He had lots of time. Days. Weeks. He wasn't going anywhere. Now: was he sure that's where he'd first seen her? Near the castle?

He had first visited the castle when he was a child. He had gone with his mother and had scratched his name on a broken Norman arch. He remembered that because she had been cross with him and she hadn't often been cross. He couldn't remember if they had been going to the tennis club or coming away from it but he was sure it was his idea to visit the castle, his mother would never have volunteered to climb the steep path that wound up through the shrubbery to what had once been the outer bailey.

Although it had a real name most people didn't know it. As far as they were concerned it had always stood on the South Downs in West Sussex and had always been known simply as 'the castle'.

It was not difficult to see why it had been built on its hill above the river: it guarded the ford and was easy to defend against enemy bowmen.

The town which had grown beneath it had originally been called King's Toun, then Kingston, but there were so many of those that in the nineteenth century it had been changed again to Kingstown. By that time the castle was a romantic ruin, much of its stone carted off by speculative builders.

But Kingstown honoured it. There was Castle Street and the Castle Hotel, a Castle Motors, several Castle View bed-and-breakfast places, the Castle Tea Rooms, a Castle Museum, a Castle Brewery, and a Castle Tandoori take-away.

Once there had been a Castle Tennis Club, but that no longer existed.

Kingstown owed much of its prosperity to the castle. It was built on a southwestern slope – some said on the site of an old Roman fort – and tourists flocked to it in summer to picnic on the soft grass beneath its ruined walls. On clear blue days they could see the sea shimmering in the distance.

All the streets of the town seemed to start at the castle and flow down to the river. Some were narrow and cobbled, some wide and lined with Georgian houses. It was said that Kingstown had more Georgian houses than Chichester, its neighbour to the east, or Winchester, its neighbour to the west.

It was listed in the *Domesday Book*, and Daniel Defoe had once said of it that it was a 'pleasant and prosperous place'. A description that served today.

From the castle walls you could see a jumble of red tiled roofs, the cathedral, three churches, a functioning cinema, the law courts and the library. The prison was tucked away behind its screen of trees as though the town considered it something to be ashamed of.

There were also other things to be seen beneath the walls: empty sherry bottles and beer cans; used syringes and condoms; crushed styrofoam cups and empty cigarette packs.

Few of these would have been there when he was a child climbing up to the old battlements with his mother.

Keleti, they had said, that's a foreign name.

Hungarian.

He didn't sound foreign.

He'd been brought to England as a baby. Gone to school here.

Did he speak Hungarian?

A few words.

Why didn't he say something, a couple of words, so they could hear.

He'd rather not.

Rather not didn't come into it.

Okay, Buda Pest. That was a couple.

Highly amusing. He'd need a sense of humour where he was going.

But—

Hang on. Lots of time for buts. What they wanted to ask him was if he'd ever used stuff.

What sort of stuff?

Well, for a start, how about smack?

No.

No?

Absolutely not.

Acid?

No.

Speed?

Once or twice.

Coke?

Sure. But they knew how it was at parties.

No they didn't know how it was at parties. Maybe they went to different parties.

It was a social thing, that was all.

Like smoking. Did he want a fag?

He didn't smoke.

He just did drugs, was that it?

No, no. A few times. That was all.

Had he ever been picked up for drugs?

No.

Had he ever heard of the Holmes computer?

No.

They used the Holmes computer. If he farted in a dark room in China the computer would know. So . . . they would ask him again . . . had he ever been nicked for drugs? Had he been a naughty boy?

Well . . . there had been one occasion.

One?

Maybe two.

Or three?

No, two. Possession.

What?

Grass. He'd got off with police warnings.

That was better, wasn't it? Much better to tell the truth. But they'd ask the computer anyway, just to check.

Pause.

Right then . . . Janos, was it?

Jason. His father had changed the name.

Kind of an anagram.

He supposed so.

There he went again. Supposed. Never mind. Did he want a rest?

No. He was okay.

Tea? Coffee?

Nothing.

That wasn't very bright. He'd learn to think differently. Where he was going you took everything you were offered whether you wanted it or not. (Pause) Jason . . . kind of a tv name . . . Okay Jason, why didn't they start from the beginning again. He'd parked his car in the square . . . seen the girl and followed—

Bullshit! He'd never said that!

The truth will make you free. Had he heard that expression? No? Religious. But not free of the nick of course. Didn't mean that. Free inside himself more like. He'd feel better afterwards.

But for Christ's sake it was the bloody truth!

No, it wasn't, they said. He was lying, they said. He was a bloody rapist who chose his victims with care. Young girls, maybe even kids. Certainly the seventeen-year-old girl he'd picked up on the tennis court.

Tell us, they said, how did a really big bastard like Jason get it in? With a shoe horn?

They asked that question before they knew who he was, before they could guess what he might do.

2

'Annie! Annie!'

The sound of her name brought her jerking upright out of sleep.

'Wake up! It's six o'clock!'

She looked at the clock on her bedside table.

'No it isn't. It's *five* o'clock!'

'Oh.' Her father's voice was not contrite, only irritated. 'My bloody clock must be wrong.'

He didn't apologise, but then he never apologised. She heard him stumping off to his own part of the house. She lay back against the pillows, listening. She tried to relax but with her father up and about she knew she wouldn't be able to.

Bang! A door slammed.

Whoosh! The lavatory.

Then voices. Probably the BBC Overseas Service. The news at 0500.

Oh, God.

She had not slept much. Half the night she had lain stiffly in bed worrying. Was she making a terrible mistake? But what was the alternative?

Crash! Crash!

Father making his early morning tea.

That was part of his African legacy. She had got over hers years ago, but she remembered the childhood ritual as though it was yesterday. Every morning she would be wakened by Watch, her father's clerk, confidant, cook, friend, and guardian. Just remembering how Watch fussed over her father made her smile.

For years – most of her childhood in fact – and as far back as she could recall, it had been Watch she had seen first thing every morning; she could hardly remember her mother being in Africa at all. She would open her eyes and there, hazy on the other side of the mosquito net, would be Watch's prim black face, his hand holding her cup of early morning tea; a brick-red liquid that tasted of metal polish.

'Half an hour blekfas,' Watch would invariably say and she would take the tea and wait for him to leave, then pour it from the window or through an opening in the tent, depending on where they were.

Then breakfast, a proper breakfast of bacon, eggs, fried bread, sausages if they had them, lamb's fry, perhaps even a chop, with Watch hovering over her making sure she ate up.

When she read Kipling's *Jungle Book* she realised that Bagheera and Baloo, who had with loving grumpiness seen to Mowgli's upbringing, had been reincarnated into her father and Watch.

And after breakfast they would load the truck and get going before the sun grew hot; Watch driving, her father sitting in front with him, Anne occupying the rear.

Another day, another small town. And Henry Vernon in

black gown and grey periwig would vigorously prosecute the unlawful in the name of Her Majesty across the water.

She became aware of a different sound, a faint breathing near her face. She opened one eye. A small figure dressed in Mickey Mouse pyjamas stood by her bedside.

'Can I come in?' Hilly said.

'Just for a little while.'

The autumn morning was cold and Anne moved further over in the bed. 'You have the warm place.'

Her five-year-old daughter backed up against her breasts and stomach.

'Better?'

'Yes.'

'Couldn't you sleep?'

'Grandpa woke me.'

'He woke me too. I'd be surprised if he hasn't woken most of Kingstown.'

'I don't like Kingstown.'

'You will. You're just not used to it yet.'

'Clive doesn't like Kingstown either.'

'Did he say that?'

'When he took me to the zoo. He says it's too far from London.'

'Well, I'm sorry about that, but it doesn't change anything.'

'I like Clive. I like his Mercedes.'

'Do you?'

'He loves you.'

'Does he?'

'I don't like school.'

'You said you did.'

'Well, I don't.'

'It's because it's new and you're new.'

'Why can't we live in London like we used to?'

'Because there's Grandpa now . . . I explained all this to you. It's not just the two of us any more.'

'I liked it when it was the two of us.'

'So did I, darling, but things change. Anyway, you love Grandpa, don't you?'

'I suppose so.'

'He loves you.'

'He bangs things.'

'I know.'

'Did he bang things in Africa?'

'All the time.'

'When is he going back to Africa?'

'He's living with us, sweetie. He's part of the family now.'

'Oh.' Hilly did not sound convinced.

'You'll get used to him being here. And you'll get used to Kingstown and you'll get used to your new school. It's got a lovely playground. Better than the one in London. You'll see, in a couple of weeks you won't even remember London.'

'But—'

'What?'

'I don't want you to go to prison.'

'So that's what this is all about. I have to, darling. I've explained it over and over. Here . . . come closer. Now listen, you have to be a big girl. You'll have Grandpa.'

'But who'll take me to school?'

'I'll take you this morning. But Grandpa will fetch you.'

'And tomorrow?'

'Grandpa will do both. He'll be looking after you and you'll be looking after him. So – no more tears . . . I've got to get up now but you can stay while I get dressed.'

'Can I choose?'

'I've already chosen.'

'What?'

'My dark green trousers. Yellow blouse. That biscuit-coloured pullover. Okay?'

'Okay.'

She showered and towelled herself, viewing her body in the partially steamed-up mirror. She was long-legged with squarish shoulders. Her waist had almost returned to what it was before having Hilly and she was pleased with that, all things considered. She gave her bottom a cursory glance. Physiologically, she knew why women's bottoms were larger and softer and rounder than men's but that didn't help. But she comforted herself with the fact that Clive seemed to like it.

Her right shoulder and arm always looked to be slightly more muscular than her left, which irritated her. But there wasn't much she could do about that either.

She wore her dark hair short and her faded-blue eyes were widely spaced. Her skin was pale and as a child she had had to wear hats in the African sun. But if she was careful she could tan to the colour of a golden biscuit.

When she and Hilly came downstairs the noise was louder.

'My God, what's happening?' she said.

The kitchen looked as though it had been vandalised.

'Breakfast is happening,' her father said.

The table had not so much been laid as loaded with feeding implements. Henry was waiting at the stove, a fish slice in his hand.

Even in Africa where the people among whom he had worked wore tribal scars, wrapped themselves in blankets, smoked pipes two feet long, and looked out from under conical hats of basketwork – even among those people, Henry Vernon had been thought to dress eccentrically.

He was wearing a collarless white shirt, not the kind affected by pop stars, but the kind worn by men who have lost the collars, and knee-length khaki trousers, once known as Bombay bloomers, which left his powerful knotted calves bare. On his feet he wore, without socks, a pair of patent leather dancing pumps now covered in dust and ancient African cowdung. Around his waist was Anne's short and frilly apron.

He was in his late sixties but was still a formidable figure; short, broad and muscular. His head was bald but for a white tonsure of hair. His face was round and in the middle of it he wore a small white moustache. His steady grey eyes – eyes which had turned a thousand bowels to water as their owners stood in the dock waiting for him to open the case against them – peered out over half glasses.

He began to serve up. There were two fried eggs each for Anne and Hilly, a mound of bacon, a pork sausage, fried tomatoes and fried bread. It was, Anne thought, as though Watch had joined the household.

'That's what Tiggers like best,' he said, shovelling a mound of food onto Hilly's plate.

'Just eat what you can, darling,' Anne said hastily when she saw the expression on her daughter's face.

She turned to her father. 'This is far too much. We never have more than cereal and toast.'

'Nonsense. You can't do a day's work—'

'Father!'

'—without a cooked breakfast.'

Anne stared hard at her father. Her father stared hard at her. Hilly looked back and forth from one to the other.

'Very well,' he said. 'You know best.' It was said in a way which gave it precisely the opposite meaning.

On the way to school Hilly said, 'Best about what?'

'Things.'

'Are you and Grandpa having a row?'

'No, darling.'

Not yet, she thought, but it was getting closer. And the whole business momentarily depressed her. But it was only momentarily, for she was essentially an optimist and now she said out loud, 'Sufficient unto the day . . .'

'What day? What is sufficient unto?'

'It has to do with your grandfather.'

'Oh.'

One of the 'things' that had to do with Henry was shopping.

'If I'm going to be – what do they call it, a housemother? – then of course I must do the shopping,' he had said.

'But—'

'Don't be silly. I've shopped before.'

She had often helped Watch push a trolley round an African supermarket but could never recall her father being there. His shopping had been the occasional selection of a new shell briar pipe at Alfred Dunhill or a visit to his shirtmakers when he was in London on home leave. She simply could not visualise him buying toilet paper and lavatory cleaner.

'How d'you think I managed when I retired?' he said.

She gave him a list and he looked at it as though it were a statement from an unreliable witness.

'You've got two sorts of washing powder down here,' he said. 'If we're trying to save money then—'

'They're for different sorts of washing.'

'I don't see why—'

'Father, please, if you're going to help then don't argue.'

Now, as she drew up at Hilly's infant school, the shopping list was wiped from her mind. Hilly was being brave and clingy at the same time. 'Look, there are lots of other little girls like you.'

Hilly didn't seem to find this much of an argument.

The teacher was sympathetic. 'Come along, Hilary. We're building a bird-table. You'll like that.' Then to Anne. 'She'll be fine. Don't you worry.'

'Her grandfather will fetch her,' Anne said. 'He's—' For a moment she thought of describing her father and then abandoned the idea.

As she drove away she briefly felt she had committed a criminal act by leaving Hilly, but Kingstown was in the throes of the morning rush hour and she had to concentrate on the unfamiliar streets.

The prison was on the same slope as the castle but a mile further west. First there was a screen of cypress trees, then the grim Victorian walls with razor wire on the top. For a moment her nerve failed her. She drew up and sat with her hands on the wheel. She wanted to turn round, pick up Hilly and go back to London, but there was no way back.

She drove up to the barrier. A prison officer dressed in black looked at his clipboard and then at the number plate of the car.

'Dr Vernon?'

'Yes.'

'That's your parking area over there. Don't forget to lock your car. Then go to the main door and knock.'

'Knock?'

'That's it, doctor, just knock.'

3

The door was huge and arched. At shoulder height she saw a small black circular doorknocker which might have been found on any door in Kingstown. She took a deep breath and gave two firm knocks.

The results were appalling.

The knocks turned out to be crashing blows and instantly a small door, cut into the larger, snapped open and a uniformed officer said, 'Gently, miss, or you'll have the whole place down.'

'I'm sorry, I had no idea—'

'You a visitor? 'Cause it's not time yet.'

'I'm Dr Vernon. Dr Melville's expecting me.'

'Sorry, doctor, didn't know who you were. Mind the step.'

She found herself in a narrow, gloomy entrance hall, at the far end of which was a steel barred gate. There were several uniformed men in the hall and a duty officer in a raised cubicle to her left which was cut into the old walls and protected by heavy glass. She was announced to him and he said, through a speaking slit, 'I'll let Dr Melville know.'

The hall was full of movement and the jangle and rattle

of keys. Some bunches of keys were being handed in to the duty officer by staff going out, and some were being retrieved by staff coming in.

There was no human contact. A numbered tally was dropped into a slot in the wall, scooped up by the duty officer in the cubicle, who in turn dropped the matching bunch of keys into a return slot. It looked simple and foolproof. But she reminded herself that nothing was foolproof in here.

The rattle of these keys and the long chains by which they were attached to the waist, was constant, a kind of counterpoint to the clanging noise of the opening and closing of the barred gates that echoed through the building.

Bang! Bang!

Someone else had used the doorknocker. The noise in the stone-floored entrance hall was deafening. An elderly woman stood in the doorway.

'I come to see Billy,' she said. 'Billy Sweete. I'm his grandmother.'

'Visiting hours aren't till this afternoon, love,' said the same officer. 'Unless he's on remand.'

'I come in the bus.'

'Yeah, but is he on remand?'

She stared at him.

'He burns things.'

'Yeah, but has he been convicted?'

An officer came up to Anne. 'Dr Melville's on his way.'

'Thank you. What does Special Black mean?' She pointed to the words in large type on a notice board.

'That means normal. It means—'

'It means,' a voice said behind her, 'that we might have a quiet time for your first day.'

She turned and saw a tall man in a white coat. He was thin and angular with thick black hair in which there was an occasional silver glint. She estimated his age at late thirties.

As he spoke bits of him moved: hands, shoulders, feet. He never seemed to stand still but was like some charged particle, so filled with kinetic energy that only its partial release stopped him from fizzing away.

'Come on,' he said. 'I'll show you the nick.'

She followed him to the great barred gate. He opened it with a key in the bunch on his chain and she noticed that he did so in one fluid motion and wondered if she would ever reach a point where she would also do it like that, without thought, without registering the obvious symbolism. And then she realised she would have to or she might as well quit right now.

They walked down a long corridor, Melville slightly ahead of her. 'This is really your induction week but since you're staying on permanently at the end of it and I'm one short in the hospital, I'm afraid I may have to throw you in at the deep end . . .

'Oh . . . and by the way, if you'd like me to call you Dr Vernon I will or I can call you Anne . . . and you can call me Tom or Dr Melville whichever you like though I'd prefer it if you called me Tom. We don't stand on ceremony; there are more important things to do.'

'Please call me Anne.'

'Right.' He flung an arm at several doors. 'This is all Admin. And over there is Reception.' A thumb jerked.

'Security in there. Don't try to remember it all. It'll come in its own time. So will the names and faces. So will the initials. We go in for lots and lots of initials . . . And you'll see the Governor later, of course . . . And the Deputy Governor, except he isn't called the Deputy Governor any more but the Head of Custody, or HOC . . . and then there's the Head of Management Services, or HOMS . . . and the Head of Works, HOW . . . and the Head of Activities and Services, HOAS . . . and I'm no longer the Senior Medical Officer but the Head of Medical Services. Another HOMS, I suppose. Big changes in the service. But the more we change the more we stay the same.'

'It all sounds a bit like Nancy Mitford.'

He stopped and turned and his thin face broke into a smile. 'The Hons cupboard! Wasn't that marvellous!'

Then he was off again, long striding, coat flapping. 'Here we are.' He unlocked a gate. 'This is what it's all about.' He locked the gate behind her. 'This is the nick. This is where it happens.'

It was the first gaol Anne had ever been in. There had been a few times in Africa when she had accompanied her father to police cells to bail out a servant who had been drunk the night before, but she had never been inside one of England's classic Victorian houses of correction. She had seen interiors often enough on tv and what surprised her was how much like tv it seemed, with its cream-painted brick walls and the anti-suicide nets on each landing and the iron walkways.

But somehow she had not bargained for its busy-ness.

She had imagined it as a place where the demarcations were neatly drawn; the prisoners locked away in their cells, the prison officers – she must remember not to call them screws – in the freedom of the wings.

It wasn't like that at all. It was more of an ants' nest with people moving in all directions and officers chatting with prisoners, and prisoners cutting other prisoners' hair, and vacuum cleaners humming, and everyone seeming to be on the move. And she saw others, men in civilian dress who waved casually to Tom Melville and who were identified as a HOW or a HOAS or some other member of the 'management team'. This was also something she had read in the bumf that had been arriving in the post for weeks. Man management, business management, financial management, health management: it all sounded very different from 'slopping out' and 'doing your bird'.

Were the prisoners 'clients' now? Where was the danger, she wondered? Where were the shivs and the knives she'd seen so often at the movies? And a voice inside her head said: They're here. They're invisible, but they're here.

As they moved through the wing Melville was constantly greeted by prisoners with, 'Watcher, doc!' and 'Hi, boss! Got any drugs today?' And there were muttered colloquies about headaches and valium.

'Well?' he said, coming to a stop at last.

'It's not . . . I thought . . . well, that the prisoners would be locked up and . . .' She shrugged. 'It's just not what I imagined.'

'We mix as much as possible. From the Governor down. We try to be visible. It lowers the level of stress. It's called dynamic security.'

They had stopped where the four wings met; the very centre.

'It's one of D.S. Hill's prisons,' he said, waving his hands at the interior. 'He also designed Lewes Gaol. Built in the 1850s.' He stabbed the air. 'Four wings: A, B, C and D. Built in the shape of a cross. Can't you just see the Victorian ecclesiastical mind at work? The image of the Cross? Redemption through punishment?'

He turned. 'This is A wing. Young offenders wing.' He pointed to a dark, shut-off area. 'Closed while they put in sanitation. And thank God for that. YOs are a terrible nuisance, they disrupt everybody in the prison.'

'B wing.' He flung out an arm. 'Convicted men. Same as C Wing. You know where you are with them. Not like those over there in D wing: remand prisoners.'

Unlike those in B and C wings who were dressed in light blue prison clothing, the men on D wing wore their own clothes. Melville led her past them. Some were watching tv, others playing pool or table tennis. He said, 'Aggressive, edgy, macho, yet inside they're probably terrified of what's happening to them and what's going to happen. Watch yourself in D wing. They've got a lot to prove.'

As if to underline what Melville was saying, an unidentified voice from a group of young men said, 'Fucking quack! Quack! Quack!' Melville ignored the voice and let Anne out into the prison yard.

'Does that sort of thing bother you?' he asked. Before she could reply he went on, 'If it does you'd better think twice before joining the service.'

'I'm a big girl now.'

'Right. Fine.'

They walked past the exercise yard with its high chain-link fencing. He pointed to several wires which were tautly stretched above the yard.

'In case of helicopters,' he said.

'Helicopters?'

'For lifting an escapee.'

'Oh.'

'There's a good reason for everything in here. Prison's a state of mind. It'll come. Here we are. That's us.'

He was pointing at a small red-brick building two storeys high and dwarfed by the immensity of the prison wings.

'A world within a world.'

It was like a cottage hospital but with major differences. There was a ward with five beds, seventeen single rooms with tables, chairs and hospital beds, and three unfurnished rooms with suicide-proof windows.

'Just the opposite to the NHS,' she said. 'You've got more private rooms than ward beds.'

'That's because most of my patients can't get on with each other. I suppose eighty per cent that come in here are psychotic.'

There was an X-ray unit, a laboratory, a dispensary, and an administrative block.

'We try to keep things simple,' Melville said. 'Anything complicated goes to Kingstown General. This is your room.'

The hospital had recently been refurbished with a new sanitation system and paint job. Her room was small, but light and got the morning sun. It contained a desk, two chairs, an examination couch, a washbasin, bookshelves and a metal cabinet.

'Basic, but it's all you can expect from the Home Office. Do you like the colour scheme? I chose it.'

It was pale green and white.

'Yes, I do, very much.'

'I suppose you had to say that. Anyway it'll look less bleak when you get your things in.' He paused and then said, 'You'll have to make allowances for us. We've never had a woman doctor in this prison. There are some female prison officers but you're a first for us. Come and meet—'

A middle-aged man in black trousers and a dark blue regulation jersey with two pips on his shoulder-tabs came into the room.

'Hello, Jeff, I was just coming to see you. This is Dr Vernon. Anne, this is Jeffrey Jenks. The Head of Nursing Services. Used to be called Hospital Principal Officer and I still call him my PO.'

They shook hands and she found herself looking into a pair of cold blue eyes. He was thin-faced with iron grey hair parted in the middle.

'Pleased to meet you,' he said, but the words lacked warmth.

'I was just telling Dr Vernon that we haven't had a woman doctor here before and it's all new to us.'

'That's right,' Jenks said. 'Very new.'

'Jeff's something of a misogynist, aren't you Jeff?'

'That's right.'

It was said lightly but Jenks's smile was as cold as his eyes.

He turned away from Anne and spoke directly to Melville. 'We've got someone for you.' She felt as though he had closed a door in her face. 'Les says he's worried about one of last night's receptions. Claims he was beaten up by the police. Dr Symes recorded his injuries.'

'Where is he?'

'Over in D Wing.'

'I'll have a look at him in the medical room.' Melville started to walk away, remembered Anne and said, 'I'd like you to be in on this.'

She followed him across the yard to the main prison where an officer, a few years younger than Jenks and with only one pip on his shoulder, met them.

'This is Les Foley,' Tom said, introducing her once more. 'Mr Jenks's number two and my left hand. Isn't that so, Les?'

Les smiled. This smile was warm, dimpled, almost motherly. He was plump and his hair had been lightened. His hand was soft and moist.

'What's it all about, Les?'

'Don't like the look of him, doc. He's been in the thick of it with the police. Apparently he went berserk in the station and they had to restrain him.'

'I love that phrase,' Tom said, dryly.

'I know. Probably went over the top. His face looks like it was trodden on. The police sent in their usual warning. Lots of boxes ticked off and Dr Symes two-ed him up.'

Tom saw the look of incomprehension on Anne's face and said, 'Prison-speak for the police sending in a form detailing his violent behaviour – which gets them off the hook for any injuries – and the fact that Jack Symes put him in a cell with another prisoner for his own safety. Go on, Les.'

'He's very down. I'm thinking suicide risk.'

'What's the charge?'

'Attempted rape.'

'Okay, I'll see him in here.'

Anne followed Tom into the medical room. 'This is where the daily sick parade happens,' he said. 'This is the real world. Don't let the hospital fool you.'

The last time she had seen such a room used for medical purposes had been at an African clinic in Lesotho. There was a scarred grey lino-block floor, a stained washbasin, a metal table which served as a desk, and an examination couch.

Melville sat behind the desk/table, Anne sat in a corner to his left. Les brought in the prisoner, gave Tom Melville his medical records and left the room.

'Sit down, please,' Tom said and studied the file.

Looking at the prisoner, Anne felt as though she had received an electric shock. He was in his late twenties and was big; six feet five or six, she thought, and as wide as a door. He was dressed in a dark green silk shirt, a pearl grey sweatshirt, black cords and dark blue boat shoes. Everything looked expensive.

His hair was short and dark and slightly curly and sat close to his skull. There were contusions on his face, one eye was almost closed, his lips were swollen and in some places the skin was broken. His huge hands were also badly lacerated.

There was a kind of muscular, highly strung, animal quality about him and she thought immediately of one of the old Tarzan films. She could imagine him swinging from jungle vines and out-swimming crocodiles.

But his eyes worried her. They were a deep brown, the

whites were bloodshot and they were swimming with tears.

'Keleti,' Tom said, 'Janos Keleti. Czech?'

'I was born in Hungary.'

The words were shaped by swollen lips but Anne could hear that the timbre of his voice was low and that he was English and well-spoken.

Tom rose and looked closely at the battered face. 'Dr Symes made a careful record of your injuries. How are you feeling now?'

'Sore.'

'According to the police you damaged ... let's see ... two chairs, a table, a filing cabinet, a typewriter ... as well as a couple of detectives. You've got every right to feel sore.'

'They started it.'

'Okay. Sure. Now when you came in you chose to be segregated under Rule 43.'

'They said I should.'

'Who? The prison officers?'

'For my own good. But—'

'They were right. Alleged sex offenders have a hard time in prison.'

'But I'm *not* a sex offender.'

Tom held up his hand. 'I'm not here to judge you. Just to help you and—'

There was a sound of running feet and the door burst open. Les said, 'Quick, doc, someone's tried to top himself in C wing.'

Tom threw back his chair. 'He's all yours,' he said to Anne and then he was gone. The door slammed. Then burst open again. In a moment Les had locked the door in the open position. 'Just in case. Can't be closed now,' he said, and ran.

Without thinking Anne moved to Tom's chair behind the desk. She said, 'It's not Janos Keleti, is it? I mean, that's not the name anyone would know you by.'

He shook his head.

'It's Jason Newman, isn't it?'

'Yeah.'

She leaned back in her chair. 'Once upon a time I'd have given you my right arm if you'd asked me for it.'

He frowned. 'Do I know you?'

'No, but I know you. Do you remember playing in the South of England Junior Championships at Winchester, oh, ages ago? You won it.'

'Sure. I beat Shackleton six-one, six-two in the final.'

'But after that you played a mixed final. Your partner was Ruth someone. You were only thirteen, I think. I was fifteen at the time and one of your opponents. And you beat us six-love, six-love, and that was the time I decided that tennis wasn't for me as a serious career. You don't really remember, do you?'

'Not really.'

'But you remember your score against Shackleton to the very game.'

'Nobody remembers mixed.'

'Anyway, that's how I know you.'

He tried to smile but the swollen lips were too painful.

'And after that,' she went on, 'I was never on the same court with you. Never in the same tournament. God, you went round the tennis sky like a comet. Specially the British sky. I remember a few years later reading in *The Times* –

that was after you'd made the Davis Cup team – that you were the greatest thing to hit British tennis since Fred Perry. And I said to myself: *I played with him!*

She stopped abruptly. Tears were spilling out of his eyes and running down to his injured mouth.

'I'm sorry, Jason. I didn't mean to upset you. Listen, I don't know why you're here – it's my first day – but let me try to help you.'

He sat in front of her, a huge man completely obscuring the chair. He lowered his head into his hands.

'Oh, Christ,' he said. 'I need help so badly.'

4

The King's Arms was in one of the narrow cobbled streets that ran down into the town from the castle. It was, as Tom Melville said, 'A proper pub; no music, no formica, no one-armed bandits.' There was a coal fire in the saloon bar, scrubbed pine tables, red velvet curtains, and the place smelled richly of ale.

'But the great thing about it,' he said as he carried their drinks to a corner table, 'is that none of the prison staff use it.'

They made themselves comfortable.

Tom said, 'Your cv said St Thomas's. It was a pretty high-powered place when I was there. Now there's talk of scrapping some of the teaching hospitals. Do you think it'll go?'

'I hope not. It's a big part of my life.'

'The problem is that these days you've got to know as much about financial control as gall stones, and we were never taught that. Human relationships. Man management. These are the buzz words now.'

They were both drinking white wine and he held up his glass and said, 'Here's to your first day in wonderland.'

She smiled. 'Why wonderland?'

'Because nothing is as it seems. We all appear sane enough on the surface, but underneath . . .'

'Is there something I should know?' It was said half jokingly.

'Only that you need to be slightly crazy to work in it unless you're doing some monograph on the Psychiatric Assessment of Dangerousness or Recidivism in Sexual Offenders.'

His voice had taken on a cynical tone she had not heard before and she said, 'Is that why you joined?'

'Lord, no. Simple pragmatism.'

She waited for him to continue but he sipped his wine and looked over her shoulder at the bar which, at six o'clock, was beginning to fill up.

He seemed restless and she half expected him to start pacing the floor.

He said, 'Sorry it's been such a jangled first day. Did you get the school thing sorted out?'

The 'school thing' had happened while she was talking to Jason Newman. Les had put his plump face round the door and said there was an urgent telephone call for her.

It was the head teacher of Hilly's school warning her that a person looking like a tramp but purporting to be Hilly's grandfather had arrived an hour early and was demanding his granddaughter.

It had taken Anne some minutes of explanation and apology before things were put right. By that time the attempted suicide from C wing had been brought to the hospital. She was needed there and could not return to Jason.

'It *was* your father, then?' Tom said.

'It was my father all right.'

'In your cv you mentioned being brought up by him in Africa. Was he farming out there?'

'He was in the Colonial Service. The very last of it. He'd gone out from England with a law degree and joined the legal section. When I was little he spent much of his time in court as a public prosecutor, later as a judge. Then when the sun finally set on the Empire he stayed on until the independent countries had their own judiciaries.'

'Whereabouts?'

'Lesotho mainly. I was born there, in Maseru. But we were also in Botswana and Malawi.'

'I don't know Lesotho but I've visited the Okavango a couple of times and travelled in the Kalahari.'

'Wild life photography?'

'That's what most people think. No, just being there. Trekking in the wilderness. Sleeping rough. Beholden to no one.'

'By yourself?'

'My ex-wife came a couple of times. But she didn't like it much.' He grinned at the memory.

They spoke about Africa for several minutes and then he said, 'Is that where you learned your tennis?'

'My father was keen, but with all the travelling he hadn't anyone to play with. As soon as I could hold a racquet he used me as a kind of tennis wall.'

'What made you give it up? I mean you seemed to have a terrific future. Pots more money than you can make here.'

She was silent for a moment, then said, 'To be a

champion you've got to sacrifice everything, and I mean everything, including books and theatres and social life. In fact you shouldn't even know you're sacrificing them. You shouldn't even know you're missing an intellectual life. But growing up with my father gave me a side most players don't have. Maybe you'll meet him one day. Most people think he's dotty but he's pretty clever. And better read then anyone I know. All those years without tv, I suppose.'

'Would he have wanted you to?'

'Never. He wanted me to have a degree behind me; a profession. But it was my own decision to stop playing. It happened all at once. I thought ... well ... that there simply had to be more to life than hitting tennis balls and ending up—'

'Like Jason Newman?'

'No, Jason's a one-off. I meant ending up teaching on some "tennis ranch" in Spain or Portugal where you talk tennis from breakfast to bedtime.'

'How long is it since Jason stopped playing?'

'About five years, I think. He burnt out early.'

'Incredible that he wasn't recognised by the police.'

'Maybe they never watched tennis on tv. Not everyone does. And then the name Keleti. It didn't mean anything.'

'And it doesn't take more than a day or two to become yesterday's man. I'm no tennis buff and the only thing I remember about him is that he was a loud-mouthed brat on court. Some said he was worse than McEnroe.'

'That's a tragedy.'

'What is?'

'That he should be remembered only for his bad behaviour.'

'It's true, isn't it?'

'Yes, but he had everything. He was *the* complete player: grass, clay, cement, it didn't make any difference. And he had the one thing that every champion needs: a killer instinct.'

She told him about the time she had played Jason in the mixed final in Winchester. 'He was only thirteen but he wanted to win so badly you could smell it ... No, not win ...' She paused, trying to produce an exact image. 'It was as though he was trying to annihilate us ... destroy us ... But then afterwards we all met in the players' lounge for a party and he was shy and gentle ... It was strange.' She took a sip of wine. 'And today I watched him cry his eyes out.'

'Prison does that to some people. Simple despair.'

'He told me he'd had a row with his wife before he left the house. I think that's what's causing the anguish. I'm glad he's ... what is it? ... two-ed?'

'It's two-ed up. You're getting the jargon. You think he's feeling guilty about his wife, rather than the girl he attempted to rape?'

'I didn't get on to the criminal charge. Should I?'

'Why not? We're supposed to evaluate him. Anyway, what you've got so far is the row with his wife and then he gets into a car, comes into Kingstown ... where does he live, by the way?'

'In a village about twelve miles from here. I can't remember the name.'

'Okay, he comes into Kingstown, wanders down to the playing fields beneath the castle and what then?'

'I don't know.'

'Have you been down there?'

She shook her head. 'I've hardly been anywhere. I've been trying to get the house to rights.'

'Of course. There are tennis courts too. Public ones. Do you think he might have gone down specially to pick up a girl?'

'It wouldn't have been to play. I mean he wasn't dressed for it and public courts wouldn't be his style.'

'Any girl would have been flattered if she recognised him.'

'I suppose so.'

'Another?'

'No, thanks. I'd better check on what my father's been up to.'

He walked her to her car. She said, ' I told Jason I'd try to help, talk to him again. Perhaps ring his wife. Is that okay? God knows he needs it.'

He thought for a moment. 'This is supposed to be a new era in prison management. Openness is the watchword. He's your baby. Do anything you want. Just let me know how things progress.'

She let herself into her house and thought once more what a beautiful place it was; Georgian, in a quiet terraced street, with its own walled garden at the back. She had never lived in a house like it and, without the money her father had put up, could never have expected to. Nor, to be honest, would ever have wanted to, not if it meant leaving London. A house like this in Westminster, yes. But not in a cathedral city. Its one blessing was that it wasn't in deepest

Shropshire, but only an hour from London.

Her father's share had come out of his savings, hers had come from the sale of her flat in London plus an interest-free loan from her lover.

Even thinking about her flat, perched on the top of a five-storey house in Eccleston Square, brought a feeling of deep nostalgia. From one side she had a view of the square and the tennis court on which she had never played. On the other there was a view over Victoria, to the Grosvenor Hotel with its onion domes that would have looked more in place in Moscow. It was like living in the clouds.

And that, of course, had made it untenable when her father returned from Africa. The stairs would have killed him. So forget it.

Apart from missing London the main snag in her new life was sharing the house with her father. But again, like her job, there had been little room for manoeuvre. Even now, remembering how she had found him in his retirement cottage near Cape Town made her feel panicky.

'You mus' come quick,' Watch had said on the phone. And she had. It had been a close run thing.

She discovered that her father had recently collapsed three times at the remote cottage. Each time Watch thought he was dead, but after a series of deep gasps and a change in facial colour from lilac to suffused pink, which scared Watch out of his wits, he had recovered. The local doctor had diagnosed the attacks as Stokes-Adams.

Anne knew that any one of them could have stopped his heart for good. The surgery and medical care to check the condition were out of sight financially. But his contributions had been paid to the NHS all the years he was abroad so Anne worked fast. She put the cottage on the market and brought him back to England to have a pace-maker inserted. He seemed to accept that the African adventure, which had lasted for most of his adult life, was over. That wasn't the problem. It was the parting from Watch. There was talk of him coming over but it came to nothing and he returned to Maseru to live with his widowed sister.

That was the past. That was finished.

She gave a metaphorical shrug as she closed the door behind her. People were always saying what a pity it was that the nuclear had replaced the extended family. She had said so herself to Paul when she knew she was pregnant. Now she had a chance to put her feelings where her mouth was.

'I'm home,' she called.

There was no response. She put her head into the sitting-room and the kitchen. No one. Halfway up the stairs she heard her father's voice. She moved closer and was able to look through the partly-open bathroom door. Hilly was in the bath pouring water from one small plastic mug to another, her father was sitting on the loo, a book in his hands. He was reading aloud.

'"Good heavens!" exclaimed the archdeacon, as he placed his foot on the gravel walk of the close' – That's the land near the cathedral, her father explained – 'and raising his hat with one hand, passed the other somewhat violently over his now grizzled locks—'

'What are grizzled locks?' Hilly said.

Anne had probably asked the same question when she was a child, for her father had read *Barchester Towers* to her once a year until she almost knew it by heart.

He had always travelled with a full set of Trollope which he read to her and which she then read herself. The back of the truck contained not only her school books but his library as well. There were no children's books other than *The Wind in the Willows* and *The House at Pooh Corner* and some Kipling which had been included not because her father thought she might like something lighter but because he loved them.

All over southern Africa, on bridges over rivers like the Zambesi and the Limpopo, the Kunene and the Orange, she and Watch had played pooh sticks.

By the time she was fifteen she had read most of Trollope, several of the Icelandic Sagas, some Conrad and a selection of Kipling's verse. She had not read a word of Enid Blyton and did not feel deprived.

She rescued Hilly from her bath and put her to bed. School had apparently not been as bad as expected and had been considerably brightened by her grandfather's rumbustious arrival.

'Then we went shopping at the supermarket,' Hilly said as Anne got her into her pyjamas. 'Grandpa made a fuss.'

'Oh? What sort of fuss?'

'He wanted someone to pack the groceries. He said they always did that in Africa.'

'And?'

'The lady said he wasn't in Africa.'

'And?'

'He said he was going to stand there until they bloody well did – that's what he *said* – and lots of people were behind us and the lady shouted at him.'

41

'The checkout lady?'

'She said he was a stupid old man and Grandpa called her a silly twist. What's a twist?'

'I don't know. And then?'

'And then a man came and packed Grandpa's things and we came home.'

Her father was pouring himself a whisky and soda when Anne came downstairs. The autumn evening was mild but he had put on a heavy sweater and an old pair of striped morning trousers. He often said that the African sun had thinned his blood.

'Drink?' he said.

'I had one with my new boss.'

'That sounds chummy. What's he like?'

'I don't know. He could be nice. He's certainly restless.'

'Are you going to enjoy yourself?'

'I'm not sure "enjoy" is the right word.'

She told him about the suicide drama. 'They're paranoid about suicides because they always get into the press. How was Hilly?'

'She's been marvellous. I don't think much of her school though. The head teacher's a bloody twit.'

Anne decided not to go into that. 'She says you had a problem at the supermarket.'

He opened his blue eyes very wide in the look of mendacious innocence which she knew of old. 'Problem? No problem at all. Just another bloody twit who didn't known her job.'

He lit a pipe and began to suck at it. It sounded as though he was under water.

'What would you like for supper?' she said.

'I had mine with Hilly. Smoked haddock and poached eggs.'

'Sounds wonderful. Is there any haddock left?'

'Enough for you.'

He came into the kitchen.

'No one could make this like Watch,' he said.

She ate with relish and when she'd finished she filled the sink with hot water.

'What are you doing?'

'Washing up, of course.'

'No, you're not.'

She gestured at the piles of dirty dishes stacked neatly on a work top.

'I'm going to do them in the morning,' he said. 'One good burst a day. The problem with women is that they're always wiping things and washing things. No organisation. Once a day!'

'But—'

'Annie, if I'm going to be a housemother then let me be one.'

'I hate you doing this sort of thing.'

'Fair's fair. You go out and win the bread. Anyway it's good for the character. Now, I want you to show me exactly how you work the dishwasher and the clothes washer.'

She felt a sudden sense of alarm. 'Wouldn't it be better if I—'

'Annie!'

'Okay, okay. If you really want to learn.'

She showed him, and then they took their coffee into the sitting-room. She told him about Jason Newman.

'The tennis player?'

'I played against him once.'

'I know. You wrote me about it. I thought for a moment you had met God.'

'I had in a way. But today I was in shock at first. You don't expect a childhood hero to turn out an attempted rapist.'

'You're making a hell of an assumption aren't you? You've got him guilty and he hasn't even been tried yet. A word of advice. Rape cases are notoriously difficult. Attempted rape even more so. There's gang rape and marital rape and date rape and male on male and female on female – don't look surprised, there is – and anal and oral and now the bloody feminist lobby has grabbed the rape question and is running with it when anyone who can rub two thoughts together knows that it's partly the feminists who are responsible for the increase.'

She opened her mouth but he held up his hand. 'So be careful with your assumptions.'

'I don't—'

He made a gurgling noise on his pipe and began to bang it out on the side of the fireplace, the sound of which effectively drowned what she was saying.

'I remember once in Maseru I had a chap up before me for rape. Big chap. And the plaintiff was big as well. Had a backside on her like a mare. Anyway, it was supposed to have happened in a car. So I adjourned for an inspection in loco. Car turned out to be a Fiat Topolino. You remember them? About the size of this armchair. I said no one was going to be raped in a thing that size unless she cooperated and I dismissed the case.' He stood up. 'I've got work to do.'

'How's the book going?'

'It's coming along.' He kissed her.

'You're a tendentious man,' she said. 'You only say these things to annoy me.'

He grinned at her. 'Nonsense. Anyway, you're the boss now. You can tell me to shut up.'

'Thanks for nothing.'

He paused in the doorway. 'Oh, by the way, that chap what'shisname, the one with the flashy car . . .'

'Clive?'

'He phoned. Said would you ring him back?'

'When was this?'

'When Hilly and I were having our supper. Just after six.'

'He said he was going to. I completely forgot! You might have told me earlier.'

'Sorry. But it didn't sound urgent. I'll lock up.'

She lay in a foam bath and dialled Clive's number. She got the answering machine. She began a message. 'Clive, it's me. Sorry I wasn't in when you phoned but it's been a hell of a day and I've only just got back . . .'

Why was she lying?

'I'll try to ring you early tomorrow or from work if I get a chance. 'Bye, darling.'

5

'I'm not saying it was your fault, squire,' Billy Sweete said. 'Not saying that at all.'

He was lying on the top bunk, Jason was still fully dressed and sitting on a chair at the small square table. The cell was dark, the lights had gone off a long time before, now there was only the ghostly blueish glow of the nightlight, just enough so the screws could look in at the prisoners.

Sweete said, 'You going to sleep sitting there or what?'

Jason hardly heard him. He was just a voice; words; no sense to them. They mingled with the night sounds of the prison; the coughing and the hawking, the whimpering in dreams, the tapping of messages, the calling of names, the crying, the shouting.

Jason heard Sweete turn over on his bunk and knew he was looking down at him.

The terror – wild, hysterical – had quietened now to an all-pervasive fear. He could feel it as a permanent knot in his bowels.

'I couldn't blame you,' Sweete went on in his gloomy, nagging voice. 'I'm not saying that. What I'm saying is it was a liberty.'

There was one thought hammering away at Jason's brain until he felt sick with it: why hadn't she come?

'You know *why* don't you?' Sweete said.

That penetrated. 'Why what?'

'Why they two-ed you up? Put you in with someone else. Me for that matter. Bloody liberty.'

'I thought they always made you share a cell.'

'Not no more. Single cells now. All done up with toilets. You wanted to be here when we still had slop buckets, mate. Na, the reason's safety.'

'Safety?'

He spoke the word but only half registered the meaning.

'They done that because they was afraid you'd top yourself.'

'Me?'

'Listen, you're Rule 43 remand, right? One of the *worst* places for it.'

'Not me.'

'You *say* that. But you never know.'

Jason shivered. No, he thought, you never knew.

'I was in Winchester nick with a bloke who topped himself. Sharing a cell with him. That didn't stop him. Waited till I was asleep and then he done it. I woke up. There he was.'

Sweete sat up and swung his legs over the bunk.

'People have got rights. That's my way of thinking. If a bloke wants to top himself that's his right. I ain't going to stop him. I mean, say I was you. Famous tennis player once. I might say to myself: what's it worth, all the aggro? They going to crucify me for what I done, so why not do it first?'

He came down from the bunk and sat on the other chair. A match flared briefly as he lit a rollup. Jason had the impression of a woman; long hair, thin face, medium build.

'You know how they do it?'

'What?'

'Top themselves.'

He shook his head. He did not want to know. A fearful scenario was beginning to run through his mind.

'On the central heating radiators. People think you got to go high to tie on a window bar or something. Then step off a chair. That's not the way. Watch, I'll show you. See these? Shoelaces. That's all you need. You tie 'em together, so. Then you ties the ends to the radiator, like that. Then you kneels down and puts your head through the loop . . . I ain't going to, just in case . . . then all you do is lean forward and the laces, they cut into your neck, here and here, and it's like turning off a tap. Doesn't take more than a minute. And no strangling. They say it's gentle, just like going to sleep.'

He stood up and untied the laces. 'Any time you want to borrow them, just say.' He gave a snuffling laugh and climbed back onto his bunk. 'You ever going to sleep?'

Jason lowered himself onto the hard mattress. He kept his eyes wide open because whenever he closed them he saw her; mouth wide open; the scream ripping the silence.

'You *was* famous once, wasn't you?' Sweete said.

'I suppose so.'

'I hear the press boys are at the gates.'

Jason had heard that too.

'You going to sell your story?'

'No.'

49

'You must be soft. I would. Fifty grand, I'd tell 'em anything they wanted. Then you know what I'd do? I'd . . . I'd buy . . . Jesus, I'd get hold of . . .' His voice was suddenly hoarse.

'What?'

'Never you mind, old sport.'

He was silent for a long time.

Then he said, 'I never reckoned tennis much. Not like football. What makes a person take up tennis? I mean it's not a proper sport is it?'

No one would have said that to his father.

I die for tennis, he used to say. You die too. Otherwise you nothing. No good for nothing.

That's when his father still had the club. It was one of the most beautiful clubs in the south of England. Once they'd played championships there. That's when Jason was a kid. He'd been a ball boy.

Not everyone would die for tennis. Not his grandfather. He hadn't been much impressed. Nor by Lajos. It's only a game, he had said to his son-in-law. It's something to enjoy. It's not a profession for the boy.

And his father had said, What the fuck he know about it?

Four grass courts. Six hard. A clubhouse. Hot showers. A bar. His father had always wanted to put in a restaurant like a club he knew outside Budapest.

It give class.

But he never had the money.

Crack . . . crack . . . crack . . .

Jason could hear the sounds even now. The tennis wall.

Hour after hour. Day after day. Weeks . . . months . . .

You practise, his father had said. You stay until I say you stop.

For God's sake – his mother talking – look at his hands. They're bleeding.

You mind your business. He my son. He my business.

And the ball machine.

Plock, plock, and the balls would come shooting out.

Swing – swing through – No! Not like that! You not controlling racquet. You must have strong hands. Fast hands. Exercise make strong.

Plock, swing through, plock, swing through . . .

The sun beating down . . . dizziness . . . Come on! You never going to be great player unless you practise.

He practised.

What about other things, Lajos? School? Learning?

This is better than school.

He's going to grow up knowing nothing about books or music or anything.

He going to be great player.

What for?

Because I say so.

His sister had watched angrily. She was bright. She studied hard. No one gave a damn.

At meals, his father's voice: You say he ignorant? Listen. Tell your mum: what is Eastern grip. Here is racquet. You show your mum.

Like this.

How you know?

Like shaking hands with the racquet.

What it do?

Good for ground strokes and volleys.

Where you use it?

Grass. Fast courts.

Okay, show your mother Western grip. Say what you learn.

The palm of the hand behind the handle.

What for?

I . . .

Come.

I . . .

And then the slap and the tears and his mother protesting.

Shut up! Now, say. What for? Is for heavy top spin. Say it.

Heavy top spin.

And where you use?

Slow courts. Clay.

You see?

But his mother watched with pain-filled eyes. She cried a lot, he recalled, in those days.

Winter.

Sweeping frost from the courts. And always his father's voice. Bend knees . . . bend! Lock wrist! So . . . volley . . . and volley . . . no! Not so weak! Stiff. Otherwise no control.

And the legs going . . . and the feet going . . . and the arms going . . . and the hands going . . .

Tears.

You seven years old! You not baby no more!

Anne was woken by the phone again. This time she was

flustered, panicky, because she had only recently got to sleep. For a moment she thought she had the duty, then the present reasserted itself. She was in her bed in the new house.

As she picked up the phone she saw the time was 12.15. Only one person would ring as late as that.

'Darling?'

'Clive?'

'Did I wake you?'

'It's a quarter past twelve.'

'I've only just got in from—'

'—from a meeting.'

'How did you know?' He laughed.

'I guessed. It's not difficult.'

'I phoned earlier.' There was an edge to his voice. Clive didn't like people not being in when he wanted them.

'I know. My father told me.'

'I don't think he likes me.'

'Of course he does.'

'Strange way of showing it. "She's not here!" That's all he said.'

'Telephones aren't really his scene. They rarely worked well in the bush and they were mostly party lines with people listening in half the time. So he used to make Watch do the answering.'

'It's a bit off-putting. Makes me feel like a kid again with parents getting in the way – and all that that implies.'

'Well, don't let it. Anyway I'm sorry I wasn't here. First day at work.'

'How did it go?'

'Fine, considering.'

'Considering what?'

'That it was my first day.'

'First days are always a bugger.'

She thought of Clive in his penthouse apartment at Chelsea Harbour and suddenly wished she was there. No need to get up early. No need to worry about anything. Let Clive take care of things. He liked taking care of things. Liked organising, arranging. There were times when she liked being taken over, times when she didn't. And that confused Clive.

In her mind's eye she saw his reflection in the glass wall of the apartment: tall, powerful, prematurely bald. There was something slightly dangerous about Clive. On the surface he seemed normal enough, but if you weren't dangerous you didn't make the sort of money Clive made, or control the lives of so many people.

She imagined him, mobile phone in hand, looking out over the tiny marina with the floating gin palaces, to the dark slick of the Thames. She found it difficult to visualise him without the phone. He used it everywhere like a spare hand: walking about, in the car, even in bed. She had got to the stage now where she would not go to a restaurant with him unless he left it in the car. He had grudgingly agreed.

'How's Hilly getting on in her new school?' he said.

'Fine.'

'What are you wearing?'

Sometimes he liked to play sexual games on the phone but tonight she was too sleepy.

'A nightie. I'm in bed.'

'The black one?'

The black one was a present from Clive and had come from Janet Reger and had cost more than Anne made in a month.

'That's special.'

'I wish I was in bed with you, darling.'

'I wish you were too.'

There was a pause. She knew he was waiting for her to continue this line of talk but she couldn't think of anything to say. So she said, 'I bet you're standing by the windows.'

'Right.'

'Did you take over anyone today?'

'You make it sound like a criminal offence.'

'It was only meant as a joke, darling.'

'I suppose I did in a way. Basically, I bought a substantial share in a foundry.'

He told her about a new acquisition for the Clive Parker Group of Companies. Something about die castings. She could not keep up with Clive. He was into so many things: building, property, shipping, fast-food restaurants, haulage, bottled gas, even video cassettes. Now die castings, whatever they were.

He said, 'Listen, darling, I've got to go. I've got to call New York. Are you working this weekend?'

'No, but I promised to take Hilly out on Saturday.'

'Sunday then. I'll pick you up around eleven.'

'What shall we do?'

'Have a bloody good lunch for a start.'

'And then?'

'What d'you think? Jesus, I wish I was in bed with you right now. We could be—'

'Watch it. Remember what happened to Prince Charles when he talked dirty on the phone.'

'But who would be listening to us?'

'God?'

'More like his opposite number. See you at eleven.'

It was to be a regular Sunday. They always did the same things. Sometimes she wished . . .

In a couple of seconds she was asleep.

6

'Well, this *is* nice,' Tom Melville said, as he entered Anne's room. He was holding two steaming mugs of coffee. She took one gratefully. It was now mid-morning and she had not stopped since arriving for work a little after eight.

'I was scared stiff you mightn't like it,' he said, indicating the green pastel walls on which the autumn sunlight was falling. He went over to her shelves. She had brought in a few books. He flicked a finger against the spine of one. 'A new Cecil & Loeb. You *are* being good! And a Bluglass.' He touched a huge tome on forensic psychiatry.

'I thought I'd better have that as a backstop,' she said.

'We've got a reasonable basic library here,' he said. 'Don't spend your own money. That thing costs a fortune.'

'A friend asked me what I'd like as a present for my new job.'

'I wish I had friends like that.' He picked up a framed photograph. 'Your daughter?'

'Yes, that's Hilly.'

'How's she settling down?'

'She's missing London, or says she is.'

'Her father's—?'

'Dead. It was in my cv.'

'Yes, of course. I'm sorry.'

He sipped his coffee and began to pace slowly up and down the confined space. She was reminded of a tiger in London Zoo and retreated behind her desk to give him more room.

After a moment he said, 'How was sick parade?'

Dr Symes was away at a course on financial management and taking the parade was part of her being tossed in at the deep end.

'There seems to be an epidemic of sore feet.'

'That's our standard problem. It's the prison shoes. All you do is give them a chit that says, "Shoes to fit" and they go off and change them. Insomnia's the other fashionable ailment.'

'I had a couple this morning wanting tablets. I said we'd see.'

'If they're coming up for trial and need a couple of good nights to get their heads together, I'm usually sympathetic. But not otherwise. Though it's pretty hard on them. How the hell anyone gets to sleep after being banged up most of the time I don't know. The other problem is IBS. Lots of that around. A good hospital officer can spot irritable bowel syndrome a mile away. We call it worry guts, and it's a fair description. They're *all* anxious, especially the remands, no matter how macho they appear on the surface. Once they're sentenced they tend to settle down a bit.'

He pulled a letter from his pocket and gave it to her. It was from a firm of solicitors and addressed to the Governor. The writer asked about the nature and severity of the injuries sustained by their client, Mr Jason Newman, at the hands of the police.

'He's talking about possible damages,' Anne said.

'Has Newman given you any indication he wants to sue the police?'

'None. Anyway, according to the notes he started it, and he's never denied that.'

'Then it's just an attempt to make a case for bail. Not a chance on a charge of attempted rape. Would you like to deal with it? I usually give them a ring, though I don't think I've dealt with this particular firm before.'

'I'll see Jason first, then phone them.'

She had lunch in the canteen then walked down the hill into the town. She strolled in the High Street, now a pedestrian precinct, and let the sunshine warm her face. She had suddenly begun to feel claustrophobic inside the prison walls and had decided to go walkabout to prove to herself that she did not belong there except by her own choice. Smiling slightly she wondered if the large book which Clive had given her had anything to say about gaol fever.

Jenks was in his small cluttered office in the hospital when she returned. His door was open and he was smoking a cigarette. It seemed to her that with the exception of Tom Melville, everyone, staff and patients, smoked. Jenks was bent over a diary and several printed forms and did not appear to hear her.

'Hello, Mr Jenks.'

He looked up. He did not quite mark his place with his finger but only seemed to.

Anne said, 'I'd like to see the remand prisoner, Jason Newman. Is that possible?'

'If you go over to D Wing one of the officers will bring him to the medical room.'

'I'd rather see him here, in my own room.'

'I'm sorry, miss, but we make the appointments a day ahead.'

'But what if we don't know a day ahead who we want to see?' It was said as sweetly as she could manage and hid the irritation she felt.

'In that case you go to the medical room. I mean I can't go fetching prisoners. I got to do these transfers for tomorrow.'

'Well, what do you suggest then, Mr Jenks?'

'I don't know, miss.'

'I'd rather you didn't call me "miss".'

'Sorry?'

'The word you used. Miss. I'd rather you didn't use it. Since I'm a doctor I prefer to be called Doctor. Do you think you can manage that?'

There was a pause as they stared at each other. She knew she was being irrational but she sensed that now, at the beginning, was the time to make her stand. She had met people like Jenks before: staff sergeants in the army, petty officers in the navy, union officials: unqualified people who controlled little empires, who had power without much responsibility and were forever guarding their dignity.

She had probably made an enemy of Jenks, but from the moment they had been introduced she had felt his hostility. Far better have it out in the open so they both knew where they stood.

'Mr Jenks, I'd like to see Mr Newman. I'd like to see him now. And I'd like to see him here.'

She had really no idea whether or not she was in the right or whether she was breaking a set of sacrosanct prison rules, but she had gone too far to turn back.

Jenks put down his pen and shuffled the papers in a gesture of exasperation. Then he stubbed out his cigarette and called, 'Les!'

'Yes?'

Les, his dimples showing nicely, came down the corridor, smiling at Anne.

Jenks said, 'Dr Vernon,' the word doctor was emphasised, 'Dr Vernon would like to see a remand called Newman.'

'Oh, yeah, the tennis player. You want to see him here, doc?'

'Please.'

'Right. I'll have him over in a jiffy.'

'Thank you,' Anne said.

In her room she found herself trembling slightly. 'That'll teach him,' she thought. But at the same time she thought she might regret what she'd done.

She was calm again by the time Jason arrived. 'How are you feeling now?' she said as he lowered himself onto the small metal-framed chair.

She could have answered the question herself; his eyes were bloodshot and there were purple smudges below them. His skin had a greyish pallor.

'I can't sleep.' His voice, coming from such a big frame, was filled with a childlike anguish.

'I'm not surprised. Are you getting any exercise?'

He shook his head.

'If it goes on I can give you something for it. I'd like to

61

look at your face.' With the solicitor's request in mind, she made a careful inventory of the damage.

'Can you tell me what happened?'

He frowned, as though to say: whose side are you really on? 'About what?'

'About what happened at the police station.'

'My lawyer—'

'It's because of your lawyer I'm asking.' She mentioned the letter. 'I'll have to ring him. He'll want to know about the injuries. I may have to give evidence. And you've never denied starting the fight. Did you?'

'The questions were pretty rough.'

'But only questions. They didn't start anything?'

'No. They just took it for granted I was guilty. They said I was a rapist. They even talked about me and kids. It was disgusting. I mean I didn't do anything like—'

'Don't tell me any more now, Jason. I'm not sure whether I'm supposed to know things like that. Not about what you've been charged with. Have you seen your wife yet? What's her name by the way?'

'Margaret. No, she hasn't been.'

'There may be all sorts of reasons. She's pregnant, isn't she?'

'Eight months.'

'Well then, she might not be feeling up to it.'

'She hasn't written or phoned.'

'It's a bit early for a letter. Have you tried phoning her?'

'A dozen times. I get the engaged sound all the time. It's as though she's taken it off the hook. Maybe the press got hold of her. Is there anything in today's papers?'

'Not that I've seen.'

'Thank God for that.'

'There's another royal scandal. It's wiped everything else off the front pages, and it's five years since you stopped playing. That's a long time these days when everyone wants to be famous for fifteen minutes. Anyway, you're sub judice now.'

He was silent for a moment and then said, 'It's horrible.'

'What is?'

'Being here.'

'I can imagine.'

'Can you?'

'Well . . . no, not really.'

'It's being in with the Rule 43s that's worst.'

Shame was written all over his face.

'It's for your own safety, Jason.'

'That's what they say. But it's like being in . . . I don't know, some sort of private jungle where we can eat each other but have to be protected from everyone else. We're called nonces. Did you know that?'

'I've heard the word.'

'On my landing there are rapists and paedophiles and flashers and God knows who else and they talk about it. They talk about what they've done all the time and how they're going to do it again when they get out. One man talks about buying kids. Little girls. Another guy married a woman because she had two little boys. He planned it that way. Months and months of planning just so he could get near them. And when he did—'

'I can guess, Jason.'

'But I'm not like that. I want to get out of there. Can't you get me into an ordinary cell?'

'I suppose I could speak to someone if you really wanted me to. But think about it. At least you're protected where you are. Talk to your lawyer about it.'

'I've hardly seen him.'

She was surprised.

'He was appointed by the court,' he said.

'But I thought—'

'That's what everyone thinks. That I'm as rich as Croesus. The fact is I'm broke. I lost everything in the Lloyds insurance crash. I was in one of the syndicates that went bust. They took my house, the cars, everything, even my tennis racquets. They said they might have some value at auction because I'd played with them.'

'I'm sure he'll do his best, Jason.'

'All he wants to know is did I follow the girl? Was it in my mind? Did I plan it? I told him no, I didn't, but I don't think he believes me.'

Anne was still feeling slightly battered from her encounter with Jenks when she left the hospital at 5.45 and walked across the yard to the main gates. It had been a long day and a tiring one.

''Night, doc,' the duty officer called as she stepped through the opening in the huge wooden doors. It was still daylight on a crisp autumn evening.

'Good night,' she said.

The greeting had been casual, friendly, and for a moment she felt a slight spasm of warmth at the knowledge that she was beginning to belong. But did she *want* to belong? As she walked to her car in the reserved car park she knew this was a question that was going to haunt her and she sensed that it was still not quite resolved in Tom's mind either. The prison service – even the phrase – had bad vibes, and yet the people she had met, with the exception of Jenks, did not seem to bear any resemblance to those depicted in tv documentaries. As with everything, she thought, you saw what you wanted to see.

As she unlocked the car door a voice said, 'You better look sharp. Don't let them catch you.'

She looked up and saw an elderly woman with a small round red face who was wearing a long fawn coat with fur trim that had seen better days. On her head she wore a cheap polyester scarf. Her eyes were almost black and shone like a bird's.

'You want to be careful,' the woman said.

'I'm sorry, I—'

'Visitors ain't allowed here. I saw them tell a bloke off for parking here. I seen you before, ain't I?'

Anne had a faint recollection of the woman but could not place her.

'You was visiting yesterday, when I arrived.'

'Were you . . . did you bang on the door?'

'Didn't it make a clatter? Thought I'd woken the dead.' She gave a throaty giggle. 'You'd best move it.'

'I'm allowed to park here. I work in the prison.'

'Oh . . . I'm sorry, dear, I thought you was a visitor like me.'

'No, I'm one of the doctors.'

'Excuse me.' There was a sudden change of attitude.

'Whatever for?'

'For talking to you like that.'

'Nonsense. It was kind of you to warn me.'

'Only, they *do* make a fuss.'

'I'm sure they do.'

Anne pulled the car door open. The woman came closer.

'Excuse me,' she repeated. 'Are you one of them psychitratist doctors?'

'No, just an ordinary one.'

'I only asked because of Billy.'

'Billy?'

'Billy Sweete. I'm his grandmother.'

Now Anne recalled her more closely. She had spoken about her grandson to one of the officers. What was it she had said? Something about burning?

'Please, can I have a word?'

'I don't think this is the time to—'

'I need help, doctor.' There was something about the way she said it that reminded Anne of Jason's cry for help and she felt immediate sympathy.

'Okay, go on.'

'Doctor, he needs to go to a hospital. He burns things . . . and he does other things, mad things, and they had him in a hospital . . . His mother's dead, see, and his father abandoned him. So I'm the only relation, see, and that's what they done . . .'

'What?'

'Released him. To his only relation. That's me. Care in the community, they says. No more keeping people in hospital. Well I says it's not fair. I mean who has to cope? Not them as lets them out. It's us what has to look after them.'

'Mrs—'

'Tribe. Ida Tribe. And him with matches and lighters. You know, doctor, once he made a bomb. A bomb! I says to him, Billy, if you let that thing off in my house I'm going to call the police.'

'Mrs Tribe, I—'

'You got to get him into a hospital, doctor. You got to tell the judge. And then *keep* him there. I know what you're going to say. You'll say that's cruel. But what about *me*? I'm frightened to go to bed with Billy in the house. I ask myself: what's he going to do? I listen to his mumbling and mumbling. He says it's praying. But who's he praying to? I mean, God ain't going to listen, is he? Would God listen to someone like Billy with his burnings and his . . . well, his other things? Never. God ain't got time. 'Course he ain't. There's all the rest of them in here. If God had to listen to all the people in gaol he'd have no time for people who weren't in gaol, if you follow me. No, it's them foreign heathen gods he's got. And the *smell*. I says to him, Billy, no more lighting that filthy incense. It goes right through the house.' She paused for a moment. 'But he never listens to me.'

The torrent of words stopped as abruptly as it had started.

Anne said, 'I'll make inquiries. Leave it with me.'

She got into the car.

'What's your name, dear?' Mrs Tribe said, the social gap between them suddenly closing.

'Dr Vernon.'

'I'll remember.'

Anne drove off. As she turned from the prison she

looked into her rearview mirror. Mrs Tribe in her moth-eaten coat, a white plastic carrier bag in her hand, was standing in the middle of the empty car park. She looked like someone who had been abandoned on a coral atoll.

7

'Grandpa and me are writing a book,' Hilly said.

'I,' Anne said. 'Grandpa and I. Let me dry your ears.'

'Not you. Me!'

'Okay, you. Now the other ear.'

Anne had come home early enough to give Hilly her bath and had also planned to make the supper.

'*I* was going to,' her father had said.

'I'll do it for all of us. I'd like to.'

'I had it planned.' He sounded petulant.

'What had you planned?'

'Smoked haddock and poached eggs.'

'But you had that last night.'

'I like it. Watch used to make it.'

'You can't have it every night. I mean Hilly can't.'

'Oh?'

'She'll get sick of it.'

'Have it your way.'

He took *The Times* and a whisky and soda and she watched him go out of the kitchen towards his basement flat. He was wearing an old grey sweatshirt and the long wrap-around skirt – this one in blue and brown – called a *kikoi* which both men and women wear in East Africa.

Anne thanked God they were not expecting visitors.

She made Hilly a toasted cheese sandwich and hot chocolate then took her up to bed. After she had read her a story Hilly said, 'What's a fang thief?'

'A what?'

'Something like that. Grandpa told me but I can't remember.'

'Never heard of it. When Grandpa picked you up at school was he wearing his *kikoi*?'

'No.'

'That's a relief.'

'Mummy . . . am I ever going to have a father?'

It pierced her like a knife.

'I don't know. Why?'

'Everybody at school has fathers.'

'Lucky them. Maybe one day. You've had a father.'

'Paul.'

'That's right, sweetie, your real father. The one who made you.'

'But he's dead.'

'That's right.'

'And he's never coming back.'

'No, darling, never.'

'Not even one day.'

'Not even then.'

They had had this conversation before.

Hilly turned on her side. Her thumb came up to her mouth. Anne started to reach forward then thought: if it comforts her then let her have it. Anyway, she was doing it less frequently.

When Hilly was asleep Anne went down to the large

sitting-room and dining-room which still had the original sliding doors between them. She closed them and made the sitting-room cosier. She turned on the news but it was politics and economics. She knew she should be going through prison service briefings on her role in the new management era but she couldn't face them. She also knew if she sat staring at tv and not taking it in she would think about Paul. She was able to forget him for days at a time, after all it had happened nearly five years ago, but when Hilly brought it up it all came swirling back.

She wandered down to Henry's basement flat. His sitting-room was untidy in a masculine way: full ashtrays, pipes littered about. And the room was also full of African artefacts waiting to be used as decorations but now simply standing in piles against the walls. There were Masai spears, carved birds from near Lake Ngami; tiny 'love' bows and arrows made by the Kung Bushmen of the Kalahari; Ovambo drums; Ndebele beadwork; woven beer strainers from Pondoland; necklaces made from ostrich eggshells; basketwork hats from Lesotho. He had collected widely.

He was working at his desk in the corner of his room. 'Listen to this,' he said. 'In the seventh century under Kentish law if you cut off a man's thumb you had to pay him twenty shillings. That was a lot then. I suppose because it harmed his work. It only cost six to lacerate his ear. Twelve to smash his thigh. You could murder him for a hundred shillings. And if Jason Newman had been a freeman and raped the female slave of a commoner it would have cost him five shillings. But if he'd been a slave and she was free he'd have been castrated.'

'Well, there you are then,' she said. 'That solves that.'

She wandered about the room picking up bits of Africana and putting them down again.

'You're making me nervous,' he said.

'Sorry.'

She sat down in one of the canvas safari chairs that had accompanied them on their travels.

'Is Hilary asleep?' he asked.

'Just. What's all this about fang thieves?'

'Not fang thieves. *Infangthief*. Old English law giving the right of taking and fining a thief in one's own jurisdiction.'

'That's just the kind of knowledge that'll help her with her drawing and numbers.'

'Don't be ironical. You knew what a tort was when you were seven and it didn't do you any harm.'

'I certainly don't know now.'

He ignored her. 'So what about your alleged rapist? Did you see him today?'

'Alleged *attempted* rapist if you want to be accurate. Yes, I saw him. I really feel sorry for him. I think he feels abandoned. And he is. No one seems to care about him now.'

'People can hardly remember who was famous the day before yesterday. It's not surprising they're not interested in someone who was a tennis star five years ago.'

'But his wife's abandoned him too.'

'Some women don't like their husbands trying to rape other women.'

'Now who's jumping to conclusions?' She picked up a Masai spear and felt its point. 'The problem with tennis players is that if they're going to be champions they've got to start when they're not much older than Hilly. And that means giving everything to it. It follows they don't have much to fall back on. Intellectually, I mean.'

'I understand that most of them have IQs that border on cretinous.'

'Well, maybe not that bad, but they have to forget about a decent education. When I was playing it was impossible to have a real conversation with anyone. No one read a book. All they talked about was tennis, vitamins and injuries. And when they weren't talking about those things or sleeping or playing, they were watching tv. Something called "The A Team" was considered to be intellectually challenging. You see how you wrecked me with all that Trollope and all those torts.'

'You should be bloody glad. What about Newman?'

'It's just possible I may be getting out of my depth with him.'

'Why should you?'

'It's my job to evaluate him. I'm not a trained psychiatrist and this job calls for a lot more psychoanalysis than I'd bargained for. After we've dealt with the sore feet and irritable bowels much of the rest of the day is spent with people who have personality disorders of one sort or another.'

'That shouldn't surprise you, should it? After all they committed crimes, which means they're anti-social. If you're anti-social you're not normal and if you're not normal you're dotty.'

'You make it sound simple.'

'You can bet it's not as complicated as it's made out to be.'

'You'd better come in and do the evaluations then.'

He smiled and tapped his papers. 'Too busy with crime and punishment.'

She rose and kissed him on his bald head. 'I'm off to bed.' At the door she paused. 'Hilly was asking about Paul again.'

'It's only natural. She sees other children with fathers.'

'Thank God we've got you. At least she's got a grandfather.'

'That's a very nice thing to say, but what little children need most are good mothers. And Hilary's got one, so you don't need to worry there. I used to worry about you, though. It may not have seemed like it but I did. If we hadn't had Watch I don't know what would have happened. Have you heard from your mother recently?'

'Not for months. Goodnight.'

'Who are you writing to Jason, old chap, old bean, old sport?'

Billy Sweete lay on his bunk and stared at the ceiling of the cell.

'Cat got your tongue? You must be writing to someone. You been writing ever since association. You ain't just going to sit there writing . . . Oh, wait, I get it, it's your diary is it? Dear diary, another lovely autumn day for my holiday. Now, let's see, what did my friend Billy and me do today? Can hardly remember we was so busy. There was tele to watch. Basket-bloody-work. Painting by numbers . . .'

They were banged up now. Lights off in fifteen minutes. Jason wanted to finish before that. Wanted to tell her how sorry he was, how desperate he felt. Maybe that would help.

Thoughts came fast. Writing slow. It had always been like that.

What for you want books? his father had said. How you going to learn to hit tennis balls from books?

Reading... Writing... Not much time for either.

Now when he needed the skills they were rusty, like old penknives that couldn't cut.

'If you don't want to talk, don't,' Billy Sweete said. 'You may have been famous once, old fruit, but you ain't famous no more. You're in the nick now, not in some plush hotel. You're a nonce, that's all you are. Like me. You're a Rule 43. You like young girls. They're going to crucify you. You know that? Crucify. You read the papers? There have never been so many rapes. Lessons to be learned, the judge will say. Example to be set. Take him down.'

Sweete came across from his bunk. 'You think this is prison? This is remand, mate. This is the Savoy. You're going to a proper nick. Maidstone. Dartmoor. Maybe even the Scrubs. Four years. Maybe five. Then every day is going to be the same. Day in and day out.'

He began a slow shuffling dance. 'Dear diary ... it is seven thirty ... UNLOCK! ... Hear them noises? Steel on steel. Doors opening. In other nicks the smell's bad. It's happy time. Slop out time ...

'M-y ... bl-ooo ... hea-v-en... Can I have the next dance darlin? ... Promised? ... Oh, dear, how embarrassing...'

Jason tried to ignore him. The sudden mood swings bewildered and irritated him. Billy Sweete seemed two or three different people.

'Okay, so off we go to the servery . . . Just Bil-ly and me, and-baby-makes-three . . . I love the golden oldies, don't you?

'Heavy food. Starchy food. Wholemeal bread. That's for the bowels, old chap. So you take the stuff back to your cell . . .

'Slow fox – watch the turn – you ever see "Come Dancing"? Best programme on the tele.

'You eat in your cell, Jason, dear boy. You know why? Because there are too many riots in canteens, that's why. It's flying-tray-time. So they bangs you up in your cell while you eat, safer that way . . . You listening to me? You hearing what I'm saying?'

He sat down opposite Jason, who covered his letter with his arm.

'I don't want to read your frigging letter.'

He rolled himself a cigarette and lit it. The cell was pervaded by the sweetish smell of Old Holborn.

'UNLOCK!' Sweete suddenly yelled. 'Nine o'clock. Labour to shops. Everybody on the move. Transfers. Discharges. But not you, old cock. Oh, no. You've still got years to go. But you see them others. The discharges. You been seeing them for weeks. Shaking. Sick with worry. Called gate fever. Will I make it? Will something go wrong? Will I lose some of my remission? Yeah. They're shitting theirselves.'

He suddenly stuck the red hot tip of the cigarette onto the soft skin on the inside of his forearm. There was a wisp of smoke and a sickening smell of roast pork. Jason stared at him in horror and incomprehension.

'You wind me up,' Sweete said. 'You sit there not talking. It ain't natural and it ain't friendly.'

Jason was staring at the angry red mark on Sweete's arm. The centre was a tiny brown crust.

'I'm sorry,' Jason said at last.

'Christ! It talks!'

'Why did you do that?'

'Me to know, you to find out.' He nipped the end off the rollup and put it back in his tin. He suddenly went into a boxer's crouch, his hands balled, his long hair falling over his face. He threw a series of punches in the air. 'Left ... jab ... left ... jab ... then wham! Right cross. Ooooh! Aaaah! Nine ... ten – Yer out. Billy Sweete done it again.' He turned to Jason. 'That's real sport, mate. Not yer frigging tennis.'

He got up on his top bunk again. 'Take a letter,' he said. There was something almost hysterical now about his whole demeanour. 'A letter to Dear Diary. My Day, by Jason Tennisplayer. At 11.45 we partake of luncheon, and then the prison is in patrol state. And what is patrol state? Patrol state is when everyone is banged up again and quiet so the screws can go and have their midday meal.

'And then, old pal – wait for it – in the afternoon ... VISITS! Only you ain't ever going to get a visit, Jason. She's going to forget you. She don't want no rapist in the family.'

Jason stood up and walked over to the bunk. He was tall enough to look down on Sweete.

'If you say that again,' Jason said, 'I'll kill you.'

8

Anne knocked on Tom Melville's door.

'Come in.'

Jenks was sitting on the opposite side of Tom's desk. There were papers in front of them.

Anne said, 'I'll come back later.'

'No, no.'

'It's not important.'

'We were just finishing.'

Jenks ignored her, instead he said to Tom, 'We should get on to—'

'Not now Jeff, we can do it later.'

Reluctantly Jenks left the room.

'I didn't mean to interrupt,' Anne said.

'Nonsense. He's getting to be an old woman. Coffee?'

'Thanks, I've just had some. I've organised myself, you'll be glad to hear. I don't have to cadge from you. And it's really about organisation I wanted to talk. I've been going through the prison service briefings and—'

'You *are* being good. No, that wasn't patronising. I mean it.'

She smiled, 'I hadn't even considered it. There's a

section about "command position" in an emergency and I'm not sure what that means exactly or where I'm supposed to go.'

He said, 'I think it's time for the alternative tour. Not the one you had on your first day. That probably made the place seem like a holiday camp. This will redress the balance. I'll tell you about command positions on our way.'

She followed him down the hospital corridors and out into the grey autumn day. The great wings of the Victorian house of correction reared up ahead of them.

Tom said, 'We usually hear on the grapevine when something is going down, like a riot or a hostage-taking or just something bloody minded. And you can bet it's on your Sunday off. The whole place goes onto a war footing.'

'That sounds ominous.'

'It's the nearest analogy I can think of. The Governor becomes the commander with a direct line to the incident room at the Home Office. And we're his staff officers, if you like. Our command position is more a state of mind than a "position". The hospital becomes a forward operating unit as in battle. We clear the place of patients, get them into Kingstown General, warn the management there that casualties might be arriving. And we get our own unit ready – bandages, dressings, drugs, that sort of thing. That's our command position.'

'I'm not sure why but I thought I'd have to put on one of those armoured suits and a helmet and—'

'They're out of date now. You've been looking at tv documentaries. Give me your hand.'

She put out her right hand and he took hold of her thumb. He exerted light pressure downwards. She experienced a stab of pain and felt herself suddenly bending at the knees.

'I didn't hurt you, did I?'

'No.' She rubbed the base of her thumb. 'I thought you were going to, though.'

He grinned and said, 'I'm not that much of a feminist. I do believe there are certain differences.' Then he grew more serious. 'It only needs two officers to immobilise a prisoner if they can get a grip like that. Much easier than the old method.'

She followed him to Reception. 'This is a dangerous place,' he said. 'They come in from the courts. They've just been sentenced and some are pretty desperate. The police have searched them but that doesn't make them safe. Weapons may have been smuggled to them. Some may be high on drugs. So be very careful here. You'll examine them once they've showered and changed into prison clothing but never, never underestimate them.'

'Nothing excepted? In the examination, I mean.'

'Absolutely nothing. The Home Office long ago decreed that male and female staff were equal. The only thing you won't do – and it is the *only* thing – is strip search a male prisoner.'

He led her through the wings and down a short flight of stairs. They were partly underground now and the air was dank and smelled of human waste and disinfectant. He indicated a row of cells. 'Segregation unit. The really bad lot.'

There were the usual sounds of coughing.

'Everyone here has broken prison rules. But that's not the only problem. There's a small group called 10/74s – which only means Circular Ten of 1974 – who are subversive. No other word for it. They lead us all a hell of a dance. Wear out the prison staff. And themselves for that matter. So it's policy to move them from prison to prison. Gives us a rest and them a chance to make a fresh start. But watch out for them. They've got nothing to lose.'

'BASTARD! BASTARD! BASTARD!'

The voice was close enough to make Anne jump.

Another voice shouted, 'Who's there?'

'The doctor,' Tom said.

'Hey! I want to talk to you.'

Tom opened the sliding panel on a cell door. Anne had a glimpse of a bare room with only a foam mattress on the floor. Then a face appeared above a thick, muscular neck. The prisoner wore a short, elaborately trimmed beard and his eyes were almost black.

'Listen, doc, I'm doing weight training. I'm on a high protein diet, see, and these sodding – Christ! What's a woman doing down here? You come to visit, love?' He put out his tongue and made an obscene movement with it.

Tom closed the window.

'Don't you do that to me you sod!' the prisoner shouted.

They moved away. 'We've all had to get used to that sort of thing,' Tom said.

He took her to the Centre Office, the glass-encased room at the very centre of the prison with views along each wing and up onto the landings.

'Like the bridge of a ship,' he said. 'From here the duty officer can keep an eye on things.'

He introduced Anne to an officer then took down a canvas bag hanging from a wallhook. He took out a pair of scissors. They were like none Anne had seen. One blade was turned at right angles to the other, like anvil secateurs.

'For suicides,' Tom said. 'They usually use shoelaces or something thin. You can't get your fingers under the ligatures so the drill is that someone, whoever gets there first, will hold up the body to relieve the pressure. Then you push the bottom blade under the string and cut down with the top blade. Okay?'

There was a gravitas about him she had not seen before.

A bell went off stridently nearby. A voice shouted, 'Some bastard's set his cell alight.' There was a smell of smoke.

'You'll get used to cell fires,' Tom said. 'This is the other occasion when we take up our command positions.' He led her through the jostling throng of remand prisoners and discipline officers. Smoke was drifting down the wings and then being sucked up into the atrium. By the time they reached the hospital the first – and only – casualty was on his way.

'How are you feeling now, Jason?' Anne asked.

'My throat's like sandpaper.'

'That'll go in a day or two.'

Two prison officers had brought him to the hospital, coughing and retching. Tom had given him a shot of hydrocortisone and prescribed steroids for the next five days.

'Apart from that?'

'Okay. They got to me fast, apparently. I mean the mattress had only just begun to smoulder.'

'Just as well,' Tom said. 'Foam is pretty deadly when it's on fire. Creates phosgene and cyanide. Any idea how it happened?'

'My cellmate smokes. And he's in for arson.'

Tom said, 'The officer on duty says he wasn't in the cell at the time. He was out on the landing watching tv.'

Jason said, 'I wouldn't know. I was asleep.'

Anne said, 'It must have been his cellmate. Who else could it have been?'

'It happens all the time,' Tom said. 'Anyone could have flicked a cigarette into the cell hoping it would set something alight. It's part of the whole business of their frustration and tension.'

He left Anne alone with Jason.

She said, 'I've spoken to your lawyers. A Mr Brinkman was handling your case, wasn't he?'

'Yeah. Kenneth Brinkman.'

'I'm sorry to tell you, he's been made redundant.'

'Redundant? Oh, Christ!'

She waited for him to say something more but he remained silent. She had the feeling that his psyche, like a burrowing animal, had gone down deep into his subconscious leaving only part of it in her presence.

She said, 'Don't you think it might be a good idea to sell your story? You've had offers, haven't you? It would give you money to pay for a good defence lawyer.'

He clenched and unclenched his hands.

She said, 'I heard there was a posse of press people at the gates wanting to get in touch with you.'

He said bitterly, 'All they want is the dirt.'

'Has your wife been to visit you yet?'

He shook his head.

'Listen, Jason, would you like me to contact her and tell her about the lawyer?'

He's your baby, Tom Melville had said. Do anything you want.

'God, yes! The phone's still engaged all the time.'

'Then give me her address as well as the telephone number.' She took them down then said, 'Isn't there *any*one else who could help? Didn't you mention a sister?'

'Clare? She'd never help. Hates the sight of me.'

'Are you sure you're not exaggerating?'

He did not reply.

After a moment she said, 'Anyone else?'

'Only my mother. Oh . . . and my grandfather . . .'

'There you are, you *have* people who could help.'

He pulled a letter from his pocket and handed it to her. 'It's from my grandfather. Read it.'

'Dear Jason (she read), This morning's paper mentioned your problems. I realise this is a bad time for you but it comes as no surprise. I always thought something would happen to you on the basis of your past behaviour. Your mother makes no progress nor will she ever. God knows who will look after her when I'm gone. Clare certainly won't, she's said so often enough and I believe her. So this letter is really to say to you: don't look to us for help, and don't involve us in any way. You have brought this upon yourself and now you must live with it, just as we must live with our tragedy. Thank God your mother will never know.' The letter was signed M.R. Thorpe.

'That's your grandfather? He doesn't sound like any grandfather I've ever known.'

She was fishing but he did not rise.

Instead he said, 'Are you going to send me to a hospital?'

'Of course not. Your lungs will feel tight for a few days and your throat will be raw. But there won't be any permanent damage.'

'I don't mean that sort of hospital. I mean a mental hospital.'

'Why on earth would we do that?'

'For tests?'

'But we're doing the evaluations here.'

'Yeah, but—'

'What makes you think a thing like that, Jason?'

'I was told that sex offenders often go to mental hospitals.'

'We don't call them that any longer . . . secure hospitals.'

'Okay. Secure hospitals. Same thing isn't it?'

'Well, anyway, why would you think—?'

'What if you thought – or what if the court thought . . . You have to give evidence of mental problems don't you? I mean they won't just send me without . . . I don't . . . I'd rather die . . . I know how to—'

'Jason!'

'—kill myself!'

'Stop it!'

His hands were shaking.

She said, 'What's started you worrying about a secure hospital? Have you been listening to other prisoners? Well don't. You're you. People have looked up to you, hero-worshipped you – me included. No one's ever looked up to the others. You're not like them. At least I don't think you are.'

Later, when she went to report to Melville, he said, 'They get like that sometimes. Simple paranoia. It comes from fear and desperation and rumours and misinformation and God knows what else. It'll pass. It comes in cycles, sometimes they overlap, sometimes they follow on. All we can do is what we're doing.'

He was looking at a spread of photographs on his desk.

'Deshka River, Alaska,' he said, indicating a rushing stream and snow-topped mountains. 'I was there in the summer when the king salmon were running. Wonderful place. Never saw another human being, but lots of black bears and moose and even a grizzly. And a billion mosquitoes. That's me in a beekeeper's veil and gloves.'

He was a different person from the one who had taken her on the alternative tour and acted so decisively with Jason. But it was about Jason she wanted to talk, not about mosquitoes in Alaska.

As though sensing this, he looked up from the photographs and said, 'Don't get too involved. It doesn't do any good.'

Henry Vernon, BA LLB Cantab., sixty-seven years old, late of the British Colonial Service in Africa, was making a kite. Hilly was hovering, giving advice.

'That won't stick,' she said.

'Won't stick? What d'you mean won't stick?'

'You're using paper glue.'

'You're an expert on glues, are you?'

'We make things at school.'

'Have you ever made a kite before?'

'No.'

'So much for *your* advice.'

'Have *you* ever made one before?'

'Of course.'

'When?'

'A long time ago. But kites don't change. They are immutable. Hand me the string, please.'

'What's immutable?'

Anne's voice came from the kitchen, 'Breakfast you lot.'

It was Saturday morning, the sun was shining brightly, and there was no work and no school.

As they sat down in the big warm kitchen, Anne said, 'What's the wind like?'

'Not bad,' her father said. 'Could be better.'

'I don't like muesli,' Hilly said.

'I don't blame you,' Henry said. 'Bloody health food will be the end of us. All my life "experts" have been telling us this is good for you and that is bad for you and then a few years later, just the opposite.'

'It *is* good for you,' Anne said.

'Bosh and piffle.'

Hilly began to stir the spoon round and round in the milk. 'Did you ever fly a kite?' she asked her mother.

'When I was little. There's a mountain near Maseru called the Mountain of Night. Its African name is Thaba Bosio, and Grandpa and I climbed up there and flew kites a couple of times.'

'Where will we go?' Henry said.

'What about near the castle?'

They set off about ten and drove past the prison. 'That's where I work,' Anne said to Hilly.

'It looks pretty grim,' Henry said. 'But those old Victorian gaols all do. How's Newman taking it?'

'Badly. He thinks we're going to put him in what used to be called a mental asylum.'

'And are you?'

'I shouldn't think so for a moment. Some of the other prisoners have filled his head with worries. If only his wife came to see him he wouldn't be quite so ... well, paranoid I suppose. I've promised to try and contact her.'

'Do you think that's wise?'

'It's only fair.'

'I don't see that it's got anything to do with you. You shouldn't get involved.'

'That's what Tom Melville said. Look, I'm supposed to evaluate him. I'm not a trained psychiatrist. I need all the help I can get – and so does he.'

She told him about the letter from Jason's grandfather.

'That only reinforces my view. They sound like a rum lot.'

'But don't you see; I've got a reason, a personal reason. I *know* him. I can't just abandon him when he's got no one else.'

'He's got a solicitor, hasn't he?'

'Hardly.' She told him what had happened.

Henry said, 'And so you come riding up on your white charger.'

'It's not the first time!' Her tone was acid.

He knew what she meant. Without her prompt arrival in South Africa he might have been dead by now. 'All right, have it your way.'

They came to the municipal park below the castle. It was a large space with tennis courts, three soccer pitches and an area of equal size set aside for informal activities like walking and jogging – and flying kites. One side was bounded by the river, another by the rocky buttress on which stood the castle.

There was a slight northwesterly breeze blowing and the three of them went to the far side of the park near the tennis courts. Anne and Hilly ran the kite back and forth and at last it climbed groggily into the air.

'Lord, I'm unfit,' Anne said. 'I'll have to do something about that.'

'Take up tennis again,' her father said. Then he and Hilly moved away as the kite dipped and climbed. Anne turned to watch the tennis players. There were six courts and all were in use. The players were across the age range from a middle-aged mixed four on one court, to two small boys slugging it out on another.

Ever since she had parked on the road that ran under the castle walls and strolled across the grass, Anne had had the feeling she had been here before.

She walked round the courts to an area of nettles and blackberries. They covered what looked like large broken slabs of concrete and small piles of broken bricks. But they were not obvious under the trailing arms of the blackberry bushes.

Frowning, she turned away and found herself being stared at by a little old man with a mongrel dog.

'Lost something, love? Jack'll find it, won't you old chap? He loves finding things.'

The man was short and gnarled and gnomish.

'No, nothing. I thought . . . I was wondering about these concrete slabs. Was there a building here once?'

'Tennis club. But that was years ago. People came from all over.'

'That was the clubhouse?'

'Castle Tennis Club. Smart. Oh, yes. Very smart. Grass courts and hard courts. Even played competitions here. They played the Sussex Championships one year.'

'Did it . . . was the clubhouse painted white with wide steps?'

'You remember it? I thought you'd be too young.'

She smiled. 'That's a nice thing to say. I think I came here once with my school. But I seem to see . . . did it have a thatched roof?'

'Indeed it did. Oh, yes. And that was the trouble. When the fire started, up she went! All over in an hour or so.'

'When was that?'

'It only seems like yesterday to me. It does when you're old. But to someone like you it would be a long time ago. Twelve . . . fourteen years . . . I don't know. Could be more; could be less.'

'And the club never started up again?'

'Never. There was some story at the time but . . .' he tapped his head. 'Memory. Jack's got a better memory than me. Never forgets where he buries his bone. Do you, old chap? All I know is the council took it over. Now anyone can play. Better I suppose. Except...' he lowered his voice, 'the people who came here had real style. Not like this lot.'

She thanked him and was about to turn away when he said, 'Is that your little girl?'

She followed his gaze. Hilly was running with the kite to the far side of the playing fields. She couldn't see her father.'

'Yes.'

'I saw you come. Three of you.'

'My father's with her. He's somewhere over there.'

'You want to be careful, miss. Specially after what's happened.' He turned away and pulled on the dog's lead.

She looked again at the weedy growth. Some of the bricks beneath it were blackened. Her memory was sharper now. She could remember playing in a junior competition but she could not have won or the memory would have been clearer. It must have been soon after she started school in England.

She began to walk round the courts the way she'd come. She could no longer see Hilly. Her father was standing behind the stop-netting, watching.

'Where's Hilly?' she said.

'I thought she was with you. She said she was coming over.'

You want to be careful, miss. Specially after what's happened.

'Oh no!'

She ran round the side of the courts. The playing fields were suddenly emptier than they had been. There was no sign of Hilly.

She saw a group of boys with a football. 'Have you seen a little girl with a kite?'

They shook their heads.

She ran on. The noise of the weir was loud now. The river was high and the water foamed white as it dropped into the weir pool.

'Hilly!'

The river bank was lined with tall trees and there was a good deal of secondary growth.

'Hilly!'

She ran up the line of the trees in the direction of the weir.

'Have you seen a little girl with a kite?' she said to a fisherman on the bank.

'Sorry.'

She ran on.

And then, out of the corner of her eye she saw something move. She whirled. Hilly was running diagonally across the field with the kite trailing in the air behind her.

Anne raced towards her. 'Where have you been?'

'Here!' Hilly was affronted. 'You left me. So did Grandpa.'

Anne was about to fling her arms around her and then thought better of it. There was no need to overdramatise something the child wasn't even aware of.

'Let's find Grandpa,' she said.

On the far side of the playing area, under the castle, a large white Volvo drew up. It had a stripe on its side and she realised it was a police car. A man and a young woman got out and began to walk across their line in the direction of the tennis courts. They passed about thirty yards away. The girl was in her teens. She was small but full-breasted, and pretty with dark hair. Her face was spoiled by a petulant mouth.

'I know that lady,' Hilly said.

'Don't point.'

'But I do.'

'Where on earth do you know her from?'

'The supermarket,' Hilly said. 'Grandpa called her a twist.'

9

Heat drained him. He hated it; hated playing in it.

You were born in a heatwave, his mother always said.

The day was hot, tropical. Sussex burned. The concrete courts were like furnaces.

Playing the tennis wall, hour after hour. Another hour with his father. The heat making him light-headed.

Swing through the ball . . . place feet properly . . . look at feet . . . You not preparing . . . feet is everything . . . feet . . . balance . . . swing . . .

Hands covered in band-aids, each finger a white cylinder, racquet grips slippery with sweat . . .

You lazy, now I make you run.

Backwards and forwards, side to side, whipping across the court.

Bend knees for backhand! Think! Use brains!

Plock . . . plock . . . plock . . .

Over and over again.

Goodnight, Lajos.

Goodni', Mrs Johnson. Goodni', Mrs Powell.

Don't keep Jason too long in this heat. He looks tired.

We finish now.

And then the boy standing at the stop-netting. A boy from the town. Not a member's son. A nobody.

Would Jason like a game?

No. He was going home now.

Was he scared of getting beaten?

Lajos listening.

You know who is this? This my son, Jason Newman. He going to be Wimbledon champion. You still want to play?

Yes.

Okay. You play.

That's how it had started. It was clear in the memory bank. The heat. The fading light. The empty courts. Just the two of them.

And his father.

The boy's name was Gary. He was half Jason's size. Jason had never seen him before. Later he found out that his father was caretaker at a school. There was no court at the school. No tennis wall. There was a garage door with a painted netline. His father called it a lower-class school.

Jason could not handle Gary. He didn't play properly, not the way he, Jason, had been taught to play. He didn't serve and come to the net. He dinked and cut and lobbed and spun and sliced and dropped.

It was like cheating.

He was small. Jason's serve was big. Gary stood back and jumped in the air and pasted the serve down the lines.

His legs were short, Jason's were long but dead. Gary ran down everything.

Try! Jason's father shouted. You not trying!

He was angry. At the change-overs he flicked Jason with a towel. You are coward.

The harder Jason tried the worse he played. Gary beat him easily. They didn't play a third set.

Jason's father said: You tanked. I teach you not to tank. I beat it into you. You not my son.

When his mother came to search for them it was nearly midnight. Jason was sweeping the courts. His father was sitting in the umpire's chair, smoking and watching the boy under the bright halogen lights.

For God's sake what are you doing to him? He isn't ten years old!

She began to shake the chair.

Her husband jumped down and struck her in the face. It was the first time Jason had seen that.

Don't, he cried. Oh, don't . . .

'What's all the noise about, Jason old cock?'

Jason opened his eyes.

'Don't what?' Billy Sweete said. 'What don't you want them to do?'

'I don't know.'

'You don't know? Make a note of that please, doctor. Punter here doesn't know . . . Ho ho ho . . . Doesn't know? Bring a straitjacket. We'll teach him to know.'

'Leave me alone.' Jason turned away on his bunk.

'I'll leave you alone all right. It's them as won't. Listen, let me tell you what they do. You ever see that film *Cuckoo's Nest*? Something like that. Well, that ain't nothing to Loxton, mate. I done time there. You can't tell me nothing about Loxton. Worse than Broadmoor. Couldn't even look out a window. Couldn't even *stand* by a window.'

'I told you before, I don't want to hear about these places.'

'Don't want to hear? Gent doesn't want to hear. What's that? Oh. Doctor says you got to hear. Do you good. Maybe you're going to a place like Loxton. Maybe even Loxton itself. Listen, when I was there you had to get permission to go to the toilet. Even to cross the room. You been crying in here. Oh, yes, I heard you. And in your sleep too. I seen people cry at Loxton for weeks, *months*. This is the Savoy, mate.'

'For Christ's sake I don't want to hear! If you don't leave me alone—'

'What? Put the boot in? Maybe you can and maybe you can't. You got big hands, Jason. You can do some damage with those – if you know how. But I don't think you do, see? I think you're a cream puff. And I think you should ... What's that, doc? Yeah. Listen and learn. Right.'

Sweete put his hand to his head in a two-fingered salute. 'Boy scouts be prepared.'

Then he said, 'We're on remand, right? So we got privileges. But in Loxton you got to earn them. You even got to earn the right to work. And the only way to do that is to get in with the nurses and the only way to do THAT is to grass on your mates. Someone got a shiv – you go and tell. Someone got some dope – you go and tell. Anything – you go and tell. Then they let you work.

'But if you get snotty with them, it's solitary, old sport. And not just for a couple of days. I knew blokes who were in solitary for weeks and weeks. When they come out they couldn't talk properly.

'They take your clothing away from you in solitary. And you become an animal . . .'

Jason was pressing his fingers into his ears.

Sweete stood over him. Then he said, 'Sleep well, Jason old fellow. Nightie night.'

Anne stood at the big windows of Clive's apartment and looked south across the Thames. The view from the penthouse of the Plaza Tower in Chelsea Harbour was the kind enjoyed only by the seriously rich. Looking down now, as the bright autumn afternoon turned to pearl grey dusk, she could see a series of famous international names and logos in the mall below. The discreet neon glowed expensively in the half light.

And then, past the mall, was the tiny marina with the huge motor yachts moored so closely together that she imagined there would be a general post when one wanted to manoeuvre into the Thames.

Or perhaps they never moved. In all the times she had been in Clive's apartment she had never seen one leave the marina. Maybe they were only there to be looked at by their owners. And who were their owners? Who had money these days for floating gin palaces? Arabs? Japanese?

She sipped her champagne and listened to the low hum of Clive's voice on the bedroom phone. At last he hung up and came to join her. He had the Veuve Cliquot in his hand.

'Let me top you up.'

'No thanks. Clive, that's a minimalist marina.' She pointed with her glass. 'The most minimalist marina I've ever seen.'

She felt slightly floaty.

'What do you mean?' Clive said.

While in the bedroom he had changed into his maroon and blue silk dressing gown. So, she thought, they were getting down to the business of the afternoon.

'Small. Tiny.'

'Well you wouldn't expect them to build a huge marina here. Not enough space.'

'You've taken it literally, darling. It was only an observation.'

'Okay, but have you any idea how much the square footage is here?'

'Not a clue.'

She felt his fingers in her hair.

'A fortune.'

'The boats are . . . well, they're not exactly round-the-world racers, are they?'

'I like them. I'm thinking of getting one when a mooring comes up.'

His fingers were on her bra strap.

'Why don't we go into the bedroom,' she said. 'Then we won't spill our wine.'

His bed was soft and luxurious. Clive was hard and energetic, and made love, not with indecent haste, but without loitering. He came like a jack hammer and she was glad the mattress was soft. Then he slowly deflated, a spent balloon, and lay with his head next to her shoulder.

She thought he had gone to sleep but he moved slightly and said, 'Well?'

'Very nice.'

'No, not that. But thank you. Have you thought about it?'

'You know, darling, I've had a lot on my mind. Father. New school for Hilly. New house. New job.'

'I realise that. I'm not pressing.'

The phone rang. He sat up.

'Clive . . .' It was a warning.

'Okay.'

The answering machine whirred into action and he lay back again. But he did not relax completely.

'Tell me something,' she said. 'I've often wondered: why me?'

'Well . . . I love you . . . And I want you . . .'

'Thank you. But I'm not a good bet, you know. There's my father. And there's Hilly. And I've got a profession I want to continue with. I mean I'm not God's gift to anyone, much less a tycoon.'

'You make the word sound squalid. Anyway I'm not a tycoon.'

'You're supposed to say yes you are God's gift. But never mind. And of course you're a tycoon. You buy and sell companies. You have a flash apartment. That's tycoonery.'

'My apartment isn't flash.'

'Come on, darling, just look at it. All tinted glass and

chrome steel. Plants brought in from a contract gardener.'

'You don't like it?'

'I didn't say that. To tell you the truth, part of me just loves it. All the luxury and the security . . . But part of me says it's too much. Not this apartment, but the whole Chelsea Harbour development. There are so many wretchedly poor people in the world and—'

'Oh, for God's sake.' He rose on one elbow. 'What about your own Georgian house in Kingstown? You're like the French socialists: vote to the left, live to the right. Don't you understand that if there weren't people like me—'

'You'd have to be invented. Okay, Clive. It's too nice an afternoon to argue.'

'Jesus Christ!'

'Don't be huffy.'

He lay back with his hands under his head. 'If you married me you could furnish it how you liked *and* practise your profession. I mean you don't really want to go on in the prison service, do you?'

She had never thought of the prison service as permanent, but now, hearing the disparagement in his voice, she bridled. 'Maybe I will, maybe not, but I'm going to give it my best shot. Just remember that when I came back from Africa the job in London, the super job in the super practice, had been given to someone else. They simply blew me away because I had to fetch my father. I had no choice. I'm not just going to dump the prison service like I was dumped. They're short staffed as it is.'

The phone rang again. This time she did not stop him. He swung his legs off the bed and padded into the drawing-room. He had a good body, she thought.

Through the half-open bedroom door she could hear his voice; not the words but the tone. It was the tone he used when speaking to his mother.

She wondered if the first call had also been from Mrs Parker. Trust her not to trust the answering machine. When she wanted Clive it was NOW.

The first time she had met Mrs Parker was in her flat in Richmond. It was in a 1950s block, redbrick with metal-framed windows and a flowery name: something like Clematis Court. She had invited them to lunch: tinned tomato soup, tinned steak-and-kidney pudding, tinned peaches, tinned cream. Clive very serious. Anne on her best behaviour as befitted someone being displayed as a possible future daughter-in-law. Clive had not put it that way, of course, but that's what it meant.

Mrs Parker was stick-like and had what looked to Anne like a thyroid condition. She was in her late seventies and wore heavy make-up and an auburn wig, which sometimes slipped to one side giving her an abandoned appearance.

She had been a widow for many years. Her late husband, who had worked as the accountant in a firm making chutneys and pickles, had left her with the flat and a modest income.

She was a coaster-and-doily lady. There were coasters everywhere: on the arms of chairs, on small nests of tables, on the drinks trolley, on the display cabinet. Anne even found one in the bathroom under the soap dish. She also had a large supply of teaspoons with coats-of-arms on them from places like Carmarthen and Inverness and Exeter – spoils of her annual beano on a coach tour.

But it was her treatment of Clive that Anne remembered best. At that time he was in his late thirties – he was forty-one now – and a successful businessman. To Mrs Parker he was still young Clive aged eighteen.

Before they had their lunch Mrs Parker had various 'little jobs' she had saved up for him to do: like changing the plug on her electric blanket, mending a window catch, getting her suitcase down from the top of her wardrobe so that she could put away some of her summer clothing.

Clive did these things without comment and without resentment. It was clear he had done them for many years. While he was thus occupied Mrs Parker talked to Anne, or rather complained to her. She complained about friends who did not come often enough to visit her; she complained about the weather, crime, the television. A long list.

Then she seemed to focus directly on Anne for the first time. A doctor? Wasn't she a bit young to be a doctor? What experience had she? If she didn't mind her saying so, Mrs Parker preferred male doctors; men with long experience; who specialised in internal medicine.

When they left, after that first meeting, Clive said, 'I think she likes you.'

'How can you tell?'

The acid in her voice caused him to come to his mother's defence. 'Don't judge her too harshly. My father put her on a pedestal. Did everything for her. It's not her fault.' He paused, then said, 'And she's bloody lonely.'

Now, in the penthouse, Clive put down the phone and padded back to the bedroom. He looked preoccupied.

'Mother thinks she's eaten something,' he said. 'I told her to take some Milk of Magnesia. Okay?'

'Why not? It can't do any harm. Listen, I think I'd better be getting home.'

'Don't be silly, it's still early. Have another glass.'

'No thanks.'

He poured himself another and bent down to kiss her.

She said, 'Do you ever think of going to a concert or something?'

'No. Why?'

'It's just that we do the same things most Sundays and now that I'm not in London—'

'The same things? Don't you like what we're doing?'

'Of course I do. But it's just that I feel I'm missing things now. French movies and music and that kind of thing.'

'French movies? Yuck.'

'Some of them are good, darling. Very good.'

'I like taking you to a restaurant then coming on here.'

'Yes, I know.'

His face was beginning to tighten. He was a man who did not like to be challenged, she thought.

He said, 'There's something I meant to say. It's about the money. I want you to stop the payments. It's ridi—'

'If you say that once more I'll never see you again. We agreed. End of story. Now I really must go.'

This time he made no protest. While she was dressing she heard him on the phone again. This time his voice was brisk, peremptory. Business, she thought.

At home she decided to go to bed early. It had been a tiring week. Hilly was already asleep and her father was in his flat. The house was quiet. She leaned out of her window. There was a faint acrid smell of coal fires. Kingstown was silent.

She would have to do something about Clive. She couldn't go on stringing him along forever. But WHY did he want to marry her? Was it because he feared the loneliness which he saw his mother experiencing?

For that matter so did Anne. But was it a good enough reason for marriage? He was in his forties, she just thirty. There was time . . . That's what she always told herself.

And did she *want* to get married? Why share her life with someone she wasn't sure of just for security? She had security. She had a job, a house, a daughter – indeed a family.

But Hilly would grow up and leave home. Her father would die. And then, when she was at her most vulnerable, there would be no one.

And didn't Hilly really need a father?

Clive said he was fond of her and Hilly certainly liked him. But what if she married Clive and it didn't work and they broke up? Wouldn't that harm Hilly even more?

And anyway women were not supposed to need men any longer.

Oh?

She put on her dressing gown and went down to her father's flat. He was puffing at his pipe and reading.

'You all right?' she said.

He made a gurgling sound which she took to be yes.

'I'm sorry about yesterday,' she said. 'I shouldn't have shouted at you. It wasn't your fault. It was just that an old man had said something to me and then I didn't see Hilly and I panicked.'

'No, it was my fault. It's . . . well, things have changed. When you were little I lost you twice. Once in a fruit market in Nairobi you wandered off and I went round calling your name and then a large black man brought you back to me on his shoulders.'

'I remember that.'

'The other time was in Maseru. I thought you were in the back of the truck and Watch and I drove off and we'd gone about twenty miles when we found you weren't. So we drove back and you were playing in the street with a couple of little chaps. The point is that at no time was I worried that anything would happen to you. I knew I'd find you, that it was only a matter of time.' He paused. 'I realise that it doesn't seem to work like that any more.'

'No. It doesn't. These days kids who wander off are sometimes never found again or if they are they're dead. And women who break down in their cars – same thing.'

'The time is out of joint,' Henry said.

'It is a bit. Goodnight.'

10

It was early in the afternoon. Tom Melville was at his desk going through a medical file, Anne was sitting next to him.

His room in the prison hospital was like a monk's cell in its austerity, she thought. It was painted white, had an old scarred desk, an examination couch, and a bookcase with a mixture of textbooks and the odd blue paperback denoting serious sociological intent.

Her own room with its fresh green paint and sun-splashed walls, was infinitely preferable. Then she caught herself wondering, somewhat guiltily, if he had overspent on hers to the detriment of his.

There was a knock at the door. Les's plump face appeared and he said, 'Ready when you are, doc.'

'Okay, wheel him in.'

The man who was ushered in was of medium height with long brown hair and small eyes. He had a shuffling walk and his whole demeanour was deferential. He stood at the vacant chair on the other side of the desk until Tom said, 'Sit down, please.'

'Yes, sir.'

Anne was concentrating hard. This was a case in which

Melville was doing an evaluation prior to a psychiatrist coming from Loxton Special Hospital to see the prisoner. Tom had asked her to sit in.

'William John Sweete,' Tom said. 'Is that what they call you – William?'

'No, sir, Billy.'

'Okay, fine. Do you know why I asked to see you, Billy?'

'No, sir.'

'I've got to make an assessment about your mental state. You've been assessed before, of course.'

'Yes, sir. Last time, sir.'

'So you know the ropes. You go back to court for remand, let's see . . .'

'Next week, sir.'

'Have you been given a date for the court hearing?'

'Not yet, sir.'

'Right. So . . . you're charged with arson, same as last time.'

'Yes, sir.'

'And . . .' he turned over the pages, '. . . and you were in Loxton for four years and a bit. Then you went to Middleton and from there you were released into the care of your grandmother. Is that right?'

'Yes, sir.'

'It may be Loxton again, Billy. You realise that?'

'They said Granton, sir.'

'Who said?'

'Police doctor, sir. When I was arrested.'

'Yes, well . . . we'll see about that. And there's no need to call me sir all the time. Would you rather go to Granton?'

'Yes, sir.'

'Why?'

'It's a psychotherapy unit, sir. They help you there. In Loxton they never did nothing for you, sir. I mean they gave us drugs to shut us up but, well, I don't think it did me any good, sir.'

'Why do you think that?'

'I'm in the nick again, aren't I, sir?'

Tom smiled. 'You've got a point there. Okay, well, let's take it from the beginning. Just pretend we know nothing about you.' He turned to Anne. 'Billy likes burning down things. Isn't that so, Billy?'

'Yes, sir.'

Anne was remembering the old woman in the car park.

He burns things.

'It's mainly barns, isn't it? Why barns?'

'Burn nicely, sir. Usually full of hay or straw.'

'When did you start?'

'When I was fifteen, sir.'

'But you weren't caught for a long time, were you?'

'When I was twenty, sir.'

'And all in Sussex?'

'Some in Hampshire, sir.'

'Okay, we'll come back to the barns. First of all let's hear about your childhood. Where did you live originally?'

'London, sir.'

'Parents?'

'Never knew my father, sir. They was never married. I mean my parents. My mother died when I was a baby.'

'What did your father do?'

'Lorry driver, sir.'

'So . . . ?'

'Well, sir, when my mother died I went to live with my grannie on the farm near East Marden.'

'That's pretty much cut off in the middle of the Downs, isn't it?'

'Specially in winter, sir, with the snow.'

'Go on.'

'My grandmother works there as a housekeeper, sir. She keeps for Mr Gillis, has her own cottage near the farmhouse.'

'So you grew up on the farm. Did you enjoy that?'

'It was all right.'

'What did this Mr . . . Mr Gillis farm? Sheep?'

'And cattle.'

'Do you like animals?'

'Not much, sir.'

'What did you like doing on the farm then?'

'Blowing things up, sir.'

'I see. And what did you blow up?'

'Blew up part of a wall once. An old car. A broken trailer.'

'What did you use to blow up these things?'

'Gunpowder, sir.'

'Where on earth did you get gunpowder?'

'I emptied it out of shotgun cartridges, sir.'

'Whose? Mr Gillis's?'

'Yes, sir.'

'Did he know?'

'Yes, sir.'

'Did he give them to you?'

'No, sir.'

'You stole them?'

'Yes, sir.'

'And did he find out?'

'Yes, sir.'

'And?'

'He used to give me a hiding, sir, with a whip. Said it came from South Africa, sir. Called a – can't remember exactly what it was called, sir.'

'A sjambok,' Anne broke in.

He turned to look at her directly for the first time. 'That's the word, miss.'

'This is Dr Vernon,' Tom said.

'Sorry, doctor.'

'All right,' Tom said. 'Let's get onto something else. School. It says in your file that you got seven O levels. You must have been pretty bright, Billy. Did you like school?'

'No, sir.'

'Why not, you were doing well?'

'Dunno, sir.'

'But the work itself. You must have liked that or you wouldn't have done well at it.'

'Yeah. Quite liked it, sir.'

'And apart from that?'

'Not sure what you mean, sir.'

'Well, did you have any friends there?'

'No, sir.'

'Enemies? Were you bullied, for instance?'

'Yes, sir. At the start. But I hit back and they stopped.'

'Did you make friends after that?'

'No, sir. I didn't want no friends.'

'What about the teachers? How did you get on with them?'

'If they left me alone I left them alone.'

'And did they?'

There was a momentary pause. 'Yes, sir, afterwards.'

'After what?'

'After I ... well, there was one of them, sir. Always picking on me. Couldn't do nothing right. So I tells him to stop it. And he says don't be cheeky, he'll do as he pleases. So I hit him. After that he left me alone.'

'You hit him? What with, Billy, your fist?'

'Piece of two-by-four, sir.'

'You mean you found a piece of wood lying on the ground and picked it up and—'

'No, sir, took it with me.'

'So you had planned to have a showdown with him?'

'Yes, sir.'

'Just because he picked on you?'

There was silence.

'Is that right? Because he picked on you?' Melville repeated.

'Not only that, sir.'

'Go on.'

'Interfered with me, sir.'

'Sexually?'

'Yes, sir.'

'How old were you when you hit him?'

'Fifteen, I think. But it started when I was a lad, sir.'

'The teacher interfered with you when you first went to the school? Is that what you're saying?'

'Yes, sir.'

'What did he want you to do?'

Sweete glanced at Anne. 'Don't like to say, sir.'

Anne said, 'Would you like me to leave, then you can discuss this with Dr Melville?'

Tom said, 'No, don't leave. We won't go into it at the moment if he doesn't want to, but eventually you must, Billy, you understand that, don't you?'

'Yes, sir.'

'And Dr Vernon is here to help, just as I am. Anyway, leave the details for the moment. Did you ever report this "interference"?'

'No, sir.'

'You just decided to deal with it yourself, is that right?'

'I told him to stop, sir, and he started picking on me.'

'So you dealt with him. Tell me, Billy, did anyone interfere with you before the teacher?'

'Mr Gillis, sir.'

'The farmer? The one your grandmother keeps house for?'

'Yes, sir.'

Tom began to tap his pencil lightly on the desk. 'You never said any of this the first time. Why was that, Billy?'

'Didn't like to, sir.'

'Too embarrassed?'

'Yes, sir.'

'But this time?'

'Don't want to go back to Loxton, sir.'

'So you've decided to tell everything.'

'Yes, sir, everything.'

'Okay, Billy, thank you. We'll talk again later.'

After Sweete had gone Tom began to pace up and down the small room.

'What do you think?' he said.

'I don't know what to think. I don't know whether he's telling the truth or not.'

'I don't know either. It's all a bit glib. I think friend Billy knows how to play the system.'

He threw himself into his chair. 'He knows the score about Loxton. He's been there. And believe me it's a . . . well, you wouldn't want to end up there. What he could be doing is allowing us to believe that he's just a *little* bit psychotic. And then he's letting us drag the reasons out of him. Now your turn. You play devil's advocate.'

'Well, the first thing I'd say is you're crediting him with a Machiavellian brain.'

'Oh, he's bright. Seven O levels. And he's learned from previous experience. What he wants is to go to Granton which is a relatively free-and-easy psychotherapy unit compared with Loxton.'

'But he said straight out that that's what he wants. At least he's being honest.'

'Mmmm. But perhaps dishonestly honest. It's like someone playing quadruple bluff. He says this and this knowing we'll think that and that. He's trying to manipulate us.'

'You can't blame him for that. You can't blame him for not wanting to go back to Loxton.'

'Of course you can't. My point is he's showing us what we want to see; telling us what we want to hear. Sexual abuse of kids is the hot favourite at the moment. We've no way of checking this at all. May just be a pack of lies.'

'Lying about something like sexual abuse?'

'Why not? They lie about everything else. No . . .' He began to tap his pencil on the desktop again. 'I think Billy has drawn the curtains on part of his mind so that we can't see into it. You'll discover this yourself the more assessments you do. There's always a secret place in people like Billy where the real personality hides and they only show you what they want you to see.'

She told him about Sweete's grandmother, Ida Tribe. 'She's terrified of him. Wants him put away for keeps.'

'A lot of relatives do.'

Anne drove down into the village of Leckington in the dusk of an autumn evening. It lay in a river valley and mist was gathering in the water meadows. For a moment, when she first saw the village of old brick and flint houses with the smoke from their chimneys rising on the still air, she thought she might be looking at countryside painted by Constable or described by Jane Austen; a never-changing England. It was only when she saw the tv aerials that the twentieth century reasserted itself.

'Keepers' stood at the end of the village. It was a small cottage three up and three down set in its own garden of half an acre. The wicket gate was broken and hanging by a single hinge and the brick path leading up to the front door was slippery with moss. There were a couple of half barrels on either side of the door but whatever had been planted in them had long since expired and, like the rest of the garden, they were filled with grasses and nettles.

The curtains were drawn and the lights were on in one of the downstairs rooms. But the moment Anne pressed the doorbell the light went out. She pressed again. She thought she heard a child cry, then silence.

'Mrs Newman,' she called through the letter flap.

Silence.

'Mrs Newman, I'm Dr Vernon from the prison. I've been talking with Jason. May I come in?'

Silence.

'Mrs Newman, I know you're in the house. I saw the light. Won't you please let me in so I can tell you how Jason is? At least you can do that much.'

There was a subtext to her words which hinted at the wife's neglect.

The light came on and a voice from within said, 'Can you prove who you are?'

Anne pushed her driver's licence through the letter slot. After a moment the door opened.

The figure standing there was backlit with a halo of gold round her blonde head. Her face had a ghostly beauty.

Anne stepped inside, Margaret Newman closed the door. She was heavily pregnant but the rest of her was so thin as to be almost anorexic. Her beautiful pre-Raphaelite face was hollow-cheeked. She held a child in her arms.

She turned away and led Anne into a sitting-room/kitchen warmed by a large Aga cooker. There the light was stronger.

'You've seen Jason?' she said.

'A couple of times. His physical health is all right but I'm worried about his mental state. He misses you dreadfully.'

'Does he?'

Margaret reached for a packet of cigarettes and lit one. Her hand was shaking violently.

'Sit down.'

The chairs and sofa, of brown uncut moquette, were covered in toys, bits of clothing and unidentifiable stains. Margaret made as though to clear a space and Anne said, 'It's all right, I've been sitting all day.'

Margaret turned away, comforting the baby in her arms. 'I was about to feed her.'

'Let me hold her. What's her name?'

'Julie.'

'Hello, Julie.' Anne took her while Margaret began to prepare the feed. 'She's lovely. I've got a little girl of five.'

Margaret did not respond. Anne thought she was like someone coming out of an anaesthetic, aware of the world but not sharp enough to respond to it.

She took the child back and began to feed her from a tin of baby food.

'He's been trying to phone you, but you're always engaged,' Anne said.

'It's off the hook. The press never let me alone.'

'Jason's been hoping you'd come to visit him.'

Margaret swung round. 'How can I? How can I get there? Don't you see what my life is like? This bloody place is a worse prison than Jason's. At least he has someone to talk to. Who is going to look after Julie if I go? I don't even know if I can take her with me.'

'Of course you can.'

'Don't patronise me!'

'I'm sorry, I didn't—'

'I heard your tone of voice. I heard what you said. You blame me, don't you? Yes, you do.'

'No I don't blame you. I don't even know you, how can I blame you?'

'Everybody else does. I hear it in the village. In the street. In the shop. That's his wife, they say. You know, wife of the chap who raped the child. And I can sense what they're thinking: must be something wrong with her for him to do a thing like that.'

'It isn't like that! No one's proved he raped anyone. He isn't even charged with that. And it certainly wasn't a child.'

'What does she look like?' The question came like a volley at the net.

'I don't know.'

'Young and pretty, I bet.'

'She's young all right. Seventeen, I think. But I don't know if she's pretty.'

'Not like this!' she pointed to her large stomach. Then she said, 'He just couldn't wait!'

Anne said, 'I know it's difficult for you but I suppose it's difficult for Jason, too.'

'Why are you taking his side?'

'I'm not taking anyone's side.'

'Yes, you are. That's why you've come here.'

'I've come here to try and get you to see him. If you don't,

I feel he might ... well, he's in danger of becoming mentally unstable. It's largely because he misses you and Julie and feels that you've rejected him.'

Abruptly Margaret sat down in one of the armchairs and buried her face in the baby's clothing. When she looked up tears had coursed down her cheeks washing away some of the make-up on the left side exposing mottled yellowy-brown skin. Anne looked more closely and Margaret put up her hand to hide it.

'What happened?' Anne said.

'It's nothing.'

'Yes, it is. I've seen it often enough before. Jason?'

She nodded.

'Have you told the police?'

'No.'

'Are you going to?'

'I don't know. Sometimes I think ... Why are you asking these questions? You're not his lawyer.'

'No I'm not. Do you know the one the court assigned to him has been made redundant?'

'They wrote to me.'

'That's making it even worse for him. He really needs a good lawyer. Do you know anyone?'

'No. Even if I did we couldn't afford it!'

There was a moment's silence then Anne said, 'Would you like to tell me what happened?'

'What good would that do?'

'Something shared. And it might help me understand Jason better.'

Margaret did not reply. Anne studied her. Even with eyes red from weeping she retained her fragile beauty. She lifted the spoon to the child's lips and against the light Anne could see the bone structure of her hand as though in an X-ray. She said, 'How did you and Jason meet?'

'Photographic session. We were modelling for the same clothing manufacturer. I was modelling swimsuits. Jason was modelling tennis gear. He was under contract.' She stopped.

'Go on,' Anne said.

'He asked me to have a drink with him afterwards. I didn't really want to. I mean, I knew nothing about tennis. I'd read about his brattish behaviour on the court. Everybody had. But he wasn't like that when he was being photographed. He was nice. So I thought, why not? I mean he was pretty famous then. We had a drink and he asked me out again. I started going to watch him play. And I realised there were two Jasons. The one on court and the one I knew.'

'And—'

'Look, I don't want to talk about it, okay? Anyway, I've got to put Julie to bed.'

Anne knew she had got as far as she was going to get for the first meeting. She said, 'And I've got to put Hilly to bed. But, listen, will you visit Jason? I think it's vital.'

'I've told you. I can't. I can't drive, if you must know.'

'That's unusual these days.'

'That's why it was so crazy to come here. I said to Jason at the time it was crazy but he said we had no option. The rent's low. Because the roof leaks. Jesus!'

Anne said, 'What if I could organise a lift for you?'

'I'll think about it.'

'He needs you, Mrs Newman. He's totally lost.'

'For God's sake, so am I! I said I'd think about it.'

'That's fine. But how do I get in touch if you keep the phone off the hook?'

'Phone the shop. They'll give me a message.'

11

Like so, he said. One knee on ground. Like sprinter in starting blocks.

Do it, he said.

They did it. Six of them. Six young boys from Jason's school. No girls. He wouldn't have girls. The school had said why not three girls and three boys and he had said no.

What could the school do? It was his tournament.

You ballboys, he had said to the six of them. Not ballgirls. Not ballpersons. I teach you. Okay?

Jason had been one of them.

So, okay, like sprinter. Two at net. One each side. So nearest one runs for ball near net. Do not drop ball. If you drop ball you get less money, okay? So, you don't drop. Not in my tournament.

They watched him carefully. White shirt, long white trousers, white tennis shoes, tanned face, black hair.

This is what some wanted to be. This was a famous tennis player. But he had no name in tennis. Not to them, anyway. The big names were coming tomorrow; from America, from Sweden, from Germany, from Australia. But not from Britain. No big names here.

Hallstrom, Vickers, Benton, Schellberg, Voigt . . .

Five out of the top ten on the computer.

It had taken Lajos more than two years to set up the tournament – the Southern Grass Court Championships sponsored by the South of England Tourist Board. Twenty-five thousand pounds. But it wasn't the money that brought the best; it was the grass.

Grass meant Wimbledon. All year they had been playing on clay and concrete. Here they could prepare for the Big One; here they could shake off the red dust of Rome and Roland Garros.

But no women, Lajos had said. Okay? And the tourist board had said okay. Men were a stronger draw for tv anyway.

So, now, ballboys.

Now I show you how to throw.

The six pairs of eyes watched him.

You, netboys, your job is pick up on court near net then get balls to boys at ends. Like so. Rolling ball on ground. Okay?

So . . . you at back. When Schellberg or other players want balls for service you hold high above head. You throw down, like so. One bounce in front of him. Okay?

Last thing – be careful of Vickers.

They nodded. They knew about Vickers.

So it went.

Flaming June. Gales. Rain. Cold. Stoppages. Injuries. Tempers.

The final. The crowd thin. Anoraks. Woollen hats. Umbrellas.

Schellberg versus Vickers. Germany versus Australia. The ballboys freezing.

126

Vickers going down. First set to two; second set running out like sand in a glass.

Net cord. Query from Vickers. Overruled.

Service out. Query from Vickers. Overruled.

Overruled . . . overruled . . .

Then . . .

Vickers returning serve down the line.

Out.

Schellberg leading by five games to two, second set.

Vickers walking slowly to the chair. What?

I saw the ball long.

You what?

It was long.

Bullshit, man.

The crowd silent, the linespeople watching, the ballboys afraid.

The umpire starting the stopwatch. Mr Vickers will you please—

You're talking shit, man.

Mr Vickers, abusive language gets you—

Are you blind? Didn't you see the chalk? Vickers tapping the court with his racquet. There's the fucking mark, man.

Vickers turns to the line judge. His stiff face is beginning to collapse.

There's the mark, Vickers says to him. What do you say, man?

The man says nothing.

Vickers pushes his racquet in the man's face. You see all of Schellberg's in; why not mine?

Mr Vickers— The umpire is impatient.

Fuck you man, I want this guy changed.

I'm not going to change anyone and I'm giving you a public warning—

Shit! I want the referee. Get me the fucking referee.

The referee arrives and speaks to the line judge and the line judge changes his decision and the point is reversed and that is that. Vickers walks it seven-five; six-love.

Jason's mother said afterwards, wasn't it a pity about the final. Wasn't it a pity it was won that way!

And Lajos said what did she know? She was just a stupid woman. Winning was winning. It didn't matter how.

Jason said nothing.

'My daughter tells me you don't drive,' Henry Vernon said, as he opened the door of his car for Margaret Newman. 'Don't blame you. They don't know how to drive in this bloody country. They think they do but they don't. Here, let me take the baby.'

He held Julie while Margaret got into the car and then passed her in. Margaret took her without a word.

'Do you know Africa?' Henry said.

'I went out to Cape Town to see Jason play in the Diamond Challenge.'

He drove slowly down the village street.

'I know the Cape reasonably well. That's where I retired.'

She seemed uninterested. They were passing the shop/post office. Abruptly she stiffened. Two middle-aged women and an elderly man formed a knot on the pavement in the afternoon sun. Their heads swung in unison as the car passed them.

'Have a good look,' Margaret said and turned to stare them down.

The man dropped his eyes, but the two women looked back with unconcealed interest.

'Bitches,' she said.

'There's always talk in a village,' Henry said. 'That's the benefit of living in a city. Nobody gives a damn about you in a city. Of course that can be tricky if something goes badly wrong. No one to care.'

'That's what I'd like. Nobody to give a damn.'

'Watch where you're going you old fool!' Henry shouted out of the car window. An elderly woman in a small Metro disappeared behind them, her face frozen in fright. 'Geriatrics shouldn't be allowed to drive,' he said.

When he returned from Africa he had been scathing about the cars that thronged the British roads. 'They all look alike,' he had said to Anne. 'Bloody tin cans.'

In Africa his cars had been something of a legend. Apart from the American truck which he and Watch used as day-to-day transport, he had owned separately, and sometimes together, an Armstrong Siddeley, a Lanchester, a pre-war Jaguar and an Alvis. There was not a single mechanic in any of the countries in which they had lived who had ever seen under the bonnet of cars such as these, nor heard of a pre-selector gearbox. The result was that if anything went wrong – and it did frequently, for Henry would drive into walls and cows and sometimes farm dams – it took not weeks but months to put it right. Large spare parts, like the back axle for the Armstrong, came out by sea from Southampton, smaller items by air to Johannesburg where they were forwarded to Lesotho or Malawi or Botswana depending on where he was living at the time.

The cars, which in any case had never been built for African roads and which shook to pieces after short and unhappy lives, had ended up in African villages as hen houses. The wheels had been taken off and used on carts, the leather seats as furniture.

When he came home to England for good he bought a massive 3.5 litre Rover of nearly forty summers which he was now piloting through the narrow lanes of West Sussex.

He turned to Margaret, registering again her pale skin and fine bone structure, and said, 'Anne tells me you were a mannequin.'

The word seemed to puzzle Margaret for a second, then she said, 'We call it a model now.'

'Ah. Anyway, going back to what we were saying, don't models need publicity? I mean you wouldn't get so much work if no one gave a damn about you.'

'You do when you're starting. It becomes a nightmare afterwards.'

'After what?'

'After Jason and I – well, started going together.'

'You don't have to be on your best behaviour. I can remember what men and women do. Rows and fornication in varying measures.'

She burst out laughing. 'You remind me of my father.'

'Must be a splendid chap.'

'He's dead.'

'All the best people are.'

'He wanted me to be a doctor – like your daughter. But I wasn't clever enough. In fact I was thick. Watch it!'

A delivery van missed them by a few inches.

'Monster!' Henry shouted.

'You were in the middle of the road,' Margaret said severely.

'I have a granddaughter who uses that tone when she speaks to me. What did your father make of you modelling?'

'He died when I was getting started. I don't think he would have liked me modelling swimsuits or bras and pants.'

'He didn't know Jason then?'

'No, thank God. He hated people like Jason. I mean people who made exhibitions of themselves on the sports field. He stopped watching sport on tv, except golf.'

'He sounds better and better. I'm sorry I never knew him. What sort of behaviour?'

'The usual – abusing the umpire and the lines people. My father really hated that. He always said it was unfair because they had no comeback; they just had to take it.'

'My feelings precisely.'

'But Jason wasn't like that in real life. Off court he was the gentlest person. Until . . .'

He waited, but she did not continue. 'Anne told me he'd beaten you up.'

She did not reply directly, instead said, 'You know, if you live with a tennis player, really live, there's nothing else. He's it. The centre of the universe. He wanted me with him all the time; at courtside, travelling, in hotels. So I had to give up my own career.' She paused. 'It was pretty horrible, really. Sometimes we didn't even know what country we were in. We'd get to an airport and the courtesy car would take us to our hotel. Jason can't sleep on planes so he'd get into bed while I unpacked. Then he'd watch tv.

131

Maybe I'd watch it with him. I've seen "I Love Lucy" God knows how many times. I've seen it dubbed into Malayan and Arabic and Spanish, even Japanese. After a time you forget what it sounds like in English. Then there's the "entourage". The coach, the physio, the manager. For a time Jason even had his own psychologist. If you didn't have your own psychologist you weren't where it was at.'

'Did he really need one?'

'Didn't matter. The best players had them for motivation. Some even had security guards in case the tennis groupies threw them down and screwed them. Sorry. I shouldn't have said that.'

'I get the general drift.'

'And then you play your match and if you get through the first round you go to the press conference and have a massage and some vitamins and you drink Diet Coke. If you're Jason you eat ice-cream, though you shouldn't, and watch some more dubbed tv and have an early night. And if you don't get through the first round you're flying again and asking yourself was that Bangkok we just left? Or was it Singapore? And who cares, anyway?'

'There must be compensations,' Henry said, just missing a bus. 'Fame? Money?'

'For some. When Jason was in the top ten on the computer it was like owning a bank. Money kept pouring in: sponsorship deals, endorsements, advertising. He had contracts with clothing manufacturers, racquet manufacturers, shoe companies. Free cars. You name it. People kept coming to us with buckets of money if only he'd endorse this or that. We had a flat in London in Barons Court so he could practise at Queen's, a house in

Hampshire and a condo on a tennis complex in Florida.'

'I once had three tents,' Henry said.

She smiled vaguely, gripped by her own memories. 'Eventually things became more and more difficult. There's always pressure. Pressure to win, to go here, to open this, to speak at that, to wear this, to be interviewed here, to be photographed there. And you can't say no because the sponsors wouldn't like it. Once Jason didn't go on a photo call to a children's hospital. The sports pages called him callous. The thing was he had food poisoning. But no one cared about that. I think that was about the time the press really turned on him, when he started losing.'

Kingstown Castle showed up on the horizon and the traffic became heavier.

'My daughter tells me you got caught in the Lloyds crash.'

'That's why we're in that horrible house. Jason's financial adviser always said we should look to the future. What if something happened and Jason couldn't play? We had friends in their early twenties who couldn't play because of injuries. Well, we weren't going to be caught that way. We were going to invest our money. So we invested in Lloyds and then came the hurricanes and the *Exxon Valdez* and God knows what else and the syndicate went bust and they came to us and said so sorry and took the houses, cars, furniture – everything of value.'

'But Jason was still playing, wasn't he? Still earning?'

She shook her head. 'He began to have shoulder trouble. They said it was his big serve and starting so young that had damaged the joint. But I don't think it was. I think he simply burned out. Players do, you know. Whatever has

133

kept them near the top just seeps away; you only have to look down the list at some of the names: Andrea Jaeger, Tracy Austen . . . there are lots of them. Some had injuries but some burned out.'

Henry turned the car into the prison car park. 'Here we are.'

Her need to talk had activated a fountain, now suddenly it was turned off. He had been aware that it was a catharsis, probably triggered by loneliness and the silence of the house. Now her own silence engulfed her. He sat silent too, waiting.

He watched her hands. Her fingers tightened on the baby's clothing, then relaxed, tightened and relaxed. She lit a cigarette and he saw she had been using the clothing to cling to. Without that anchor her hands shook uncontrollably.

'I can't!' she said, softly.

'He's your husband.'

'I just can't.'

'He needs you. Think how much worse it is for him.'

'You don't know . . .'

He waited, but she did not continue.

He said, 'No matter how hard something is, once you've faced it it's not so bad.'

After a moment she said, 'My father used to say something like that.'

She opened her bag, took out a small bottle of pills and swallowed one.

'Give me a minute,' she said.

'Take all the time you need.'

She got out of the car.

'Do you want me to come to the door with you?' Henry said.

'No, I—'

A woman's voice said, 'Can't park there, dear. It's all staff parking.'

'Can't you see she's got a baby?' Henry said.

'I'm only trying to be helpful,' Ida Tribe was offended. Then she looked at the baby. 'What's her name, dear?'

'Julie,' Margaret said.

'That's a lovely name. I had a cousin called Julie. On my Uncle Percy's side. Lived near Bosham. Worked in a greenhouse that grew chrysanths. You going in?'

'Of course, she's going in,' Henry said. 'Why d'you think we've come here?'

Mrs Tribe ignored him. 'Your first time?'

Margaret nodded.

'You come with me then, dear. Boyfriend?'

'Husband.'

'That's nice. Not many young mothers have husbands these days.'

The two of them made their way towards the great wooden doors of the prison where the other visitors were waiting.

12

'Dr Melville's in court today, Billy, and he asked me to go on with your assessment. Are you agreeable?'

They were in Anne's room. Billy Sweete had been brought over from the remand wing by Les and had the same deferential air about him as last time. This puzzled her, for by his own account and by the few remarks passed by his grandmother, his attitude to life was quite the opposite.

'Yeah. Sure.'

He was dressed in jeans with rolled up bottoms, a check shirt and brown leather bomber jacket.

'Would you like some coffee?' Anne said. 'I've only just made it.'

She gave him a mug.

'I'd like to go back to the last interview and pick up a couple of points.'

She was looking down at Tom's notes. She was aware that doctors held all the championship points for illegibility but she had never seen anything like this. For all she could decipher it might have been written in Glagol or cuneiform. Fortunately she had made sketchy notes herself.

'Is Dr Melville not coming in, then?'

'Not today.'

'Oh.'

This seemed to mark a change in him. He leaned back in the chair and looked round at the green walls, the newly-painted shelves, the glass coffee filter on its white stand, the books, the rug.

'Nice,' he said.

'Thank you.'

'Don't usually see places like this in the nick.'

It was said in a chatty, person-to-person style.

'I'd like to go back to something Dr Melville said, about you burning down barns.'

'Yeah.'

'Because they contained straw and that made them burn better.'

'And hay.'

'Right. And you said you started when you were fifteen.'

'I burned an old car. It was in a field on the farm. Been there for years. I put some petrol in the tank and lit it.'

'I thought that would make it explode?'

His face broke into a crooked smile. 'I used a fuse.'

'Did anyone report it?'

'You ain't going to the police if something happens to something you don't want.'

'Then there was a barn?'

'Yeah.' He took out the makings, rolled a cigarette and lit it. As he did so he looked over the flame as if challenging her to make him put it out. He hadn't smoked during his first interview.

'Tell me about it.'

'It was on the farm.'

'Mr Gillis's farm?'

'Yeah.'

'Why?'

'I felt like it.'

'Just out of the blue?'

'Yeah.'

'Don't you think that was a strange thing to do?'

Sudden apprehension flashed across his face. 'What d'you mean?'

'Well, you had no motive, did you?'

'I dunno about that.'

'What had happened before that? Can you remember?'

He paused. 'I'd been with Mr Gillis.'

'Had that been one of the times—'

'Yeah.' He stared at her, waiting.

'And afterwards you went and burned down his barn.'

'That's right.'

'And you felt better?'

'Yeah.'

'Do you think he knew it was you?'

'Yeah. He could smell the petrol on me.'

'Did he go to the police?'

'Couldn't, could he? Otherwise I'd have told what he done to me.'

'So you felt better when you burned down the barn. In what way? Getting back at Mr Gillis?'

'Yeah. I felt relaxed.'

'The fire caused you to feel relaxed?'

'Yeah. The fire.'

'What was it about the fire?'

'The warmth.'

'Anything else?'

'The flames.'

'What about the flames?'

'They sort of . . . excited me. I mean you got a barn full of stuff. Terrific flames. So then I comes.

'But you'd have to be at the barn to light the fire.'

''Course I was there. That's where I comes.'

At first she thought this was some form of rural vernacular which she had not come across before.

'It relaxes me, see.'

'I'm not sure I'm following you, Billy. You came to the barn, lit the straw—'

'It was hay.'

'Okay, hay. You lit the hay and you enjoyed the warmth and the flames and they excited you. And you relaxed.'

'Yeah.'

A thought pieced itself together in her mind.

'I'm sorry if I've mistaken you, Billy, but do you mean an ejaculation? That sort of coming?'

He looked down at the cigarette.

'That sort?' she repeated.

'Yeah. That sort.'

'You mean the fire caused you to become so excited you had an ejaculation?'

'I did it to myself.'

'You masturbated?'

'Yeah. Like I said.'

'Was that the same with all the other fires? You lit them

and then masturbated? Is that why you set fire to your cell?'

He did not respond for a moment and she thought she'd gone too far. Then he said, 'I didn't set fire to the cell. I wasn't even in it.'

He pinched the glowing tip of his cigarette with his fingers and put the butt into his tin.

'Let's go back a bit, Billy.'

'I didn't set fire to no cell.'

'Okay, I believe you.'

'Well, why accuse me then? It's a serious thing accusing a bloke of setting alight his cell.'

'I didn't accuse you. I asked a question.'

'Yeah, but you don't believe me. I can tell.'

'I do, Billy. I believe you.'

He was wrong-footing her and she knew it.

'You believed me, you wouldn't ask a question like that.'

'Billy, I've only got your best interest in mind. If I upset you then I'm sorry but if you went to Granton you'd get a lot worse than that. They really put you through it. I mean the others in the unit. They make you face up to what you've done and why you did it. Do you understand that?'

'Yeah. It's just that you was trying to trap me and that's a liberty.'

'I wasn't trying to trap you. You can believe that or not as you like. Now let's get back. You went to Loxton Special Hospital last time for lighting fires. But you never said anything about the reason for lighting them.'

''Cause nobody asked. Nobody cared. All they wanted

was to get rid of me. Let someone else take the responsibility.'

'So now you're talking about it because—'

'Because I don't want to go back to Loxton.'

'You're giving us reasons for your behaviour?'

'Yeah.'

'So you'll be sent to Granton?'

'Yeah.'

'Right.' She made a note. 'Last time you were here you told us you didn't have any school friends. Were you a solitary child?'

'Suppose so.'

'And on the farm, the only company you had was your grannie and Mr Gillis?'

'Yeah.'

'Have you ever had sex with a woman?'

'No.'

'With a man?'

'You mean am I a bender? No. They had sex with me but I had no choice, see?'

'Ever had a girlfriend?'

'No.'

She closed the file. 'If you had your choice of how things would go, how would you choose?'

'About the future?'

'Yes.'

'Go to Granton for a couple of years. Get better. Then get a job.'

'What kind of job?'

'Any kind.'

'And then?'

'Buy a cottage. And—' he paused dreamily.

'And what?'

'Not be bothered.'

She smiled. 'A cottage in the country and not be bothered. That would be nice, wouldn't it?'

The house was freezing.

'The stove's gone out,' Margaret said. 'It's always going out.'

These were almost the first words she had spoken to Henry since he had watched her come through the big wooden doors of the prison after her visit to Jason. Clutching the baby in her arms she had looked like some waif in a painting by Holman Hunt. She was lost and bewildered and sad and her eyes were swollen from crying. On the drive back to Leckington he had waited for her to tell him about the visit, but she hadn't.

'Have you got any other form of heating?' he asked.

'No.'

'What do you usually do when the stove goes out?'

'Get into bed and take Julie with me.'

'Good God. Well, we can't have that. How do you start the bloody thing?'

'With wood. When that's alight you put on coke.'

He looked at his watch. 'I'm supposed to be picking up my granddaughter in half an hour. Where's the phone?'

'In the hall. It's unplugged.'

He pushed it back into the jack and phoned Anne. When he returned to the kitchen/living-room Margaret, with Julie in her arms, was still standing where he'd left her. It crossed his mind that if he didn't get things done she would go on standing there until she dropped.

Thinking that talking might help, he said, 'I knew someone in Africa who could do this sort of thing. Knew all about cooking too. Could knock you up a three-course dinner on a dung fire in no time.' He went down on his knees and lit the kindling. Margaret did not respond. 'Are you just going to stand there?' He was becoming irritated.

'I'm cold.'

'Go and put some more clothes on. *Do* something. Make some tea, I'm as dry as the Kalahari.'

He spent the next few minutes crouched in front of the stove blowing on the coke and cursing.

'How do you like your tea?'

'Strong. Two sugars.'

'That's how my father took his.'

The baby was sleeping and Margaret put her down. She and Henry pulled chairs up to the stove until they were almost touching it. Gradually the large cast-iron structure began to heat up.

'Are you going to tell me about your visit or are we going to sit here looking at the stove?' Henry said.

He had decided he could not leave her in her present mood; somehow he had to get her brain moving again. She was like one of his cars that needed pushing before it started.

'He cried,' she said.

'I don't blame him.'

'So did I. A lot of the visitors cried.' She sipped her tea. 'Sad people. A big, sad room. You can feel it in the air. Even the furniture seems sad.'

'What did you talk about?'

'Money. Julie. The new baby. He was upset that I hadn't been before.'

'My daughter told me he'd hit you.'

She touched her cheek. 'Afterwards he said he was sorry. He said he hadn't meant it. But he said that every time.'

'I didn't know there had been other times. Did you tell Anne about them?'

'No.'

'Often?'

'No, not often. He never used to when we were first married. But since he lost his job he's . . . you just can't say anything to him without him losing his temper.'

'When did he lose his job?'

'About six months ago. He'd been taken on by a sports equipment manufacturer after the Lloyds crash. In the marketing department. They were supposed to be supplying gear to clubs and leisure centres. He hated it. When they told him about it it sounded as though he'd be in an advisory capacity. But it was just a salesman's job. They thought with his name he'd be able to sell heaps of equipment. They even gave him a car. But he hardly used it after the first few weeks. Instead he'd just stay at home watching tv. I used to say, Jason for God's sake how're you going to sell anything if you sit in front of the television all day? Sometimes he'd watch a programme in the evening that he'd seen in the morning. He became a kind of zombie. I thought he was doing drugs but he wasn't. TV was his drug. He'd watch from breakfast time right through the day until long after I'd gone to bed at night.'

'Humiliation can become a kind of illness,' Henry said. 'I think I can understand it.'

'I can understand it too, but it's different if you live with someone and you haven't any money except the handouts from Social Security.'

'So you nagged him to get a job?'

'Why do you say nagged? Of course he had to get a job. We had a baby coming.'

'All right, erase the word nagged. Told him to. Suggested. Is that better? But the point is did you "suggest" often?'

'I suppose so.'

'Was that when he struck you? When you *suggested* that he go out and look for a job?'

She nodded.

'And did it work? Did he go out more often?'

'Yes, after a bit. At first I thought he'd come to his senses. But then I suppose all he was doing was trying to get away from me. So, you see, the village is right. *I* caused him to go out and rape. Isn't that what you'd like me to say?'

'Not at all. I'm trying to understand both of you. I don't subscribe to any form of violence, but there are times when it's understandable.'

'I thought you'd take his side. Being a man.'

'Oh, for God's sake let's not trot out tired old attitudes. Don't you think you could have shown him a little more understanding? After all he was looking into the abyss. Famous tennis player five years before. Now a nobody. It's enough to make anyone subject to aberrant behaviour.'

'Raping a seventeen-year-old is aberrant? Is that the word?'

'There you go again. He isn't even charged with rape but with—'

'What if he had done something worse than rape?'

The question dropped into the still air of the gloomy room like a primed bomb waiting for acknowledgement before exploding.

'What is that supposed to mean?'

She did not respond.

'What did you mean by that, Margaret?' He spoke carefully. For a moment he felt himself back in a courtroom questioning a witness. 'If you mean you really know something else that Jason's done then you'd better tell me. I haven't practised in this country but I know enough about criminal law to advise you on the next step.'

She shook her head. 'I shouldn't have said anything.'

'But you have, and you can't leave it there. A crime worse than attempted rape, you said. You've got to tell someone. The police preferably. Or his lawyer. Or me.'

She lit her umpteenth cigarette. 'It's difficult.'

'Of course it's difficult. No one said life was easy. Try.'

'I tell myself it was because . . . because I'm pregnant. Look . . . I'm not very good at this.'

'That's because I remind you of your father. I'm flattered, but young women can't talk to their fathers about intimate details. So don't think of me like that. Think of me as a lawyer; which I am.'

'Well . . . some women when they're pregnant . . . they can still make love to their husbands and some can't. I couldn't.'

'My ex-wife was like you. Not only when she was pregnant, but most of the time.'

'Really?' there was a flash of interest and mutual understanding.

'And it finally led to divorce. You're not unique, you see.'

'I knew that Jason was unhappy about that side of things and one evening I found him in the bath with Julie.'

'And?'

'Well . . . he'd never done that before . . .'

'AND?'

'Isn't that enough?'

'Good God, no.'

'I mean he was naked and he was rubbing her and she was using the soap on him and—' she broke off.

'He's her father. Why shouldn't he take her into his bath? Out in the bush I often took Anne into my bath. It was a canvas affair and there was usually only enough warm water for one bath. Doesn't mean to say I molested her.'

'But you've read the papers! There's child abuse all over the place.'

'Oh, yes, I've read them. And so has everyone else. Let me tell you something. Not long ago I was in Oxford Street and I found a little girl lost near Selfridges. She was about the same age as Hilly, my granddaughter. Crying her eyes out. And people were just walking past. Forty years ago I would have taken her by the hand and walked her along the street and gone into shops looking for her parents. But not now. Now, I stopped the first middle-aged woman who passed and told her what had happened and asked her to come with me to the manager of Selfridges and we handed the child over and God knows if she ever found her mother and father. That's what the hysteria has done. It's made all men feel apprehensive about being seen with small children not their own.'

'But you don't understand.'

'I'm trying to.'

'It was just about the time the two little kids went missing.'

'What missing children?' Anne said.

Henry drew on his pipe, thought about dropping the match on the floor next to his chair, caught Anne's eye and stuffed it back into the matchbox.

'What did she mean?'

'Apparently two little girls have gone missing.'

'Here? In Kingstown?'

'One in the city, one in the countryside.'

'When?'

'In the past few months. At least that's what she says. The baby started yelling for its feed about then so I wasn't able to get the whole thing sorted out.'

It was evening and they were in Henry's flat.

'Excuse me a moment.' Anne went upstairs, looked in on Hilly's sleeping form, then checked that the windows and doors were locked. When she returned, she said, 'Just disappeared?'

'That's as I understand it.'

'And Jason? Why . . . I mean, what does she think he has to do with it?'

'Both times Jason had left home without explanation. The first time he had come back very late. The second he'd been away the whole night and come home the following day.'

'My God, what a thing to have in your mind! I mean about your husband.'

'I should think it's certainly nonsense. She looks ill to me. Thin as a snake. She's probably a neurotic at the best of times but now with this business of Newman's ... well, it might have tipped her over the edge.'

'She didn't strike me as neurotic, but I didn't have as long with her as you.'

'It started with Newman taking the baby into the bath with him.' He repeated what Margaret had told him.

'Is that all she has to go on?'

'You don't need much if you're like her. In her mind she's already got the whole village hating her. I told her it was nonsense. You remember the canvas bath in the bush don't you? Watch pouring water over us?'

'No.'

'I suppose you were too tiny. But lots of fathers take their babies into—'

'The little old man!'

'What little old man?'

'The one at the tennis courts. The one with the dog. That's what he must have meant.'

'Stop being opaque.'

'It was when you and Hilly were flying the kite. He said I should be careful of her. Something like that. Then he said, *specially after what's happened*. I didn't register it at the time but that's what he must have meant: that I should be careful of Hilly because of the two kids who had disappeared. And the school! No wonder they were worried when you arrived to fetch her.'

He saw that her eyes were filled with unease.

'Bosh and piffle.' He sucked noisily at his pipe. 'You're getting yourself into a state for nothing.'

13

The lane ended in mud, but deep tracks filled with
rainwater continued through an open gate. Anne guided
her small car across this morass. The tracks disappeared
into a hanger of beech trees all now in glowing autumn
colours. On either side of her was a jungle of blackberry
bushes. She crossed a small stream on a rickety wooden
bridge and almost immediately saw the house.

It was a strange place to find hidden away in the Sussex
Downs. There was no formal garden just rough lawn with
half a dozen apple trees, heavy with fruit.

The house was a beautiful wooden chalet, clearly built a
long time ago, and Anne thought it would have looked
more natural in Austria or Bavaria. Outside was parked an
elderly Land Rover. She stopped on the weed-covered
drive and went up the steps to the wide verandah. The front
door was half open and she heard a voice shouting from
within.

'Up! Up! Come on, get up!'

It was Tom's voice.

'Come on darling, GET UP!'

She was about to knock on the door but this last order
caused her to drop her hand. She had turned away when a

153

voice behind her said, 'What d'you want?' A man was regarding her with frankly hostile eyes. He was middle-aged with thick grey hair that stuck out from under a deerstalker. He wore a waxed coat, carried a game bag over one shoulder and in his right hand held a shotgun. His accent was rich and rural.

'I came to see Dr Melville.'

'Is he expecting you?'

'Yes he is.' Her voice was brisk.

He passed her and went into the house. 'Tommy!' he shouted. 'There's someone come to see you.'

There was a shouted colloquy between the two men and the grey-haired man came back to the door and said, 'Are you Dr Vernon?'

'Yes.'

'Tommy says go up.'

The ground floor was one huge room, its walls faced with tongue-and-groove pine panelling which had become honey-coloured with age. She stopped at the foot of a wooden staircase.

'I'm up here,' Tom's voice called.

She went up and found a bathroom at the top of the stairs. It was a large square room. A long old-fashioned cast-iron bath on ball-and-claw feet stood against one wall. Tom, a towel round his waist, was on his knees beside the bath. In the bath itself, in six inches of warm water, was a small black-and-tan dachshund. She was looking up with huge appealing eyes.

'Come on! Up! Up!'

It was only then Anne saw that the back legs were paralysed.

He said, 'You go down to the other end of the bath.' He handed her several pieces of Ryvita. 'Give her a piece when she gets to your end. I hope Joyce didn't frighten you.'

'Joyce?' She was bewildered. 'I thought she was a he.'

He laughed. 'Harry Joyce.'

He took the dog to the opposite end of the bath and raised her onto her back legs. 'Come on. Up! She can if she wants to, she just finds it easier to drag her legs behind her. Show her a biscuit.'

He put his hands into the water and moved the dog's back legs, forcing her to walk down the bath. When she arrived Anne gave her a small piece of biscuit. Tom picked her up, put her back at the other end, and said to the dog, 'Come on now, try it on your own, you lazy hound.'

But the back legs buckled under her and she began to pull herself through the water.

'What's her name?' Anne said.

'Beanie, because she used to sleep in a baked-bean box, but I'm thinking of renaming her tadpole. Her legs look like the tail of a tadpole when she pulls herself along.' He worked her legs again as Beanie moved down the bath to get the food. 'She's a greedy little thing, that's why I have to give her slimming biscuits. Otherwise she'd put on weight.'

'What happened?'

'She . . .' He hesitated. 'She had an accident.'

'Poor little thing.'

'She doesn't think she's a poor little thing.'

155

'How long has she been like this?'

'Three months. Okay, that's enough.' He scooped Beanie from the bath, wrapped the shivering body in a towel, and said to Anne, 'Come downstairs and we'll find a drink.'

On the ground floor he waved her to a large armchair. Still clutching the dog he went off to find a bottle and glasses.

She looked round. The kitchen, with a dining table and chairs, was on the left side of the front door, and on the right, the living-room, where she was sitting. There were no lights on and the place had a chilly look and a chilly feel.

The furniture looked like a job lot bought at a car boot sale and reminded her of her father's cottage at the Cape of Good Hope: functional but lacking warmth. Once, when she had mentioned it to Henry, he had said, 'Men without women always live like this.'

She itched to get her hands on these beautiful old rooms. Soft-tone lighting like that of oil-lamps, with curtains and rugs in warm reds and yellows, would go a long way, she thought, to give the place the cosiness it lacked.

He came back with a bottle of white wine and glasses. Then he spread a towel on his lap and sat Beanie on top of it. He began to work gently on her back legs, pressing down and making her resist. 'She's got more steroids in her than Ben Johnson,' he said. 'And her muscle tone's pretty good. She's just not making the connection. But – to work. Is everything all right at the nick?'

'It's been pretty hectic but Dr Robbins has been a Godsend.'

'Oh, he knows the ropes.'

Dr Robbins was a local practitioner who did freelance prison work and was now filling Tom's shoes while he attended court.

She gave him a rundown on what had been happening and finally came to Billy Sweete.

'Well, that's certainly new,' he said.

'You still don't trust him? Why would he lie about something as intimate as that?'

'So he wouldn't be sent to Loxton.' He worked in silence for a few moments on Beanie's legs. 'Trust? I'm not even sure what that word means any more.'

She waited for him to expand on that but he didn't. She said, 'I suppose we have to trust some of the prisoners some of the time otherwise they'd all be in Loxton.'

'Arson followed by sexual release isn't uncommon, you know. But just uncommon enough. What was it Kipling wrote: the something of the something excites the tiger?'

'The bleating of the kid excites the tiger.'

'*Soldiers Three*?'

'*Stalky and Co*. My father read it over and over to me when I was tiny.'

'I'd like to meet your father some time.'

She smiled but did not comment. Instead she said, 'The interesting thing is that he didn't immediately link fire and sexual excitement. When I asked him why he set the barns alight he said he did it because of the warmth.'

He frowned. 'Sorry, I'm being obtuse. Were all the fires set in winter?'

'No, no—'

'Oh, I get it. You mean—'

'Well, his father deserted the family when he was tiny. His mother died not much later. Wouldn't that indicate a lack of parental warmth?'

'That's very good. Right, well, we'll dig a little deeper into friend Sweete.'

'I thought I'd go to see his grandmother.'

'Why not? But have you got the time?'

'I think so.'

'What about Newman?'

She opened her mouth then closed it. 'I got my father to give his wife a lift to the prison. She doesn't drive.'

He looked at her as though sensing she was keeping something back, then he shrugged and said, 'Don't overdo things. You'll make it difficult for the rest of us to keep up with you.'

That phrase was in her mind as she drove away from the house. It had sounded just a little sharp-edged.

Her thoughts were abruptly shattered. As she slowed down to manoeuvre the car through the gate a dark figure loomed up from the blackberry thicket. It was Joyce, the man with the shotgun. He placed himself in front of the car so that she had to pull up.

'Would you mind!' she said, through the open window.

He came up to her. 'You're with Tommy at the prison ain't you?'

'That's right, but I don't see that it's—'

'You be careful when you comes 'ere. You follow me?'

'What on earth—?'

But he had turned away and, in the half light, was gone in a matter of seconds.

When she reached Kingstown, the lonely house, the man

with the shotgun, the crippled dog, even Tom Melville, all seemed to be invested with an air of menace and it was with a troubled mind that she locked the car and entered the house.

It was dark and still. This, in her present mood, made her feel anxious.

'I'm home!'

All she heard was the silence. She switched on the lights and went into the kitchen. On the blackboard which she used for shopping lists was scrawled: HILLY AND I HAVE GONE SHOPPING THEN TO THE LIBRARY WHAT'SHISNAME PHONED.

She found a slice of cold pizza in the fridge and ate it while she dialled Clive's number. She was surprised when she heard his voice.

'Don't tell me business is bad,' she said.

'I don't get you.'

'You're hardly ever in to answer the phone.'

'I'm just on my way—'

'To a meeting.'

'If I didn't go to these meetings I wouldn't be able to afford my flash pad or the gin palace I'm going to buy. And you won't call it a gin palace when I sail over to France without you.'

'Have you ever sailed before?'

'No.'

'Then maybe I'll be pleased to be left behind.'

'Listen, my mother would like us to come for lunch at the weekend. You haven't been for weeks. I think she thinks you don't want to see her.'

'I've had other things on my mind, you know.'

'Of course you have and I've told her that. I just think it would be a nice thing to do. We could go a little early and get away by half past two and—' He paused meaningfully.

'That's a bit clinical, isn't it?'

'We have to plan these things. It's just a fact of life.'

'*You* have to.'

'No, we both have to. I'm busy and you're busy and unless we organise we'll never get together.'

'It doesn't sound very romantic though, does it?'

'Romantic! It's not as though we're in the first flush of youth. And with you living down in Sussex and me in London ... I mean, be reasonable. We've *got* to make arrangements.'

'I suppose we do. But it can't be this Sunday. I'm on duty.'

'Oh shit, I knew this sort of thing would happen if you went into the civil service!'

'If I was in general practice or on a hospital staff I'd only get one Sunday off in two or three.'

'Not if you married me and came to live here. You could have a practice among the locals. Pick and choose. Make your own hours. Be in charge of your own life.'

'A private practice?'

'Of course. There's enough money here to make you—'

'You don't understand. If I just wanted money I wouldn't have gone into medicine. Anyway, I don't want to spend all my time treating wealthy patients for hypertension brought on by too much rich food and too much booze.'

'You're a reverse snob, you know. Don't you believe that rich people are entitled to health care?'

'I've got to go, Clive, Hilly and my father are coming back in a minute and I want to make them some supper.'

'Was that your father on the phone when I called?'

'Of course it was, you didn't think it was Hilly, did you? Why?'

'He was bloody rude. I asked him to give you a message and he sounded reluctant. And then he said he was busy. And then he said what did I think of America. I mean what sort of question is that? And when I said I didn't know what he meant he put the phone down.'

'I'll talk to him about it.'

'Wow-eeeee . . . Sniff . . . Sniff . . .'

They were in the exercise yard. Jason tried to move away from him but Billy Sweete followed. It was a grey autumn day and above them the anti-helicopter wires hummed and clattered in a cold northwesterly.

'Smell it!'

Jason, hands in pockets, moved against a wall out of the wind. Sweete shoved up next to him and lit a rollup.

'That's your real fresh air – diesel. It's them lorries going up the hill. Grinding away, blowing out the fumes. That's freedom that is. Don't you like it?'

'No.' Jason began to move away again.

'No? Doesn't like it? Take him away, nurse, and put the boot in.'

'How'd you know, anyway?'

'How do I know? 'Cause my father was a truck driver, that's how.'

'You said he left you when you were small.'

'And so he did, old cock, so he did. But it's in the blood. Oh, yes. In the blood.'

They walked on, heads bowed to the wind. The diesel smell was mixed now with the smell of cabbage and washing-up water venting from the prison kitchens.

'You ever seen blood, Jason? I don't mean frigging scratches on your knees when you fall on the tennis court, I mean real blood . . . running blood . . .'

The eye . . . the eye . . .

'. . . running so hard you can't stop it. Let me tell you old bean, it's something amazing. I seen it at Loxton – where you're probably going. Bloke by the name of Pinker cut his throat. He was talking to me. Having a rap. Telling me about his haemorrhoids. And then he takes out this razor blade, and while he's talking, while he's telling me how sore his backside is, he cuts the side of his neck and whoosh!'

Jason remembers the eye . . .

'All over my clothes. Couldn't stop it. Dead in twelve minutes.'

'I don't want to hear.'

'Don't kid me, Jason Tennisplayer. Everybody likes to hear things like that.'

'I'm going in.'

'Listen, listen, I ain't finished yet . . . I'm trying to do you a favour, prepare you for Loxton. You'll thank me one day. Let me tell you. There was a bloke called Napp. Name like that. And he has this habit of throwing his food off his plate. Knows it's wrong but can't stop himself. I mean that's why he's there in the first place because he's a fucking loony, okay? And so they tell him to stop it but he can't, see? And he does it again and the screws – oh, yeah, they call 'em screws in Loxton, not nurses – the screws hold him down and sit on him and make him eat it off the floor, only they're sitting on him so hard they break his foot. That's Loxton, Sonny Jim.'

'For Christ's sake, stop it! I'M NOT GOING TO LOXTON. They said so.'

'Who said so? The new woman quack? What does she know?' He smiled reminiscently. 'She asked me about the fires and what happened and I told her. She wasn't expecting that.'

'What?'

'What I told her.'

'What?'

'That's for me to know and you to find out.'

Jason turned away and heard Sweete's laughter.

When he went back to his cell he lay on his bunk and his thoughts were of blood. Was there something wrong with him? Truly wrong? So wrong that they'd send him to Loxton?

He tried to sleep, but all he saw was the eye.

14

'Mummy! Mummy! We've been to the library.'

Hilly burst into the house, turning it abruptly from a cold and depressing place into a home full of warmth. Anne's bleak mood vanished. She gathered her daughter up and gave her a fierce hug.

'What's that?' Hilly pointed to the stove.

'Spaghetti.'

The front door slammed and Henry came in. He was carrying his briefcase.

'The library?' Anne said. 'Have you joined?'

'Grandpa watched tv.'

'That's a funny place to watch it.' Anne began to lay the table. She turned to Henry. 'Do you want a drink before we eat?'

'Does the sun rise in the east?'

He poured himself a whisky and soda and sat down at the kitchen table.

'Up you go,' Anne said to Hilly. 'Hands and face.' Then to her father. 'Is that what you've been doing all afternoon? Watching television?'

'Not quite.'

'I thought not.'

'Have you heard of the *Times Index*?'

'No.'

'You see I'm not completely past it. It's in several hundred volumes and goes back to the first edition in God knows when. Eighteenth century, I think. It's kept by only the largest reference libraries, and Kingstown library is one. The volumes are cross-referenced and once you find the date and issue containing what you want you can ask for the microfilm and bring up the pages on a reading machine.'

'No wonder Hilly thought you were watching tv.'

'I thought I'd try to look up the missing children Margaret Newman mentioned. No luck. They're too recent for the *Index*. But when I mentioned this the librarian said they kept *The Times* on file and also, bless them, the *Kingstown Argus*.' He opened his briefcase. 'Have you ever heard me deprecate modern science?'

'Deprecate would be putting it mildly.'

'In this instance allow me to praise it. The library has a photocopying machine and voilà ...' He handed her several sheets of paper on which he had copied news stories.

The first, from the *Kingstown Argus*, read:

CHOC-ICE TODDLER MISSING ON CASTLE FIELDS
BIG POLICE SEARCH

A five-year-old child is missing after her mother left her for a few minutes to buy her an ice-cream.

Mrs Carol Marsh, 28, of the Prendergast Estate, Kingstown, said she had taken her daughter, Tessa, to

Castle Fields today so she could have a dolls' picnic by the river.

They were leaving when they saw an ice-cream van parked near the Castle gate.

Mrs Marsh said Tessa had asked if she could have a chocolate ice-cream.

'It was a warm day and I decided to have one too,' she said. 'Tessa couldn't push her dolly's pram up the steep slope so I told her to wait on the path. When I came back a few moments later she was gone.'

Mrs Marsh's mother has come to take care of her in her council flat and both women were too distressed to answer further questions.

Inspector Rodney Davis, of the Kingstown Police, said, 'As yet we have formed no conclusion as to what might have happened.

'The undergrowth and woods below the Castle are thick and little Tessa may have left the contour path to meet her mother and become lost.'

He said he had ordered a full-scale search of the area and the use of sniffer dogs.

Tessa has dark hair, is small for her age, and was wearing a green polo-shirt and black jeans.

Anyone who might have seen her or who has any information should phone the Kingstown police.

This story was followed up the following day with one headed: CHOC-ICE TODDLER'S PRAM FOUND.

Anne read the story quickly, but the discovery of the pram in thick undergrowth below the contour path was the only new aspect of the case.

During the following weeks in late summer there were other stories but they followed an all too familiar contemporary pattern and the headings told Anne all she needed to know.

'Anguished mother makes tv appeal in missing toddler case ... House-to-house search of Prendergast Estate yields nothing new ... Police interview toddler's father in Yorkshire ... Tessa's dad blames ex-wife for neglect ... "We fear worst" says police chief ...'

Then nothing.

Anne said to her father, 'Castle Fields ... that must be where we went to fly the kite. I didn't know it had a name.'

She heard Hilly in the bathroom upstairs and hastily read the case of the second child. The headings were generically similar, the circumstances different.

Again, it was a little girl. This time two years older, called Sharon. She had gone to her local village shop to fetch a video her father had ordered. To get there she had had to cross a field. She was seen in the shop where she had picked up the video and bought a Mars Bar.

She had never returned home; had never been seen again; nothing had been found; there were no clues – not even disturbed grass to indicate a struggle.

Henry said, 'It seems that more than fifteen thousand children go missing in Europe each year. Some, of course, have got lost or run away. But a high proportion vanish without trace into paedophile rings or are sold into prostitution.'

'Or are murdered.'

'Yes. Or are murdered.'

* * *

'Busy?' Tom Melville said.

Anne was at her desk writing a report and he appeared in the doorway. She smiled and said, 'I don't know. I haven't got the time to figure it out.'

'At least it's better than being bored. I can't stand that.'

'I didn't expect you back from court today.'

'We finished early. It seems you're going to be busy for some time longer. I've had a call from Jack Symes. He's having what he calls a domestic problem. His marriage has been rocky for some time. He's taking some leave to try and sort things out. Robbins will help out and so will his partner. Even so you're going to be kept on your toes.'

'Baptism of fire.'

'That's about it.'

'Would you like a cup of tea?'

'Coffee, if you have any. I need my caffeine. I could hardly keep awake in court.'

She was feeling tired herself. Although it had been little more than a week since her arrival it seemed much longer. Kingstown gaol had become part of her world, and her domestic life had fallen into a routine. She had always said to Paul that she never wanted to get into a rut, but she was in one now.

Faithfully, as though trained by Watch, her father brought her a cup of strong tea at six o'clock in the morning – he had already been up for an hour and was full of energy.

Then breakfast. Fortunately he no longer gave them a cooked breakfast – it had taken large-scale wastage to make him change his mind about that – and Anne and Hilly now approached the table less apprehensively.

Then there was Hilly to get ready for school and the domestic rituals to be planned with her father; reminders to be written down and arguments to be settled about a host of things with both of them.

There had been one or two mornings recently when she had stepped through the great prison doors with a sense of relief.

She gave Tom a mug of coffee and said, 'How's Beanie?'

'She's all right. I'll get her walking again.'

'What happens to her when you're at work?'

'Joyce looks after her.' He walked over to the window and stood sipping his coffee. There was a brooding expression on his face. 'You want to say to her *try*. You want her to want it so much that she uses those back legs to force herself up.' She heard real distress in his voice. 'But all you can do is try for her.' He swung round. 'How's the great tennis player getting on?'

She told him what her father had discovered. He began his regular pacing and Anne had a quick look around the room to see that nothing was in his way or in danger of being knocked over.

'Did she offer any evidence at all that he was abusing his baby?' Tom asked.

'Absolutely not.'

'So there's no need to rush to the social services?'

'I wouldn't have thought so for a moment.'

'Thank God. That's all we need. After the Cleveland and Orkneys debacles the social services are the last people I want paddling about in this.'

Les Foley put his dimpled face round the door. 'Excuse

me, Dr Vernon, but you asked about Mrs Tribe. She's been visiting her grandson; she's just leaving now.'

Anne excused herself and hurried to the front gate, but she was too late; Mrs Tribe had just left. She asked the officer at the traffic barrier and he pointed down the hill. 'Is that her, doc?'

Anne recognised the long coat and the scarf round her head.

'Mrs Tribe!'

She caught up with her halfway down the hill that led into the city.

'Do you remember me?'

''Course I do, doctor.'

'I wanted to ask you some questions about your grandson.'

'Well, you see, I—'

'It's just that I need some information to help him.'

'Trouble is, doctor, I got to get back. Old Mr Gillis, he has his – Stop! Stop!' She waved her arm wildly. There was a whoosh of air, and a large bus passed them and disappeared down the hill.

'Rotten sod! And me practically at the stop.'

'That's my fault,' Anne said. 'I made you miss it. When is the next one?'

'The next one? To Sheepwalk? There ain't a next one till tomorrow.' Her face was registering panic and distress.

'I really am very sorry.'

'He wants his supper, see. He likes to eat early. Always has done.'

'How far is Sheepwalk?'

'Far enough. I ain't got the money for a taxi.'

'Let me drive you. We can talk on the way.'

But they had no opportunity for talking. Sheepwalk was ten miles from Kingstown and reached mainly by winding lanes. Their talk consisted of Mrs Tribe saying, 'Go left here, doctor. And left again. Now right, and across the junction. And a left here. And then right . . .'

The lanes with their high hedges became increasingly narrow and more winding as they went deeper and deeper into the Downs. They passed villages with names Anne had never heard of, ancient Saxon names, dating from the time when this part of England was covered by the Great Forest and inhabited only by charcoal burners and criminals. They were not picturesque hamlets of thatched cottages, village greens and duck ponds, but secretive places where, in the autumn dusk, curtains were already drawn and doors barred; smelly places where slurry ran across the road and everything was slippery with mud.

Sheepwalk was dark and dreary and from there they made for a small valley, not much more than a fold in the Downs, and reached a series of stone farm buildings. An almost illegible sign read, 'Ridge Farm'.

The place looked abandoned. The barns were empty and the tiled roofs in ruins. Fences were broken and old tractors and rusting ploughs lay by the side of the track as though they had collapsed there and been abandoned. The farmhouse too seemed derelict. It was double-storeyed, and its walls were made of flint. Behind one of the downstairs windows Anne made out a light.

She stopped the car. The front door opened instantly and an elderly man in a long brown dust coat came out onto the gravel drive.

'Is that you, Ida?'

Ida Tribe was already halfway out of the car. 'Yes, Major.'

'D'you know it's past six o'clock!'

'I'm sorry.'

He bent down and peered into Anne's window. She saw a bony face with thick hair above it and black piercing eyes.

'Who the bloody hell are you?' he said.

'Dr Vernon. From the prison.' It was said stiffly. 'I wanted to talk to Mrs Tribe about her grandson.'

'Yes, well, never mind that.'

'It's all ready, Major. Only needs heating up.' She turned to Anne. 'Do you mind waiting, doctor, then we can go to my cottage.'

Anne sat in the car listening to the six o'clock news, trying not to let the irritation get to her. Fifteen minutes later Mrs Tribe appeared. She was agitated and apologetic. 'He's an old man now and he's used to his little ways. That's my cottage over there.'

Anne followed her to a small brick cottage. Two little rooms downstairs and a narrow rickety staircase leading, she imagined, to two more. It was like entering the nineteen thirties. The floor was of red quarry tiles. There was an old black woodburning range at one end and the furniture was fake William Morris with a bakelite radio and a gate-legged table. There was a sink and a wooden draining board on which stood a small mangle, the first she had ever seen.

'I'll just put the kettle on,' Mrs Tribe said.

'How long have you lived here?'

'A long time, doctor. I came after my husband died. Before Billy was born.'

She made the tea and gave Anne a cup.

'And you worked for Major Gillis all these years?'

'That's right, doctor.'

'I didn't realise he'd been in the army.'

'Not the real army. Only the territorials. But he likes me to call him Major.'

'I've been talking a lot to Billy,' Anne said. She was finding it more and more difficult to imagine him living in this small house.

'I hope you're going to keep him. I don't want him here no more.'

'That's just the point, Mrs Tribe. He was at Loxton last time but he doesn't want to go back there. There's a psychotherapy unit at a small prison called Granton which has been operating for ten or fifteen years with good results. He wants to go there.'

Mrs Tribe looked up in alarm. 'How long do they keep them?'

'That depends on individual cases and the length of the sentence.'

'Doctor, you seen what it's like here. It's no good him coming back. Where's he to live? The Major won't have him in the house. Doesn't want him on the farm. He says if he was to come back here I can take my notice.'

It was a kind of chain reaction, Anne thought. Was she going to have to assume responsibility for Ida Tribe's future as well as her grandson's?

'It's possible he won't go to Granton. He may have to go back to Loxton.'

'Oh, I hope so. You know, doctor, my life isn't easy. You've seen the Major. He's like that all the time. And he hates Billy.'

'Why?'

'Why? 'Cause Billy burnt down half the blessed farm, that's why.'

'Do you know why he did that?'

''Cause he's not all there.'

'Do you know how it started?'

'I used to think about that often. In them days we had the stubble burning. You can't burn stubble no more. But them days, after you'd brought in the harvest, you burnt off the stubble. I can remember Billy as a little boy saying let me light it, let me light it. Then it was a working farm. Not like now. The Major doesn't farm no more. Just a few sheep to keep his hand in. But then he had a cowman and a ploughman and Billy used to go with them when they burned the stubble. Always running near the flames. Once he burnt a crop *before* it was brought in. I'll never forget that. Whole field of standing corn. You should have seen the Major.'

'He told me he'd burnt an old car. And then he burnt a barn. You say you think he burns things because he's mentally unstable. I'm trying to find out what that instability is. There's a reason for his actions. Do you think it could be sexual?'

Mrs Tribe stared at her. 'Sexual? How do you mean sexual?'

'There are cases of men who get gratification, sexual gratification, out of lighting fires.'

'You having me on, doctor?'

'Not at all.'

'I never heard of such a thing in all my life!'

Anne changed tack abruptly. 'Did he have trouble at school?'

'Billy's always been in trouble.'

'But any particular trouble?'

'What d'you mean?'

'He told me there had been some trouble with a teacher.'

'He never told me nothing. The only trouble I remember was him being caught smoking in the lavatories with another boy. Oh, and bullying. First of all, as a little nipper, he was bullied. But then when he grew up he became the bully. And there were the animals. He hurt animals. Killed the Major's cat with a bow and arrow he made.'

'Did he have any girlfriends?'

'Not that I knew of.'

'What about jobs?'

'Jobs?' She gave a short laugh. 'He never had no proper jobs. Worked for a bookie once. And an undertaker. But mostly he just drew his benefit.'

'Getting back to the fires, Mrs Tribe. Did he ever light anything in this cottage?'

'He used to sit in front of that range there and push pieces of paper in. And he used to light that incense stuff. I used to hear his voice muttering and mumbling and carrying on. And he'd play his music very loudly. What he called his ju-ju music, whatever that means. And he'd carry a knife and show it to me and say how sharp it was. Oh God, doctor, I was so afraid.'

She paused, remembering. Then she said, 'It got so bad I slept down here. I used to tell him to stop it but he said he was worshipping the old gods; the ones in the trees and the stones. Said they'd lived here when it was all forest. Said they talked to him. I dunno where he got notions like that. Maybe out of all those books. He used to read and read.'

'What sort of books?'

'To tell you the truth, doctor, I never knew. I can't read very well. But he took them with him. Cleared them out one day. Took them to his secret place.'

'He had a secret place?'

'Just like a child, he was. A grown man with a secret place. In one of the old barns, I think. I never bothered with it. I was just thankful he was out of the house.'

'Did you mention this to the police?'

She shook her head. 'Maybe I should've. But I was all he had. His mother was dead. His father was gone. What could I do? I mean, they came to take him away for lighting the fires and I thought well, that's that. I thought, no need to go into the other things.'

'Did the Major know about the secret place in the barn?'

'He never said nothing to me about it.'

'How did he get on with the Major?'

Mrs Tribe threw up her hands. 'They hated each other.'

There was a sudden banging on the door. She gave a start and got to her feet.

'Is that you, Major?'

'You can clear away now. I've finished.'

'I'm coming.'

Anne said, 'I'll be on my way.'

Ida Tribe saw her to the car. 'Now you can see how things are,' she said in a low voice. 'Please don't send him back here.'

15

Like twelve-note music or quantum mechanics, ironing had always been one of life's mysteries to Henry Vernon. For most of the time Watch had seen to it on his behalf. Not that he had actually ever ironed anything except the starched white collars Henry had had to wear in court, but he had organised it. There was no Watch to organise it now.

Yesterday, Henry had done the washing – quite successfully, he thought, no floods on the kitchen floor – and then put everything in the tumble dryer – amazing machine. Now the ironing.

But like all tyros he had come face to face with that most intractable item of domestic furniture, the ironing board. After several vain attempts at getting it to stand upright, during which it had snapped at him and hurt a finger, he had placed it flat on the floor and cautiously studied it.

It was clearly a potential hazard and he was amazed that the British Safety Council had ever allowed such a thing to be sold to the public.

Henry was not by nature a technologist. Give him a tort or a criminal libel and he was happy as a sandboy, so he soon realised that he and the ironing board – in its present form – could not co-exist.

The problem was its instability. He went out and bought several angle brackets and, by the time Anne came home that evening, he was in his right mind and ironing.

He made a strange picture in his multi-coloured *kikoi* and his grubby dancing shoes. Exotic wasn't quite the word, she thought, but didn't know what was.

'Where's Hilly?' she said.

'Birthday party. I'm picking her up at seven.'

She tried to close the kitchen door. The ironing board moved with it.

'What's happened?' There was a note of dismay in her voice.

'Clever, isn't it?'

'Oh my God!'

'Well, the bloody thing wouldn't stay put.'

'But you've—'

'Fixed it permanently.'

'This is ridiculous!' She examined the screws and steel brackets. 'And look at the door!'

'I hoped you'd approve.' He was nettled. 'It's much more rigid than it was.'

'It sticks out into the room and I can't get to the food cupboards.'

'I admit there are some minor snags but—'

'Take it down, please.'

'I think you're wrong, you know.'

'Please!'

'As you say.'

'And you'll have to fill those screw holes with something, and repaint the door.'

'I'll get a carpenter.'

'We can't *afford* a carpenter.'

She went upstairs and lay in a bath. Make your mind a blank, she thought. Relax . . .

It had been a tough day. Tom had warned her he was throwing her in at the deep end and that was precisely how she felt. He was doing his best to help but his own time was fully taken up with producing a report on prison suicides in England and Wales for the Home Office.

He had put her on to the twice-yearly hygiene inspection.

'Normally I'd come with you and show you the ropes but I'm up to my eyeballs with these reports. Les knows all about it. Probably more than I do. He and Jeff Jenks taught me when I first came.'

She was glad to have Les, she felt comfortable with him. In a curious way the natural sexual tension between male and female seemed absent when she was with him and it helped to lower a factor which was becoming more and more obvious: stress. Although the medical staff made jokes about it to try to lower their own tension, a day in which she was constantly harassed by the prisoners ('Show us your tits, doc!') left her drained. So Les was the kind of mother-figure she appreciated.

The hygiene inspection was of the whole prison and, because of lack of time and money, had to be done in one day. She had to inspect every lavatory and detail every broken lavatory seat; she had to look at and under every washbasin, examine every extractor fan, check every water storage tank against legionnaire's disease; she had to examine the kitchens and food storage rooms for mouse droppings; she had to report every broken window. And to do all this she had to climb and descend hundreds of stairs. And there was always the worry at the back of her mind: what if she missed something?

And she had.

It had been while she was checking the lavatories in the education block. She had noticed, on the floor behind one of the lavatory pans, an empty glue pot. For some reason, perhaps by this time she was tired, she had not seen it as anything but an empty glue pot in the education block, a natural place for it. She was turning away when Les bent down, picked it up and handed it to her. Only then did she see the glass tube within.

'What is it?'

'For smoking crack.'

'Oh, God, what a thing to miss!'

He smiled at her, but the dimples didn't show so obviously and his eyes were harder.

'Unless it belongs, what the hell is it doing there? That's what you have to ask yourself, doc.'

Later, when she confessed her lapse to Tom, he had laughed and said, 'He did that to me too. It's his way of changing the way we look at the world; his world.'

'He put it there?'

'He does it to everyone once.'

Her thoughts stayed with Tom and she wondered what sort of man he really was. So far he had presented her with a series of snapshots. There was Tom the cynic; Tom the loner; Tom the uninvolved; but the man she had seen with Beanie was a different snapshot entirely. Or was that just a sublimation? Did he love animals more than people? Was he so bruised and battered by the human beings he worked with every day that he had lost whatever humanising qualities he had?

She remembered his house: the room was like its owner, uninvolved. Yet Harry Joyce, the man with the shotgun who had been so rude to her, had seemed like a self-appointed guardian, and to exert that kind of emotional pull on people you had to have something to give.

The phone rang and she heard her father answer it. Clive probably. But Henry's voice went on and on and unless he had suddenly taken a violent liking to Clive – something she discounted – it wasn't her London lover.

She dried herself, pulled on a pair of jeans and a sweatshirt and went downstairs. He was just hanging up.

'Margaret Newman,' he said.

'Why didn't you call me?'

'She didn't want to talk to you; she specifically said that. She wanted me.'

'Oh.'

He poured himself a whisky and soda.

'Well? Are you going to tell me what she said?'

'In a nutshell, she's not going to see her husband in prison any more.'

'Oh, Lord. Why?'

'Too stressful.'

'What about Jason? Doesn't she think he's stressed?'

'I think she's completely egocentric. Most mannequins are, they tell me.'

'Who told you? Watch?'

'Very amusing. Anyway, I can understand what's happening. She's by herself. Cut off in what she sees as a hostile environment . . . people hating her, etcetera . . . and no one to talk to.'

'If she spent some time with her husband she *would* have someone to talk to.'

'I told her that. But she's certain he's guilty of the attempted rape and goodness knows what else. She says he was unfaithful before. Now she feels that Julie was at risk, and the baby she's carrying is also at risk if she goes on being so stressed. People are constantly whining about being stressed these days. I don't remember being stressed when I was her age.'

Anne did not rise to that.

'Anyway, she's off to Mum.'

'Is she walking out on him for good?'

'My own experience of the justice system is that once one partner goes inside it takes a very strong relationship to survive.'

'The fact is she's abandoning him.'

'True.' He held up a piece of paper. 'But she did give me names and addresses of people who might help, so she's not totally without feelings.'

'Who?'

'Newman's grandfather, for one.'

'I told you about the letter he wrote. There won't be any help from that direction. He said as much.'

'She also gave me the address of his sister and someone called his guru. I thought that was an Indian gentleman until she told me he was also his tennis coach.'

'They all have gurus now. Coaches, psychologists, gurus, lawyers, managers, agents, publicists, and after the Seles stabbing, their own minders. Damn! I was hoping she

184

might help me get through to Jason. I was on the verge, too.'

He waved the paper. 'You could see these people.'

'*When*? I've hardly got enough time to see Hilly. Where does his sister live?'

'London.'

'How on earth am I to get to London?'

'What about me going?'

'You?'

'Why not? It doesn't matter how you get the information, does it?'

'Of course not.'

'Well then . . .'

'What about Hilly?'

'You take her to school, I pick her up. Or vice versa. It's not all that difficult. Women always make things more complicated than they need to be. I'm sure it was a woman who designed the ironing board.'

'You leave the ironing board out of this.'

'Secrets, old cock. That's the secret of it. Geddit? The secret is to have secrets. Jason? You awake, old sporty tennisplayer?'

Jason listened to the voice coming down from the upper bunk. The cell was dark, the prison restless, insomniac.

'Jason!'

'Yes.'

'You ever had secrets?'

'That's a secret.'

'He's being funny. Give him a valium, doc. I mean secret

185

things; secret places. I got secrets from you. You got secrets from me. Stands to reason.'

Far away in the distant night Jason heard the sound of a train. It brought tears to his eyes.

'I had a secret place once,' Billy said. 'Still got it for that matter, because nobody knows about it. That's the whole point of having something secret, wouldn't you say old man, old bean? So that the other frigging sods don't know. That's why you got to have another secret place – up in the old brainbox. Somewhere the bastards can't get to. Oh, yeah, they think they're so fucking clever. *They* think they can get into your skull; but *you* know they can't. Not if you got a secret place.'

Billy paused for a moment and said, 'You gone to sleep, Jason?'

'No.'

'You listening to me?'

'Yeah.'

'Okay then, let's play a game. I'll tell you a secret if you tell me one. How's that?'

'I haven't got any secrets.'

'Yes you have, you lying tennisplayer. Come on. I don't feel sleepy.'

Jason had had enough. 'For Christ's sake, why don't you shut up!'

A voice called from across the landing, 'Put a sock in it!'

Billy was up in a flash and standing at the door. 'Shut your fucking face!' he yelled. There was a surge of shouting and threats along the landing. Billy turned away from the door. 'That'll teach the sods.'

He sat down on the edge of Jason's bunk. 'You want me

to stay down here with you? Keep you company for a little while?'

His hand touched Jason's leg. Jason pulled it away. 'I'll break your arm.'

'Is that what you said to her?'

'Who?'

'The kid you raped, old pal. Take your knickers off or I'll break your arm.'

Jason didn't reply and Billy climbed up into his bunk. He was laughing softly.

People did have secrets. The eye was a secret; his secret; only he really knew what had happened.

That had been the watershed. If it hadn't happened his life would have been different. He wouldn't have been in this cell with Billy Sweete.

But it had happened.

All because his father put a tiger in his tank. That was Lajos's phrase; the old Esso ad. He loved it.

I put a tiger in your tank. You too nice. You too soft.

I put in killer instinct.

That was another phrase he'd used.

For God's sake, Lajos, his mother had said, you're turning him into a monster.

But Lajos no longer bothered to insult her. His silence, his indifference, did more damage. If he wanted to be specially kind to her he spoke to her. Even lines like, 'Why you no go and get pissed?' were better than silence.

A tiger in your tank. Killer instinct. Go for jugular. Kill him.

He had heard those shouted phrases on the practice court; even from the sidelines of the major stadia where his father had been warned a hundred times for coaching.

Come on, Tiger.

Tiger. His nickname for a while. Tiger Newman. New man. You come to new country, you become new man, his father had said.

So . . . next . . . the serve . . .

You tall but you need weights to build muscle. Then you have fastest serve in world. I show you.

And so he had trained with weights. He had run up the Downs and down the Downs. He had practised and practised.

115 mph . . . 121 mph . . . 132 mph . . .

The balls slamming down from a great height; slamming down and lifting so high that his opponent was taking them round his head.

Roscoe Tanner? Sampras? Ivanisevic?

Jason Newman was faster than them all.

Wham! Bang!

But never fast enough for his father.

Cannonball. Another of Lajos's words.

Cannonball come so fast he break through your guard. Yes? Now you show. And he would have to hit cannonball aces until his shoulder became so sore he could hardly lift the racquet. The cannonball, the slice, the topspin, he learned them all . . .

Listen, you must look at service box before you serve . . . plan where you going to hit ball. Okay?

Then one day Lajos said: Now you ready – ready for the big time.

He went to Queen's to play in the London Grass Court Championships and he played a Frenchman rated 181st in the world and he won eleven points in two sets and his father spat on the grass and called him a coward.

In front of a crowd of seven thousand people.

They drove back to Sussex in silence, but they didn't go home. It was late at night and the club was deserted and Lajos switched on the big halogen lights and said, Now you practise.

He had a bag of balls and he put them on the court at Jason's feet.

First the serve.

Fuck you, says Jason, and goes into the clubhouse and Lajos says, What you say? What you say?

I'm not playing any more. You can stuff it.

What? What?

Freedom. For the first time in his life Jason feels real freedom.

He goes into the changing rooms. He is laughing. And Lajos follows him and throws the bag of balls on the floor and they shoot out and roll and Lajos says pick them up you coward bastard.

And the sense of freedom goes and instead the tiger is in his tank and he picks up the balls and begins to serve.

At his father.

The big serve. Bigger than Becker's now . . . and the balls smash into his father again and again and he shields his head and tries to run but the balls ricochet around the room and under his feet and he falls and – yes, one big cannonball zoomer connects with his right eye and there it is on his cheek

. . . *a poached egg . . . sucked out of its socket . . . blood and mucus and . . . oh, Christ . . .*

And from that moment Jason is lost.

His father tells everyone that they were practising in the lights and he didn't see the ball. No one must know, he says to Jason, it will be our secret.

And after that Jason hardly lost a match for seven years.

He is remembering the eye, and feeling the guilt that spread inside him like blood spreads into tissue. He still feels the guilt, the pain of what he did. Yes, he too has a secret.

16

Sunday morning and Anne was working. On her desk was the hygiene report. She had already worked on it for a full day and wanted to go over it one more time before handing it in to the Governor's office.

There was a knock on her door and Tom put his head round. 'Got a moment?'

'Of course.'

He closed it behind him and began his usual slow pacing. 'Les says you had your baptism of fire yesterday. The hep B prisoner. Tell me what happened.'

'It wasn't as dramatic as that. I was doing the drug throughcare clinic and—'

'What was his name?'

'Reilly. Remand prisoner. Twenty-six years old.'

'I don't think I've met him.'

'Aggravated assault on an old woman.'

Reilly had been the last patient, and from the moment he stepped into the medical room she had felt uneasy. She told herself that Les was outside the door and all she had to do was call.

He was of medium height with a shaven head and a series

of earrings. His hands were tattooed. He entered the room with a swagger.

'I come for my tot,' he said.

When she had first arrived the word had confused her. 'Tot' meant liquid to her; she had to learn that most drugs in prison were given as pills in small plastic containers, but still called a tot.

Until a couple of years earlier the prisoners would take the dose in front of the doctor. Not now. It had been decreed that prisoners needed the responsibility of dosing themselves.

They took their tots back to their cells and spaced the drugs as they needed them – and sold what they didn't need. This was well enough known, but it was responsibility versus illicit sales, and responsibility had won with the Home Office.

'I'm on sixty mils and ten of the blues,' he had said. The statement was a challenge.

She already knew that every prisoner exaggerated his dosage and Reilly had come from the Kingstown drug treatment centre whose dosages she was familiar with.

He came to stand beside her and looked over her shoulder as she wrote.

'What's this?' He pointed a tattooed finger at the prescription.

'The London Road day centre never prescribes more than forty mils of methadone and—'

'That's a lie! You got to—'

'And I'm not giving you more than forty mils of valium. You can have it twice a day.'

He suddenly grabbed her by the arm and she saw the death's head rings on his fingers.

'Fucking bitch!'

She opened her mouth to yell. He released her. She looked at her arm. His nails had pressed into her skin. 'Now *you* can worry,' he said. 'I'm hep B positive.'

Tom's face showed instant concern. 'Les never mentioned that.'

'All I told Les was that he'd grabbed me.'

'I hope you've had your shots.'

'At St Thomas's.'

He relaxed. 'Hepatitis B scares the hell out of us. And the police too. They're more scared of that than HIV. Half the tarts in London are carriers so they're extra careful when they arrest them. We'll try to persuade Reilly to let us check him. He may be lying.'

'What about Les and the rest of the staff?'

'We don't force people to have jabs, but most of them do. It's too risky not to. I had a part-timer once who wouldn't handle a case. The governor wasn't sympathetic. He said that's what the £800-a-year danger money was paid for and if he didn't like the heat etc., etc.'

'What happened to him?'

'I fired him.' He crossed to the window. 'It's raining.'

'Oh, no! And I promised to take Hilly out.'

'How's she getting on?'

'At school?'

'Generally. How are you all getting on in Kingstown?'

'Hilly's settled down but I'm not so sure about my father. I think he finds it a bit tame after Africa. But he's—' She checked herself. She did not think the time ripe to tell Tom about his interest in Jason Newman. 'He's getting used to things, or perhaps Kingstown is getting used to him. How's Beanie?'

His expression changed into a frown. 'Her muscle tone is good but—' he shrugged. 'If only one could explain to her that she should *try*.'

'I mentioned her to Hilly. She's writing a story about her. Keeps on asking me if there's any good news.'

'She'd better come and meet her then. Bring her to tea.'

'She'd love that.'

'What about four o'clock?'

'Today?'

'Why not, if you've nothing else on?'

'I was going to work on this report at home.'

'I'm the boss and I say it can wait. Anyway you've been working like hell. Oh—' He dug his hand into his pocket and brought out a bleeper. 'I've been meaning to give you this. Your umbilicus. When it bleeps, you phone in. We're not often called back at weekends once the morning's duty work is finished.'

She hesitated and he said, 'If it's Harry Joyce who's bothering you, his bark's worse than his bite.'

Hilly was at a schoolfriend's house and Anne picked her up at lunchtime. 'Can we have takeaways?' Hilly said. 'Grandpa's not at home.'

Henry didn't approve of takeaways.

'Sure.'

They went to a Thai restaurant near their house and bought a series of dishes including sweet and sour chicken which was Hilly's favourite. The day was grey and rainy and they sat in the cheerful kitchen and ate out of the containers. Anne told her about Tom's invitation and Hilly's eyes lit up.

'Can I take my story and read it to her?'

'To Beanie? Sure. Dogs love stories.'

They did the week's food shopping, and in the mid-afternoon Anne drove them to Tom's. The countryside was dark under heavy clouds.

The woods had lost their autumn colours. The reds and the golds had faded to a uniform brown and already some of the ash trees had lost their leaves and their bare branches moved in the wind. Winter was on its way. Anne drove slowly and carefully over the rutted road trying not to slip into the wheeltracks made by Tom's Land Rover.

The wooden house, which she had thought so gemütlich and Bavarian, now seemed much more like a house from which children were driven by cruel woodcutters in Victorian fairytales.

An unfamiliar car was parked outside. As Anne drew up a woman came onto the verandah. Anne didn't particularly want to talk to her but couldn't remain in the car.

'Come on,' she said to Hilly. 'Let's see what's happening.'

As they got out of the car the woman came to the top of the steps and examined them.

'Oh, I thought you were Tom,' she said.

She was about Anne's age, but short and slender. She had long black crimped hair and was wearing a black suit, white blouse, and black high-heeled pumps. Everything was black and white, smart, expensive and, Anne thought with envy, the kind of outfit not often seen in a soggy landscape or even in Kingstown for that matter.

'Isn't he here?' Anne said and realised as she spoke that it was a fatuous question.

The woman lit a cigarette. She was very attractive, with a brownish skin and huge liquid brown eyes. Anne thought she detected a foreign accent and her looks suggested that she might come from the Mediterranean.

'Do you know where he is?' she asked.

'No, I was supposed to meet him here.'

Anne and Hilly were standing in a light drizzle at the bottom of the steps. They could either go back to the car or climb the steps. Anne chose the latter.

'Is he expecting you?' The woman looked over her shoulder.

'We were invited to tea.'

'To tea? Tom?' She gave a sudden sharp laugh. 'I am Stephanie.'

She spoke her name as though it was all the identification necessary. 'I have been waiting nearly an hour.'

'He may have been called to the prison. I'm Anne Vernon and this is my daughter Hilly. I work with Dr Melville.'

'You are a doctor?'

'Yes.'

'Dr Melville! It sounds . . . so formal.'

The situation was becoming farcical, Anne thought.

'You know this place?' Stephanie indicated the house.

'I've been before.'

'Ah. But it is a terrible place to find, no?' She crunched out her cigarette. 'It is very . . . rural.' She rolled the first 'r'. 'And so like Tom, don't you think? He has romantic visions.'

Anne could have said she didn't know Tom well enough to judge whether he had romantic visions or not, instead she said, 'I think we'll take a raincheck on tea. Something must have happened to delay him.'

'You think so? What kind of thing?'

'I don't know. A flat tyre perhaps. Or delayed at the prison.'

Stephanie fidgeted with her lighter, flicking it on and off. 'You like working at a prison?'

'I haven't made up my mind yet.'

'You like working with Tom?'

'Come on, darling,' Anne said to Hilly. 'I think we'll go.'

Stephanie moved as though to stop them. Anne could see she was nervy, febrile.

'Maybe it is best that you go. I must talk with him.'

Anne did not like being dismissed yet did not want to stay; the whole scene was too much like a couple of female carnivores disputing the territory of an alpha male. She said, 'Please tell him we came, but that there's no problem. We can do it any time.'

'Any time?'

'Yes, any time.'

As she turned to take Hilly down the steps she heard the noise of a car engine and Tom's Land Rover came into view.

Stephanie said, 'Oh no, still that old thing!'

She reached the Land Rover as Tom got out. She put her arms round his neck and kissed him. Tom, with a large paperbag in his arms, could not react one way or the other. After a moment he broke away and came to Anne. 'Please

197

go inside, I'll be with you in a moment. And can you take this, it's getting wet.' He handed her the bag.

Anne said, 'Look, we can come back some other time.'

'Please go in!'

Feeling embarrassed and uneasy but unwilling to make a fuss, she took Hilly into the big open-plan room. It was cold and cheerless and she switched on a couple of lights.

'I don't want to be here,' Hilly said.

'Nor do I, darling, but there's nothing we can do about it now.'

'I don't like this place.'

'It looks better in the sunshine.'

'Where's Beanie?'

'I don't know.'

Through the window she could see Tom and Stephanie standing in the light drizzle. By the jerky movements of their hands and arms they appeared to be arguing. Then she heard a heavy footstep and Harry Joyce came into the house and placed his gun against the wall. He was dressed as before in a waxed jacket and a deerstalker hat from which long grey hair protruded. His game bag was on his left shoulder and there was something in it that she assumed he had shot. The something gave a growl and she saw Beanie's nose sticking out.

'Tommy said I was to see you comfortable,' he said in his rich, country voice. He turned to Hilly. 'You the young lady what's written a story about the little dog?'

'Yes,' Hilly said apprehensively.

'She deserves a story.'

He put the game bag down and Beanie crawled into view. She gave a series of defensive barks, bouncing up and down on her strong front legs while her back legs stuck out behind her like a tadpole's tail.

Joyce laid kindling in the big stone fireplace, lit a gas poker, and in a few moments there was a roaring fire.

'May I pat her?' Hilly said.

''Course you can,' he said.

While this had been going on Anne had kept her eye on the window. The argument seemed to be coming to an end. Stephanie took a few steps towards her car, came back towards Tom, repeated the process twice more, waved her arms about, then drove off fast, spinning the wheels on the wet grass. Tom stood looking after her then slowly turned towards the house.

He ran up the stairs and entered the room. The dog began to scream. He pulled her ears and stroked her. 'All right. All right.' He turned to Anne and Hilly. 'You'd think I was beating the daylights out of her but it's only her way of saying hello. Thanks, Harry, that's a lovely fire.' Already the room looked more cheerful.

Joyce nodded briefly, picked up his gun and clattered off across the verandah.

'My apologies,' Tom said. 'I had a sudden craving for toasted muffins.' He was rubbing his hands and pacing up and down. 'It's just the sort of day for muffins. So I went into town to buy some and got caught in a demo about those two little missing kids.'

'Are you sure you want us to stay?'

'Absolutely and positively.' He turned to Hilly and said, 'I know who you are. Your mother has spoken about you. I'm Tom.' He put his hand out. 'And that's Beanie . . . but you've met her.'

The dog had moved towards the fire. Hilly crouched down beside Beanie and began to stroke her.

'Right,' Tom said. 'Tea and toasted muffins. Very Dickensian.' From the bag he brought out a packet of muffins and gave them to Anne. 'Here's a toasting fork. You do the muffins and I'll make the tea.'

Anne sat on a cushion in front of the fire next to Hilly and the dog and toasted the muffins.

'I haven't done this since I was a kid,' she said.

'Muffins in Africa?'

'My father's clerk used to make them. We toasted them around fires in the bush when we were camping.'

They ate the muffins with melting butter and dripping honeycomb and washed it all down with tea.

'Can I give her a piece?' Hilly asked Tom.

'We've got to watch her figure if we ever want her to walk again, but I don't see why not, just this once.'

Bars of sunshine streaked the wooden panelling of the room. Hilly went to the door and said, 'It's stopped raining. Can I take Beanie onto the verandah?'

'Sure. Take another muffin with you.'

Hilly gathered up the dog and went out of the house. Anne and Tom were abruptly enveloped by an embarrassing silence. After a moment Tom said, 'How's the hygiene report going?'

'Fine.'

'When do you think you'll finish it?'

'Maybe tomorrow.'

'Good, good . . .' He was looking past her at the wall as he spoke and she knew he was not concentrating on what she was saying.

'More tea?'

'No thanks. The muffins were lovely.'

'Hygiene reports are difficult to do properly.' He rose and began to fiddle with the fire. It was just as well her father wasn't there, he hated people doing that.

'I really think we should go,' she said.

'Go? You've only just come.'

'I feel we're in the way.'

'How could you be in the way if I invited you?'

'Well—'

'You mean Stephanie? If anyone intruded she did! God, of all the things to happen on a Sunday afternoon.' He sat on the cushion by the fire, knees drawn up, and stared into the flames. 'You know that phrase, out of the blue? That's where she's appeared from.' He wasn't talking to Anne as much as to himself. 'I haven't seen her for nearly six years and she just walks in and . . .' He shook his head slowly and said, 'Sorry about this, but it was a bit like seeing a ghost.'

'It's often like that when old friends suddenly materialise.'

'Especially when you were married to them.'

Restlessly he got up and began to clear the tea things. 'I'll do that,' she said.

'No. You're a guest. It's extraordinary the damage people do to each other when they fall in love. Have you found that?'

'No, I was only ever in love once and he died.'

'Hilly's father?'

'Yes.'

'Maybe it would have been different if Stephanie and I had had children, but somehow I doubt it.' He carried the tray into the kitchen. 'His name was Paul, wasn't it?'

'How did you know?'

'You mentioned him once. What did he do?'

'He was an architect.'

'One day I'd like to hear about him if you – Jesus Christ!' He ran to the window.

Anne went cold. 'Hilly!'

'No, she's all right. Look!'

She joined him at the window. Hilly and the dog were on the grass. Hilly had a piece of muffin in her fingers and was offering it to Beanie. The dog had risen on all four legs and was stretching forward.

As they watched, Hilly moved the piece of muffin slightly further away from her. Beanie tried to reach for it, took one pace, then collapsed.

'Oh, God,' Anne said. 'Poor little thing.'

'No, no!' She felt his hand on her arm gripping tightly. 'Watch.'

Slowly Beanie pulled herself up again into a standing position and Hilly gave her the piece of muffin.

'She's never done that before,' Tom said. He ran out of the house and down the steps. Anne followed.

He went down on his haunches beside Hilly and questioned her: had Beanie done it by herself? How many times? Had Hilly lifted her up?

Hilly looked at him in surprise and said, 'She doesn't like the wet grass on her tummy.'

Tom looked as though he had been struck over the head. 'My God, of course! Dachshunds hate cold, especially on their stomachs. Go on, try again.'

She offered Beanie a piece of muffin. The dog rose to her

feet, moved forward a step or two and took the food.

'Hilly, you're a genius!' Tom scooped Beanie up. 'What a clever dachshund!'

17

The house was in a close in an outer London suburb, one of a dozen new brick-built homes which would, Henry Vernon thought, have been described in the sales brochures as 'superior' or 'Regency style' or 'executive'. They all had pillars, pediments, double garages (also with pediments) neat lawns and neat shrubs. Number 9 had all these as well as a teak-veneer front door framed by permanent-shine, brass-plated carriage lamps. When Henry pressed the bell, it chimed.

The woman who came to the door was much as he had imagined her from her voice on the phone. Even though it was a wet Sunday afternoon when most people would have been slopping about in casual clothes, Clare Blackhurst was neatly dressed in a tweed skirt and a dark green jersey, her feet encased in sensible brogues. She was of medium height with auburn hair cut short. She wore no make-up and her long face was expressionless.

'I'm Henry Vernon.'

'Did we say three o'clock?'

'I managed to get lost.'

She moved aside and he entered the living-room. The day was cold and so was the room. It was furnished in oatmeals and greys and where a fire should have been burning there was a vase of pale silk flowers. The only excess was the restraint.

Henry sat, Mrs Blackhurst stood. She said, 'I think I had better tell you right at the start that I'm not happy about this meeting. I agreed against my better judgement only because you made certain accusations on the phone.'

'I understand perfectly,' Henry said in his best judicial tone. 'But I accused you of nothing.'

'Yes, you did. By implication you accused me of having no feelings; of trying to wipe Jason out of my life; of lacking sensitivity; of . . . well, of abandoning him.'

'Did I really?'

Henry had chosen a straight-backed chair in case he nodded off. He was feeling relaxed and benignant. He had driven up to London early and lunched at his club. The first person he had run into was Sir Godfrey Border, recently retired from the bench, who had been known as Herbaceous Border when they were at school together. They had had an excellent game pie with a bottle of the club claret and had reminisced about old times.

Clare Blackhurst said, 'You told me on the phone that Jason had no one. That isn't true. What about Margaret?'

'Abandoned him too. Gone home to Mum.'

'And you've made it your business to interfere?'

'Only by proxy. As I told you I'm a lawyer and I'm here on behalf of my daughter. Madam, I explained all this.'

'You said he might be sent to a mental hospital.'

'It's a possibility, that's all. One of the psychiatrists at Loxton is coming down in a few days' time to help with the assessments.'

The doorbell chimed once more.

Mrs Blackhurst excused herself. She went to the foot of the stairs and in a low, well-modulated voice called, 'John. Neville. Your father's here.'

From Henry's chair he could see into the hall. Two small boys appeared at the bottom of the stairs. They were neatly dressed in their school uniforms and their pale faces were as expressionless as their mother's. He was astonished there were children. The house was untouched by youth. No sound had come from upstairs, no tennis racquet, skate-board, bike, tracksuit top or bottom, had been in evidence. It was as though they had come from an isolation ward.

The front door opened. He could not see the man on the step but heard Clare Blackhurst say, 'I want them back early.' There was a low response and then she said, 'Goodbye, boys, have a nice time.' The door closed.

'I didn't realise you had two sons,' Henry said.

'There're quite a few things you don't realise, Mr Vernon. You don't realise how obnoxious it is for me to have someone picking over the entrails of my life like this.'

'I haven't heard that phrase for some time. In Africa the witchdoctors pick over the entrails of chickens.'

Two pink spots of colour appeared on her otherwise monochromatic cheeks. 'In fact, I object most vehemently.'

He raised a hand as though to ward off the evil spirits the entrails had released. The claret was wearing off and he had to beware the return of his normal belligerent nature.

'Madam, please restrain yourself. I am sure you are not

so far gone in dislike of your brother that you would fail to assist even at a distance.' His orotund tone was that of a judge summing up to the jury. 'He is charged with a most heinous crime for which he could go to prison for several years. His wife has left him. His grandfather has written saying that neither he nor his mother will have anything to do with him. You are the only one of the close family who has agreed even to listen. I ask myself how it is that someone who brought fame upon a family name can be hated to the point of excommunication.'

The word 'excommunication' slurred slightly on his lips but he was proud to have got it out.

He fixed her with a glance, a special look he had developed when cross-examining witnesses.

'Did you say that my grandfather had written?'

'I understand it is a most brutal document.'

'It would be.' She cast around the room like a retriever then lifted the lid of a silver cigarette box. 'I gave up six months ago. But there are still times when I want one.'

It was the first indication that she was human and he said, hopefully, that he smoked a pipe, but she did not invite him to light up.

'What is it you want of me?' she asked.

'Anything you can tell me about your brother, anything that will help.'

'You said your daughter knew Jason.'

'She played against him when they were in their teens. Admired him tremendously. Now she is in a position to help him and that is why I am here.'

Suddenly she said, 'Do you get on? I mean does she get on with you?'

'You'd have to ask her, but my impression is that she does. We live in the same house and my granddaughter lives there too. Commonplace in Victorian times, rare now.'

'I hated my father!' She had gone across the room and was standing at the window, her arms folded across her flat chest. 'Hated him, and despised my mother.'

She stopped and the silence grew. Henry sat quite still. He knew what was happening, he'd seen it a hundred times in court; it was the need to communicate, to unload old resentments, old hatreds, old guilt.

'You know who my father was, I imagine?'

'Only that he was a Hungarian Davis Cup player who defected to the West during the uprising in fifty-six.'

'Lajos Keleti,' she said, half to herself. 'Clare Newman. It's strange how families change. If I have to talk about these things, I want a drink.' She did not bring herself to ask him whether he wanted one but raised her eyebrows.

'Perhaps a small brandy.'

She gave him one then filled a large wine glass with sherry and drank half of it.

'My father did it for the money,' she said. 'Today he might have made a decent living. Not then. All his life he was in debt. I've always thought that turned him into what he became.'

'Which was what?'

'A kind of one-eyed monster, literally and figuratively. He did only have one eye. Damaged the other playing tennis with Jason at night. At night! That's how obsessed he was. And he was obsessed with the idea of Jason doing what he had never been able to do: become a champion. He lived tennis and slept tennis. It ruined my mother's life and it ruined Jason's.'

'But not yours.'

'It would have if I'd let it. What saved me was hate. I hated tennis. Loathed it. Once my father tried to teach me and gave me a racquet. I got a knife and cut the strings from the frame. So he beat me with it.' She touched her mouth. 'Chipped a tooth. After that he concentrated on Jason. He would have anyway, no matter how I'd turned out. He had that kind of macho Latin feeling for the male child and I was totally ignored.

'Any money he made from the club went to Jason. He even managed to send Jason to a private school. I had to go to a state comprehensive. While Jason got the best in tennis gear my mother and I bought clothes at Oxfam shops.'

She fell silent and Henry said, 'I can see why you disliked your father but not why you despised your mother.'

'Because she let him do this to me. He was a bully; she was weak. A mother is supposed to protect her children. She didn't protect me.'

'Perhaps she couldn't.'

'I know that now. He was a violent man and she was afraid. So she turned to this stuff.' She held up her glass. It was nearly empty. 'Once I asked her why and she said, "My rod and my staff, they comfort me." It was only afterwards that I found out she was misquoting the twenty-third psalm.'

'Yea, though I walk through the valley of death . . .'

'Precisely.'

'How do you feel about her now that you understand?'

'Pity, but also anger. I can understand what was

happening but I can't forgive her for not trying. Am I making myself clear?'

'Perfectly.'

'You accused me of abandoning Jason. Well, let me tell you something, they abandoned me.' She came and stood over him. 'There was a time when my reaction was: I'll show you what I can do; that I'm just as good as Jason in my own way. I worked like hell at my A levels, got two As and a B. Nobody gave a damn. Jason was playing in some bloody tournament or other. That's all he cared about, and my mother was drunk. So I thought to hell with all of them and I left home and got married.'

'Was that—?' Henry indicated the front door.

'Charles Blackhurst. One of my teachers. He's decent enough but it hasn't worked out. He's given me two children, but he's weak . . . weak . . .'

'You married to get away from home?'

'Of course.' She poured herself another large sherry. 'Did you go to university?'

'Yes, I did.'

'I wanted to. I even won a small scholarship. It would have meant finding about five or six hundred pounds a year, that's all. My father said no. He said women didn't need to go to university; they would marry and have kids and it would be a waste of money. So once I was married to Charles I took an accountancy course. I worked as a waitress, as a barmaid. I did anything to get the money together for tuition fees. It took me five years of working nights and early mornings to get my ACCT but now . . . now I'm the king of the castle and Jason's the dirty rascal . . .'

* * *

'Hello, Jason, how are you feeling?'

'Okay.'

They were in Anne's room. She thought he was looking dreadful. The animal sleekness had gone, the bruising on his face had turned yellow and he had lost weight.

When she mentioned it he said he didn't like the prison food.

'It's not all that bad. Is Margaret a good cook?'

'No. We used to eat out most of the time, or get takeaways.'

She noticed that he had a slight nervous twitch at one side of his mouth she had not seen before, and his eyes were bloodshot.

'She's not coming to see me any more,' he said.

'Yes. I heard.'

'Says it stresses her too much. Christ, what about me? Doesn't she think I'm stressed?'

Anne heard her own words. 'You must try to remember her condition. This is a bad time for any woman. I know it is for you, too, but she's about to bring a new life into the world. That's a big thing.'

His eyes slid past her and she realised this wasn't the time for little homilies. She had thought of telling him of her father's visit to his sister Clare and then decided not to. The visit had achieved nothing and the rejection would only make him feel more bereft.

'Mr Foley tells me you've seen a new lawyer,' she said.

'Yeah.'

'That's something, at least.'

'He let me see her statement to the police.'

'Whose?'

'Cindy Smith's. The person I'm supposed to have tried to rape.'

She hesitated, not sure whether she should ask him what the statement contained.

'She's lying!' he said. 'The bitch!'

'If she is, they'll make that clear in court. Your barrister will certainly get the truth out of her.'

'Who's going to believe me against her?'

Recalling her father's words, she said, 'Jason, it is very difficult to prove attempted rape.'

He slowly shook his head. 'It wasn't, that's the whole point. She was all for it. I mean, a man can tell even if a woman doesn't say anything. There are looks and gestures. She even started it.'

'How?'

'She was at the tennis courts and she asked me the time.'

'What were you doing down on Castle Fields? It's miles from Leckington. If you were going shopping there were nearer places. That's the kind of question they might ask you. In other words, they might try to suggest that you went there deliberately to pick up a girl.'

'I don't really know why I went there. Okay, Margaret and I had had a row and—'

'What about?'

'The usual. Money.'

'And?'

'I walked out.'

'That's not all. Tell the truth. They could find out. They might even know already.'

'Okay, okay! I . . . hit her. But they can't get a wife to testify against her husband, can they? So what's the point? I hit her and I'm sorry and I wish I hadn't.'

'And then?'

His anger dissipated. 'It's a bit blurred after that. I remember getting into the car and driving through the lanes. I drove for a long time. Maybe an hour. Then I found myself in Kingstown. I must have parked in the square and walked down to Castle Fields. I don't know why.'

'The club used to be there, didn't it? Before it burned down?'

He swung round to look at her sharply. 'How did you know that?'

She considered mentioning the old man and the dog she had met but thought he might consider her to have been prying. 'I played there once,' she said. 'I must have read about it in the papers.'

He moved restlessly in the metal chair. 'Yeah . . . well . . . I suppose that was the reason. Just something I did subconsciously.'

She waited.

'And then?' she prompted.

'I don't remember. I think I just walked around the playing fields.'

'Jason, you've *got* to remember. What was the weather like?'

He thought for a moment, then said, 'Hot. I remember hearing the music from an ice-cream van. I was down by the river where it comes over the weir and foams and makes a rushing noise. I've always been afraid of that place. A woman was drowned there once. Threw herself into the pool below the weir. They said she'd had a quarrel with her lover.'

'What did you do after you'd been to the river?'

'I walked over to the tennis courts. The club used to be there. I think I watched the people playing for about ten minutes and then this girl came along and stood nearby. She was eating an ice-cream and I thought I'd go and get one. I was just about to walk off when she asked me the time. I told her and we started chatting.'

'Did she know who you were?'

'No, but . . . oh yes, I remember now. There was a mixed four playing and they were just finishing and one of the men, I suppose he was around my age, came over and said he'd seen me play in the Diamond Challenge in Cape Town and could I give him an autograph.'

'That was when you'd gone into the top ten on the computer, wasn't it?'

'Yeah. It didn't last long though. Anyway, I gave him the autograph and that was that.'

'Do you remember what he was like?'

'No. I must have given a million autographs. I never registered a face unless it was pretty.'

'It must have impressed Miss Smith.'

'Probably. I said I was going back into the town and asked whether she'd like to come and have a drink because it was so hot. She said yes and we went to a pub and had a couple of drinks and she asked me about the circuit, the money, things like that, and then she said would I like to come to her house and say hello to her parents because they were terrific tennis fans and always watched it on tv. So I went.'

'Did it make you feel good? I mean the recognition? The autograph?'

'I suppose it did.'

'Especially after what you'd been through: losing your job and then the fight earlier that day with Margaret. People had recognised you. And you were going to be shown off by a pretty girl. Of course it did.'

'It was one of those terraced houses in the old part of town. And her parents weren't there. No one was. So she said oh, they must have gone out. We were in the sitting-room and she lowered the venetian blind. She said the sun faded the carpet. I remember that because the light in the room became a greyish colour like when you go scuba diving.'

'You see, you *can* remember, Jason. One thing is reminding you of another. Go on.'

'Well, we started fooling around.'

'How do you mean?'

'Oh, you know.'

'Don't be embarrassed. They're going to ask you about this in open court. You'd better get used to it.'

He looked down at his big hands and said, 'I began to undress her and she undressed me.'

'Completely?'

'No. She was unzipping my flies and I was taking her bra off. Suddenly she started to scream and kick and I grabbed her. It said in the statement there was bruising on her upper arms and neck. That must have happened then. She was looking at something behind me. So I turned and . . . Jesus . . . I hadn't heard him come in! There was this man standing in the doorway. He was wearing a police uniform. And all the time she's fighting and hitting me. And I just panicked. I pushed him out of the way and ran. Of course they knew who I was so they picked me up.'

'But how had the police got there? That's what I don't understand.'

'He was her father.'

Anne entered her house, dropped the car keys on the hall table, then dropped herself into an armchair in the drawing-room. 'I haven't been so tired since I was a houseman catching babies,' she said to her father, then corrected herself: 'Housewoman? Houseperson?'

Henry said, 'If I'm a housemother, you can be a houseman.'

'My bones have softened,' she said.

'There's only one thing for that.' He gave her a strong whisky. 'I'll get you some supper. What would you like?'

'Anything.'

'What about haddock with a poached egg?'

'Lovely.'

She sipped the whisky and felt the bones in her legs begin to harden. She followed her father into the kitchen.

'Jason looks terrible,' she said.

'People in prison often do. Two eggs or one?'

'One, and can I have it on toast?'

'If you must. Watch wouldn't have approved.'

They talked while she ate. She told Henry about the

interview and Jason's recollections of the events for which he had been arrested.

'She led him on,' he said.

'That's the judicial view, is it?'

'What else would you make of it? "Come home and meet my parents." Only the parents weren't there and not likely to be.'

'She might have thought they were.'

'Bosh and piffle. What did the rest of her statement to the police say?'

'Almost precisely what Jason said. Except the vital bit. She claims he grabbed her and that they'd been fighting for a minute or more before her father arrived.'

'Is she a virgin?'

'What difference does that make?'

'It would—'

'If you're thinking that Jason can defend himself by saying: well, she wasn't a virgin so she knew what was likely to happen – then forget it. That's dinosaur territory. These days if a woman says no, even a wife, and the man continues, it's rape.'

'Thank you. I'll remember to consult you on points of law. Do you see Jason as a psychotic looking for dominance?'

'No.'

'Then this sounds like it was opportunist. She wanted sex. She lured him to the house. Her father arrived unexpectedly. She screamed rape.'

'Perhaps.'

'Perhaps is enough to start with.' He cleared the plates and began to stack them for the following day's big washup.

'Have you told him about the psychiatrist from the secure mental hospital?'

'Loxton?'

'Have you told him he's to be evaluated?'

'I was going to, but he was talking freely for the first time and I didn't want to break the flow.'

'Hand on your heart: do you think he's lying, or not?'

'I think he's probably telling the truth.'

Henry sucked on his pipe and the kitchen was filled with the aroma of latakia. 'I'm beginning to feel sorry for Newman. I think that probably started when I was talking to his sister. Poor sod, *he's* been abused if you like. Differently from what we've come to believe is the norm but I'd say probably from the day he was born – and all in the name of his father's ambition.'

'Don't tell me you've got a heart after all.'

He ignored her. 'The system wasn't created to help people like Newman. I'm talking about the judicial and the penal systems, handmaidens of the legal system. I've always been on the side of the law as a judge and as a prosecutor, because society can't function without it. But sometimes that isn't the same as being on the side of justice.'

'So?'

'So Newman needs help and, with your permission, I'll try and see his grandfather. I want to know why the whole family is against him.'

18

The following morning at breakfast there was a letter for
Hilly. She looked at it in surprise. There was her name,
Miss Hilary Vernon, there was her address, there was a
stamp with the Queen's head. It was genuine.

'Can I open it?' she asked.

'Of course you can,' her mother said.

'Have I had a letter before?'

Henry said, 'I wrote from Africa but you were tiny then.'

Anne read it to her. 'Dear Hilly, I am writing to ask for
your help. Since you were here Beanie hasn't stood up
properly by herself. I know that these things take a long
time and that one manages in fits and starts—'

'What's fits and starts?' Hilly asked.

'It means one day she'll do well and the next not.'

'Go on.'

'—but she doesn't try with me. She knows she'll get her
reward anyway. At least that's what I think. Could you
possibly come and give her some more therapy? I could
pick you up at your house or your mother might like to
bring you for tea and then you could show me exactly what
you did. Beanie sends her love and I send you my best
wishes. Tom.'

'Can I go?' Hilly said.

'Of course. Would you like me to arrange it?'

Hilly thought for a moment. 'All right. You arrange it.'

The moment Anne reached her office Les Foley put his head round her door and said, 'Newman's been asking for you. He's in a state.'

She saw him in her room after she'd finished morning sick parade. He looked worse, the facial tic was more noticeable.

'Margaret wants a divorce,' he said, even before he sat down.

'Oh, Jason, I'm sorry to hear that.'

'She regrets telling me now, but thinks it better than postponing it. *Regrets!* Christ!'

'How did you hear? Did she write to you?'

'No, her lawyer came to see me last evening.'

'Which lawyer is that?'

'He's a new one, hired by Margaret's mother, apparently. If I don't make any trouble about the divorce – in other words about the kids – they won't ask for alimony and they'll also pay his fee to act for me in the criminal case. I think he wants me to plead guilty. And there was a veiled hint that if I didn't play ball they'd smear me. I suppose he meant they'd bring up the stuff about me hitting her.'

They sat in brooding silence. It was on the tip of Anne's tongue to mention Margaret's accusation that he might have abused Julie, but he seemed too fragile.

'What will you do?'

'I don't know. Maybe it would be best to plead guilty and get everything over and done with. What's the point of fighting?'

'To use a tennis expression, Jason, now isn't the time to tank. The point is that you've got to show everyone you didn't try to rape that girl. That you're innocent.'

'But for Christ's sake, no one believes me! No one!'

'Yes, they do.'

'Who?'

'I do for one. And my father for another.'

'Your father?'

'Listen to me. Will you see him? Just talk to him. He's a lawyer and very clever. He might be able to advise you.'

Even as she spoke she knew she was getting deeper and deeper into a morass of her own making. *Don't get too involved*, Tom had said. But no one else was getting involved, at least not on Jason's side.

'Why does your father want to get mixed up in this? How does he know I'm not guilty? What's it got to do with him anyway?'

'He's a complex man. And very old-fashioned. He actually believes not only in the law but in justice. Only *you* know whether you're guilty or not, but both my father and I think that at least you should be given a chance. Look, I didn't want to mention this but he went to see Clare to find out what help she could give.'

'And?'

'She refused.'

'I could have saved him the trip.'

'I'm glad he went, because it gave him an idea of just what is happening to you. I'm not guaranteeing he'll see you, Jason, but if he agreed would you talk to him?'

He shrugged. 'Why not? If it'll help.'

After he'd gone back to the remand wing she realised she had not mentioned the imminent arrival of the Loxton psychiatrist. But the time hadn't been right.

She didn't feel like going to the canteen for lunch and wandered out into the town. The pedestrian precinct was busy and she walked into the cathedral close. Kingstown cathedral was not one of the largest in the land but with its two rose windows and its newly-cleaned façade of yellow stone glowing in the autumn sunlight it was one of the most beautiful.

She was disturbed about Jason and thought about him as she wandered through the cathedral transepts. She was also worried about her own reactions. Was this going to be the pattern? Was she going to be drawn into the unhappy lives of the prison inmates? Could she keep her cool as Tom had advised? If not she'd be run ragged. The prison was a place where emotions, anger and frustrations raged, and if she was not careful she might find herself engulfed.

She passed the tombs of thirteenth-century knights and their ladies. There was the sound of organ music and the atmosphere began to have a calming effect on her. She went back to the nave. A dozen or more local people, some eating sandwiches, were sitting near the choir stalls listening to the music. She was about to join them when she saw Tom sitting at the back, chin in hand.

He gave the impression of being part of a private world and she had no wish to intrude. She found a side door and walked quickly out into the open air.

'Huff ... huff ... huff ... And that's another king for me

. . . bingo . . . bango . . . and you're dead, mate. You want to stick to tennis, Jason, old sausage. Draughts is too complicated for you.'

Jason swept the draughts onto the cell floor.

'Oh, very macho. I'm dead impressed.'

Jason went to his bunk. Billy remained seated.

'You better pull yourself together. You let one of the screws see you do that and they'll tell the quacks that you're violent and the quacks'll tell the psychiatrist from Loxton – and quick as a flash you're in for observation. And observation can be anything – a month, six months – and then, depending on what they observe, Jason old trout, it's bye-bye.'

Jason turned his back.

'That's the spirit. You turn away. Ignore it. But don't say I didn't warn you. Because the word is it's next week.'

'What's next week?'

'Your evaluation.'

'What?'

'That's what I hear.'

Jason sat up and swung his legs onto the floor. 'You bullshitting me?'

'You don't bullshit about something like that.'

'How the hell would you know anyhow?'

'Don't be cheeky, Jason. Mustn't be cheeky to Billy. I know because I got contacts, that's how. There's people in this nick that know everything. Prisoners, screws, doesn't matter which. They see things. Bits of paper. Hear phone calls, swap snout or grass for info, they pass on news . . . You get me, Jason?'

'Yes.'

'And there's people on the outside that *think* they know everything. I got a grannie. Lovely old lady. Only she wants her dearly beloved grandson, to wit me, to be locked up in Loxton and to rot there. She don't want me home no more. Wants me kept out of the way. But I'll tell you something my son. It's not going to happen. William J. Sweete ain't never going to that bloody place again. Never . . . never . . . never . . .'

'What's your grannie got to do with me?'

'I'll tell you what she's got to do with you. The psychiatrist is coming down to e-e-valuate us. Big word for a tennis player, Jason, but it means he's going to test us. You *and* me. And a couple of others on Rule 43.'

'When did you find out?'

'Last night.'

'Why the hell didn't you tell me then?'

'Because you'd just heard about your wife and the divorce, that's why.'

Jason was shocked. 'How did you hear?'

'One of the screws. Told me to watch you extra careful in case you tried to top yourself.'

Jason collapsed. Tears coursed down his cheeks and his body became racked by sobs.

'You see why I didn't tell you? 'Cause you're in a state, that's why.' Billy sat down beside him, and put an arm round his shoulders. 'You can't do this on your own Jason. Everybody needs a friend and you haven't got none.'

Jason said softly. 'I know.'

'Not your wife. Not your family. Nobody.'

'There is one.'

'Who?'

'Dr Vernon.'

'What? The woman quack? Don't make me laugh.'

Jason shrugged off Billy's hand and crossed to the window. He put a chair under it and stood on it looking out into the cold night. The lights of Kingstown twinkled below him. The castle was floodlit but that would stop as winter increased its grip and the tourists went home. Where would he be by then?

'Listen, if she was your friend, why didn't she tell you about the psychiatrist from Loxton? Tell me that, old sporty tennisplayer.'

He couldn't answer.

'You only got one friend, Jason, and that's me.'

Billy had lit a rollup and now he pressed the tip to the inside of his left arm. The smell of roast pork permeated the cell again. Jason did not object this time. He watched the blister turn black and form a small area of vulcanised flesh.

'You want to try? It might help.'

Jason took the cigarette.

'You better draw on it, make it hotter.'

Jason put the cigarette to his mouth and drew. On top of the acrid, sweet, tobacco taste was the flavour of Billy's lips.

'Now,' Billy said.

Jason pressed the cigarette to the inside of his forearm. The pain was fierce and he cried out. But a moment later came a feeling of relaxed peace, as though he had ejaculated.

'That's better, isn't it?' Billy said.

'Yes . . . yes it is . . .'

'Here. Try another draw.'

They smoked the rollup together in silence.

Anne was in her father's flat amid the Masai spears and the Bushman bows and arrows.

She said, 'I told Jason I couldn't answer for you. You might or you might not.'

Henry's pipe produced the sound of water draining from a bath.

He was at his desk, which was covered in open research books. It looked a mess, she thought, but she would never have dreamed of tidying it up. Watch was the one person who had ever been able to keep Henry tidy and only by continuous grumblings and threats. She had long ago decided it wasn't worth the hassle.

'What about Newman, does he want to see me?'

'I think he's desperate to see anyone.'

'Thank you.'

'I didn't mean it that way.'

'I was thinking about the case after we spoke. I went back to my original feeling that we're becoming involved in something that isn't our business.'

'But it *is* our business. Mine anyway. And I'm asking you to make it your business.' The fierceness of her tone surprised Anne herself.

Henry pulled out a cardboard file and she saw the name Jason Newman on the cover.

'You've already decided!' she said. 'You've just been having me on.'

The phone rang upstairs and she went up to answer it. Five minutes later she returned and said, 'That was Clive.'

'Who's Clive?'

'You know very well who he is. He's asked me to lunch at the weekend. Will you be around to look after Hilly? I said I'd ring him back if you couldn't'

'I imagine so. Hilly and I will be fine.'

He took out a series of typed sheets and she saw they comprised Jason's police statement. She felt a sudden rush of guilt. She had borrowed the statement from Jason and had taken it to the public library and photocopied it. She had not asked permission in case she was refused and hadn't even been sure she was supposed to have seen it, which was why she hadn't used the photocopier in the prison.

When she had told her father what she'd done, he had said, 'Good girl.'

She had replied, 'I thought you'd approve. It's the kind of behaviour I learned from you and Watch.'

He turned a page and his finger stopped against a line he had highlighted in yellow.

'Number 17 Castleview Terrace,' he said.

'What about it?'

'It's where Miss Smith lives. I went there this afternoon. Attractive little houses. They date from the eighteen eighties. And there's a preservation order on them.'

'How on earth did you find that out?'

'Chatting to a traffic warden. Apparently commuters park their cars in the street during working hours to save parking costs and there's an outcry from residents. Nice woman, the traffic warden. Couldn't stop her talking once she got going.'

'That's because people hate them. Probably damages

their psyches. She'd have been thrilled to talk to someone who wasn't complaining.'

'Did you know that Miss Smith's father was a pillar of the local fundamentalist church?'

'No. What's that got to do with anything?'

'I hope I never have to come to you for a diagnosis. What it tells me is that any daughter of a deeply religious man would not want him to think she was of easy virtue, i.e. she'd yell rape even if it wasn't.'

'You couldn't prove that!'

'Of course you couldn't. But a case is made up of little bits and pieces of information, rather like a jigsaw puzzle.'

'What else did you do in Castleview Terrace?'

'I saw her house. Houses tell you things.'

'And did hers?'

He picked up one of the pages and read from it. 'She [the plaintiff] then let down the venetian blinds. She said the sun faded the carpet.'

'So?'

'There couldn't have been any sun to fade the carpet. Not that day or any other day. The whole terrace faces north.'

'Jason? You awake?'

'Yes.'

They were lying on their bunks in the dark. Billy on top, Jason down below.

'Remember what Kojak said?'

'What?'

'Didn't you ever see Kojak?'

Jason remembered the tv sets in a thousand different hotel bedrooms. He had seen Kojak first as a teenager, then in a dozen repeats. He had seen him in Spanish, in Dutch, in Italian, even in Serbo-Croat.

'I saw him.'

'Come on then? What'd he always say?'

'Who loves you, baby?'

'Right. And who does? Who's the *only* one who does?'

'You.'

'Right. Not all the fucking tennis fans. Not your wife. Not your family. No one. Except—?'

'You.'

'You want a ciggy? I'll make you one.'

'Okay.'

'I'll bring it down.'

'Okay.'

19

HAVE YOU SEEN THIS CHILD?

Henry had just absorbed the lettering and the enlarged photograph on the roadside sign when he saw the police. There were four of them dressed in heavy blue uniforms and phosphorescent yellow tunics, checking cars on both sides of the road.

'Why are we stopping?' Hilly asked.

'They want to know about a little girl who got lost,' Henry told her.

Neither he nor Anne had discussed the disappearance of the two Sussex children with her except in general terms as part of the continual warnings about strangers and cars which were now part of every child's learning process.

A policeman with a clipboard and radio bent down to the driver's window.

'Did you see the sign, sir?'

'I could hardly miss it.' He smiled but the policeman did not return the smile.

It was a cold day and the South Downs were covered by mist. The policeman's cheeks and nose had turned pale blue and the tips of his fingers, sticking out of mittens, were bloodless.

'I'll ask you again, sir, to take a look at this photograph.'

Henry looked at the features of Tessa Marsh who had disappeared above Castle Fields and whose face he had seen in the newspaper files. The policeman presented him with the clipboard which gave the date and time of her last sighting.

'I'm afraid I didn't live in Kingstown then,' Henry said.

The policeman looked hard at Hilly and said, 'Can you tell me who the little girl is?'

'My granddaughter.'

'Have you got any identification, sir?'

He checked Henry's driver's licence and spoke into his radio.

'Would you pull into the lay-by for a moment, sir.'

Henry opened his mouth, then closed it. What was the use of protesting? He drove the big old Rover into the lay-by and stopped.

'Why's he doing this?' Hilly said.

'I suppose he's checking our car number on the police computer to find out if we are who I said we are.'

A few moments later they were waved on.

'Has the little girl been lost for a long time?' Hilly said.

'Yes, for a long time. Since the summer.'

They turned off the main road and into the maze of winding lanes that pattern the South Downs.

'How on earth anyone finds their way through these beats me,' Henry said.

'You're lost.'

'I am not lost.'

'We should have turned down to the left.'

'Are you sure?'

234

'Yes.'

Henry backed and turned, the car wallowing in the lane like a stranded whale. At last he managed it. 'I hope you're right.'

'This is the way.'

'I get particularly irritated by little girls who pretend to know everything.'

'There's the track,' she said.

A man loomed out of the mist, a gun in his hands and a large black shape on either side of him.

'God save us!' Henry pulled up.

'Who are you?' Joyce said. 'What d'you want?'

'We've come to see Dr Melville.'

Joyce bent down and the two black dogs whined softly. 'Afternoon, Hilly,' he said. Then to Henry, 'You can go in so long as you're with Hilly.'

Tom Melville was in the sitting-room building up the fire. The two men introduced themselves. Beanie was in her basket and when Hilly bent down to her she gave a series of high-pitched, welcoming howls.

'Just look at that!' Tom said. Beanie was struggling to rise on her back legs to greet the child. 'The little beast never does that for me. Hilly, you're the expert, where would you like to start?'

'Outside.'

'Right. Here are the biscuits.'

At first Beanie pulled herself along, trailing her legs, but Hilly refused to give her the rewards. The dog began to bark crossly. Hilly helped her to her feet but even then she wobbled and fell. It was no better than the first time.

'Could we try the bath?' Hilly said.

They trooped upstairs.

Tom began to run the water from both taps but she said, 'Just the cold.'

The water was almost freezing. Tom put the dachshund in the bath. She was trembling and her eyes were filled with mute accusation. The moment she felt the water on her belly she stood. It was shaky but she was upright. Hilly held out the biscuit. Beanie walked through the icy water trying to reach it but trying at the same time to keep her belly clear of the water.

'Marvellous!' Tom said. 'You go on for a bit and I'll make us some tea.'

The two men went downstairs.

Henry said, 'I'm only here on sufferance,' and described the meeting with Joyce.

Tom smiled. 'When I first bought the place it had been uninhabited for a couple of years. Joyce had once worked for the previous owner – he lives in a cottage in the woods – and I don't think he was too keen on me. He had had permission to manage the woods as long as he supplied the house with firewood and I suppose he thought I might stop him from felling timber and selling it. He can be pretty bloody-minded when he wants to.'

'So I gathered,' Henry said dryly.

'One day a tree fell on him. He'd been cutting down a dead elm and somehow it twisted and came down before he was ready. I just happened to be out looking for mushrooms and found him. I managed to get him out from under the branches. He was a mess. Fortunately his spine was intact though one of his legs was broken and he'd got cuts and bruises and cracked ribs and God knows what else.

I splinted his leg and got him to hospital and ever since he's looked after me like an over-protective parent. Doesn't think I'll survive by myself. He's always bringing me eggs or wood or pheasants he's poached.'

'I used to have someone who looked after me a bit like that,' Henry said. 'I miss him like the devil.'

'Was that Watch?'

'Anne told you?'

'She's talked about him.'

Tom carried the tea things to the low table in front of the fire.

'Does he always go around with that shotgun?'

'He does since the break-in. I had a burglary some months ago. Nothing much was pinched. No respectable thief would take my tv or my stereo, they're both far too primitive for these days. But he took an old radio that meant a lot to me. It had been halfway round the world with me and in some sticky places. No, the worst thing was that he hurt Beanie. She must have tried to defend the place and he must have kicked her or maybe he even threw her down the stairs. That's where Joyce found her.'

'And her back was broken?'

'One of the lumbar vertebrae.'

'You can hardly imagine someone doing that, can you? I had bull terriers in Africa. Someone poisoned one of them. Did the police ever catch your burglar?'

Tom shook his head. 'I have a feeling he was an ex-prisoner. Occasionally they appear out of the past expecting to continue with the treatment or the therapy or just for a bed or money. I haven't mentioned that to Anne though; she's got enough on her plate as it is.'

'She seems to have.'

Tom paused then said, 'Has she mentioned Jason Newman to you?'

'Yes, she has. I think she's sorry for him.'

'I wish she wasn't.'

'She's known him since she was a teenager. Anyway she's always had strong feelings about people. And society for that matter. She was a marcher when she was younger. Apartheid . . . Homelessness . . .'

'I wonder if she'll enjoy the prison service. It's not a place for strong feelings. Not a place to become involved. Tea's ready. I'll call Hilly.'

'Who would like some tea?' Mrs Parker asked.

'We've just had coffee,' Clive said.

'Thanks, but I—' Anne began.

But Mrs Parker cut across her. 'Oh, we must have tea.'

'I should be getting back,' Anne said.

'Tea first,' Mrs Parker said.

They were in her flat in Richmond. Except it wasn't quite Richmond, more like Isleworth. They were in the actual sitting-room which had 'captivated' her with its view of the Thames so that she had simply *had* to own the flat. Since then Anne had looked at this view several times and had come to the conclusion that the faint intermittent flash of silver between the gasometer and the tower blocks must be the river.

It was mid-afternoon. They had arrived around twelve, had had a glass of sweet sherry, and then lunched off tinned grapefruit pieces, tinned steak-and-kidney pie and creamed rice pudding. Anne was feeling slightly queasy.

Mrs Parker said to Clive, 'I'll put the kettle on and you can go down to the shop and buy some tea cakes.'

Clive was dressed expensively in designer jeans, boots, and an Italian cashmere sweater which, Anne thought, might have cost what she made in a fortnight.

'For heaven's sake we don't want tea cakes.' He turned to Anne. 'Do you want tea cakes?'

'I really couldn't eat another thing.'

Mrs Parker adjusted her wig. It reminded Anne of one of the beehive huts built by the Ovambo people up near the Kunene River just south of Angola. She turned to Anne, 'What an argumentative man he is. I hope you'll forgive the way he talks to his mother.'

Anne smiled palely.

The silence was broken by Clive's watch which went bleep, bleep. It was a gold digital watch which bleeped on the hour. Anne realised it must be three o'clock. He left to buy the tea cakes. Mrs Parker tottered into the kitchen on her stick legs; Anne followed.

'How are you getting on at the prison?'

'I'm kept pretty busy.'

'I think we'll have the Worcester.'

She said it as though she possessed not only Worcester but Royal Doulton and Wedgwood and Spode as well. The Worcester had been a present to Mr Parker on his retirement from the chutney and pickles factory. Anne got out the plates and the teaspoons with their civic badges.

As she waited for the kettle to boil Mrs Parker said, 'How is your little girl?'

She rarely called her Hilary, mostly your little girl. It

seemed a way of distancing the Parkers from Anne's earlier breeding programme.

'She's fine.'

'I always hoped Clive would have a son. I think he would make a good father.'

The question mark hung in the air and Anne said, 'He probably will.'

'Probably?'

'I'm sure he will.'

'You're young enough to have more children.'

Anne began to realise why Clive had been sent out for tea cakes. This was a 'talk'. She felt irritated. Be nice to her, she told herself. She's a lonely old woman.

'Clive needs a family. I can't live forever and he needs someone.'

'The milk?' Anne said.

'Top shelf of the fridge. He needs someone to give him a background, someone at home to look after the entertaining. I used to do that for Mr Parker. He had important business contacts. One customer used to come all the way from the Isle of Man.'

Anne said, 'I think Clive usually does his entertaining in restaurants.'

'Poison; pure poison.'

'I'll take the tray through.'

Mrs Parker blocked the doorway. 'He wants to marry you.'

'Yes, I know.'

'Why won't you marry him?'

Her wig had slipped to one side and she looked demented. This was worse than Anne could have imagined.

'The time isn't right,' she said.

'That's what people always say about things.'

'Well, it just happens to be true at the moment.'

Mrs Parker burst out: 'I want grandchildren before I die! Why won't you give me grandchildren?'

'Here I am,' Clive said. 'Tea cakes.'

They left as soon after tea as they decently could. In the Mercedes Clive said, 'Jesus Christ, tea cakes!' As he started the engine, his watch went bleep, bleep. 'I suppose you want to be getting home,' he said.

'I'm sorry, Clive.'

'Three guesses, Jason. Jason?'

'I'm here. I'm not going anywhere.'

'Three guesses.'

'Okay. What's the clue?'

'It's brown.'

'Is that all?'

'It's brown and hot.'

'What sort of hot?'

'What d'you mean?' Billy said.

'Could be a woman. Jamaican. Indian.'

'You're a sexual maniac, Jason, you know that?'

He giggled.

'Brown and hot and sweet.'

'Could still be a woman.'

'It's a drink, you big, randy tennisplayer.'

'Coffee.'

'It's tea, Jason. That's what I'd really like. A cuppa. Plenty of milk and sugar.'

'You want me to get you one?'

'Would you?'

Jason got up and went out onto the landing. It was Sunday evening and they wouldn't be banged up till eight. The tea urn was at the far end of the wing. Other remand prisoners were watching tv or playing ping-pong.

He fetched two mugs and took them back to the cell.

'Ugh.' Billy made a face.

'What's the matter?'

'Too much sugar. How many did you put in?'

'Three. You said you liked it sweet.'

'Not that sweet. Sweete by name but not by nature.'

'I'll get you another one if you like.'

'Yeah. I'd like that. That would be very nice, Jason.'

20

Henry Vernon took two hours to reach Bath and almost half that again to find the house where Jason's grandfather lived. At one time the lanes were so narrow and the growth so dense that he had become lost and almost immobile. His grasp of African topography had been equally elusive, but there he'd had Watch to guide him.

The house was about eight miles from Bath on a bluff above the River Avon. He came suddenly on the property behind a high stone wall. He parked and walked along the wall but there seemed to be no entrance and he realised there must be one on the other side. He was about to turn back when he saw a small iron gate let into the wall near the edge of the bluff. He went through it and into a different world.

He was reminded of Kew with its lawns and shrubs, its paths and greenhouses. Everything was as neat as a garden could be in late autumn. He was no botanist but he identified a palm tree, several eucalypts, and a group of Japanese maples still with some of their red leaves. The house was eighteenth century and built of Bath stone.

In front of him was a belvedere perched on the very edge of the bluff with magnificent views of the river and the far hills. Part of it had been glassed in. Behind the glass and facing the view was a woman in a wheelchair who might have come out of Ibsen's *Ghosts*. She was wearing a fur coat and her face was turned to the sun. For a moment Henry thought she was inanimate, a piece of eccentric garden statuary. Then she moved slightly. She was almost bald and her skin was the colour and texture of candle wax.

An elderly, bearded man straightened up from a shrubbery almost at Henry's feet. 'What the hell d'you think you're playing at?' he said.

Henry was suddenly weary of people appearing out of the foliage and demanding to know his business. The only good thing about the gardener was that, unlike Harry Joyce, he wasn't armed.

'I'm looking for Dr Thorpe. Will you fetch him, please?'

'I am Dr Thorpe and this is private property. If you're not off it in one minute I shall call the police.'

'There's no need to do that.' Henry introduced himself and explained his presence. While the exchange was taking place he noticed that the woman did not move, yet they were not more than a few yards from her and their voices were loud.

'Why the hell should I talk to you?' Dr Thorpe said and waved a pair of secateurs in front of Henry's nose.

'Because it is what any reasonable man might do.'

It was difficult to guess whether he was going to be reasonable or not. He was a Crusoe-like figure with his beard and a woollen beanie pulled down over his ears. His top half was covered in an old dark blue Shetland jersey with leather elbow patches, and his lower half was encased in a pair of battered golf overtrousers. Altogether Henry approved of this ensemble.

'How dare you barge in here and talk of reasonableness,' Thorpe said. 'You're a bloody trespasser, no more no less.'

'I would ask you not to take such a hectic tone, sir. We are much of an age. You have grandchildren, so have I. One anyway. All I ask is that you listen for a few moments to someone who has driven half a day to see you. It is simple courtesy.' He realised he was beginning to sound a bit like Dr Johnson.

Thorpe sucked at his beard and said, 'All right. Five minutes.' He leaned over to the woman in the wheelchair. 'I'll be back in a little while, darling, and then we'll go for our walk.' The woman did not react.

'Come along,' he said to Henry. 'We'll go into the house.'

Henry followed him along the paths. As he passed the front windows he saw that the furniture was covered in dust sheets and the walls were patterned by rectangular patches where paintings had been removed.

They entered a kitchen. It was a large room in which even an eight-foot pine table seemed unobtrusive. In one corner was a screen that did not quite hide a bed. Henry saw another bed in what had been a big larder or butler's pantry which led off the kitchen.

'Sit down,' Dr Thorpe said grudgingly and pointed to a kitchen chair. 'Please be brief.'

'It's not a question of my being brief but of your being co-operative about your grandson,' Henry said.

'Why the hell should I? I hate the little sod.'

'Little is clearly not applicable now. I have no way of defining sod.'

'You sound just like a lawyer. I would have guessed even if you hadn't told me.'

'Dr Thorpe, your grandson has been abandoned by everyone including his wife and sister. The only person who hasn't given up on him is my daughter Anne, who had met him briefly years ago. Doesn't that seem shameful to you?'

'Did you get a good look at Elizabeth?'

'I saw enough.'

'She's Jason's mother; my daughter; my only child. What you see is his creation; his and that bloody father of his. And to a lesser extent Clare's. God, what a family. Now, why *should* I co-operate?'

'Apart from being your son's only supporter my daughter believes he's probably innocent.'

This was going it a bit strong, Henry thought, but what the hell; you put your best foot forward. 'And I think I probably do myself.' Dr Thorpe was fretting a piece of green garden twine, dropping the pieces on the table. 'He may be guilty of all sorts of things,' Henry waved his arm in the general direction of Elizabeth, 'which I don't know of – yet. But that still doesn't take away from the fact that he may be innocent of attempted rape and go to prison because of a lack of will by his relatives. That's not justice!'

'What about Margaret?'

'She's gone home to Mum and wants a divorce.'

Dr Thorpe was silent for a moment then said, 'I wrote to him, you know, telling him not to expect any help from me. I shouldn't have done it and I regret it. But . . . well, I didn't want someone appearing on my doorstep and involving us.'

'Now someone has.'

'Yes.' He rose. 'It's time for Elizabeth's walk.' He did not indicate that the interview was over so Henry accompanied him and discovered the reason for such well-kept paths was to enable Dr Thorpe to wheel Elizabeth from one to another without bumping the chair.

'God knows how long I'll be able to keep this up,' Thorpe said. 'And that's a worry.'

They were criss-crossing the garden at a brisk pace, as though on rails. Elizabeth Newman sat still, staring ahead of her, and Henry found himself looking everywhere except at the patchwork of skin that covered her head where hair should have been.

'I used to be able to get her up to her bedroom on the first floor but I'm not strong enough any longer,' Thorpe said. 'Sometimes she walks a little, sometimes not, so I can't take the chance and we sleep downstairs in the kitchen where it's warm.'

'Can't anything be done?' Henry asked. 'Might it not be better for you both if she was in hospital?'

'We tried that. She hated it. Didn't say anything, but when I visited her she used to cry. Silent tears. My God, they're the worst. Wrenched my heart to pieces. So I thought, this is no good, and brought her home.'

'And medically?'

'Pain killers, that's about all. She had two-thirds burns but even so she might have had some sort of life if it hadn't been for the alcohol. She was already ruined. Now she's kaput.' He spoke as though she wasn't there. 'She's got Alzheimer's. She's young to get it but people do, at least that's what the consultants say. To me it's what used to be called melancholia. It wasn't only her flesh that burned. Something inside her died the night of the fire – her soul, if that's not too fanciful for a doctor. She's only an empty husk now but as long as she lives she's my daughter and my responsibility and the recipient of my love. So you see it's a race: who dies first. Fortunately, and I say that advisedly, I don't think she can last more than a year or so. Could go at any moment. The problem is me: will *I* last. If she was a patient I might consider an injection. Potassium perhaps. Stop the suffering. But your own flesh – that's different.'

They were going round the garden at quite a lick, the wheels of the chair hissing on the gravel.

'Does Jason know how bad she is?'

'Oh, yes, he used to come to see her but that just upset her. And he used to send money but I wouldn't touch it.'

'Cutting off your nose to spite your face?'

'One does these things. Life isn't rational. He treated his mother *so* badly. All right, she drank, she was weak ... but with a husband like Lajos, who wouldn't? Clare was much the same. A selfish little bitch. Brats, both of them!'

He pushed the chair in silence for a while, stopping once to adjust the rug on his daughter's lap. As he started up again he said, 'If only . . . one goes on saying it . . . If there hadn't been a Hungarian uprising he wouldn't have fled to the West . . . But you can't think like that can you? Once she met him she was finished. Wouldn't look at another man. I tried to warn her. I said, Elizabeth, he's just escaped from Hungary. He can hardly speak English. He has no money. But that only made him seem more romantic. I've got money, she said. And she had. Her grandfather left her some; not a fortune but a decent amount. All of it went on the club.'

'Weren't they ever happy?'

'At the beginning when Lajos still thought he was going to be a new Hoad or Laver. But after a couple of years he was getting nowhere. Remember that in those days there wasn't very much professional tennis. You had to be a coach at a top club to make a decent living. So he decided to set up his own club with Elizabeth's money. And after the children were born he had another opportunity – with Jason. Poor little sod. I don't suppose he had a chance really.'

'Lajos was his Svengali?'

'It was more like Dr Frankenstein and his monster. And my poor Elizabeth couldn't cope. So she began to drink and that made everything worse. I once pleaded with her to leave him and she told me to mind my own business!'

They walked in silence for a while then Dr Thorpe said, 'Tiger! Tiger! burning bright. In the forests of the night . . . That's what Lajos used to call him. Tiger. If anyone was ever programmed, it was Jason. I remember him when he was a gentle little boy. But he became a sort of monster. His behaviour on court was appalling. You must have read about it, or seen it on tv, especially the Diamond Challenge in South Africa. I often think of that Blake poem. That's where my Elizabeth is ... wandering somewhere in the forests of the night ...'

Clouds were beginning to build up and the wind was increasing. 'Time to go in,' he said to Elizabeth.

He turned the chair away and wheeled her towards the kitchen. He manoeuvred her up a wooden ramp and started the process of getting her out of the chair. It was then that Henry saw she had been strapped in. She did nothing to help, her limbs were flaccid.

'Can I—?' Henry began.

'No. Leave it to me.'

Dr Thorpe got her out and began to walk her slowly up and down the room. 'She must have exercise. I won't be able to manage her if she becomes helpless. God knows what'll happen then. I try not to think about it.'

After about ten minutes he returned her to the chair and strapped her in. 'Now for her lunch.'

'I've intruded long enough,' Henry said. 'But there are one or two questions I need to ask then I'll be on my way.'

'You're not in a hurry, are you?'

'No.'

'Why don't you stay for a bit. Let me feed her. Then she has her rest. Have a bite with me. It'll only be bread and cheese but I still have one or two bottles of claret left.'

There was something almost pathetic in the change in his attitude and Henry was reminded of Clare. She had been lonely and carrying a load of guilt. Her grandfather was lonely but there was also deep unhappiness and anger.

Henry thought briefly of his own circumstances and touched wood.

'You go and have a stroll,' Thorpe said. 'Feeding Elizabeth isn't a pretty sight. Come back in half an hour.'

Henry went and stood in the belvedere. Below him was the railway line and the Kennet-Avon canal. People were bustling about on narrowboats. A train clattered by. It was a normal, busy world. But up on the top of the bluff there was a different kind of life.

There was no sign of Elizabeth when he re-entered the kitchen but the scullery door was closed and he assumed she was in her bed.

They ate bread and cheese and drank claret sitting on either side of the big kitchen table. Both men were feeling more comfortable with each other and chatted about the new football season and the past cricket season. Then Dr Thorpe said, 'Go on, ask your questions.'

'By the way you spoke I think you assumed I knew about the fire. I don't.'

'I thought everyone in Kingstown knew.'

'I was in Africa.'

'I see. Twelve years ago next summer the club burned down. Lajos died in the fire and Elizabeth . . . well, you can see how badly she was burned. Not even the best plastic surgeons at East Grinstead could do any better than that.'

'What was the cause?'

'No one knows. They thought wiring.'

'Do you have a theory?'

'I think Lajos started it for the insurance money. He was broke by then and Elizabeth's money had all gone. I was there that night. I'd gone to see Elizabeth. I knew she was desperately unhappy and I wanted to try one last time to see if I couldn't influence her to leave him. No one was at home so I went to the club. The fire must have been burning for about ten minutes. She was trapped in the bar too drunk to escape. I managed to get her out but it was too late for Lajos.'

He held out his hands palms down and Henry saw the patchwork of skin created by plastic surgery on the backs. 'Minimal compared with Elizabeth, of course.'

Henry waited for him to continue. Instead he lifted his glass and finished his wine. There was a kind of finality about the gesture and Henry knew that just as Thorpe had wanted his company, he might as suddenly want him gone.

'Is there anything else? Anything you can recall about Jason that might help him?'

'I try not to remember but to forget.'

He rose and Henry rose with him. 'I have to rest now. I rest when she rests.'

'I'm grateful that you saw me – and for the lunch.'

'It's not that I don't want to help,' Dr Thorpe said. 'It's . . . oh hang on, there is one chap who might be able to give you some information. Jason's coach. This was after Lajos died. He took Jason over. Became his companion and father confessor as well. I think he called himself a "sports psychologist".'

'Everyone has to have one nowadays, I am informed.'

'There is a word for it . . .'

'Guru?'

'That's it, God help us. Stegman. Leonard Stegman. I think he's a South African or an Australian but came to this country a long while ago. The Lawn Tennis Association will give you his number. I won't see you out if you don't mind.'

As Henry was closing the kitchen door Dr Thorpe was already climbing on to his bed.

21

'Got a minute?' Anne said, as she opened Tom's door and put her head round.

It had become a catchphrase to both of them.

'Of course.' He was looking down at the sheet of paper on which he had been writing. He shook his head slowly. 'Sometimes even I can't read it,' he said.

She did not smile and he examined her closely. 'What's up? You look terrible.'

'That's how I feel.'

'Are you ill?'

'No.'

'Hilly?'

'No, it's Jason. I think I—'

The phone rang. 'Excuse me.' Tom picked it up, listened for a moment, his face falling into a frown, and said, 'No, I can't speak to her now. No. And please tell her not to ring me here. Well, tell her again then. Just take her number and say I'll telephone her but that she is not to try to contact me here. Okay?'

He put the phone down. 'Sorry. Go on.'

'I think I—' she started again.

There was a knock at the door.

'Oh, Lord!' Tom said. 'Yes?'

Jenks came in, the diary in his hand. 'Can we leave that for the moment, Jeff?'

Jenks looked irritated and seemed about to argue.

'Not now,' Tom repeated and Jenks closed the door with a bang.

Tom looked at his watch. It was past five and already dark. 'Why don't we go and have a quiet drink? This place is a bit like Piccadilly Circus.'

He took her to the same pub as they'd gone to before. A bright coal fire burned in the grate and they were the only customers. 'Cheers,' he said.

'What am I drinking?'

'Brandy and soda. It'll steady the nerves.'

'Do I look that bad?'

'I'll put it as gallantly as I can: you don't look your usual self.'

'I think I've just blown Jason's case,' she said. 'And I really believed I was on top of it.'

'You thought you could solve things for him?'

'I suppose I did.' She gave a slightly bitter laugh. 'Pack up your troubles – and bring them to Annie! Except it hasn't worked like that.'

'It rarely does. All we can do is give it our best shot. Tell me.'

'This may sound odd but ... he seemed a different person today. I thought I really knew Jason. I thought he was this big uncomplicated tennis player who had been accused of something he might not have done. Someone who had been abandoned by his family, who needed sympathy and sorting out.'

'That's the mother in you.'

'Well, he *was* a bit like an overgrown baby. The first day I saw him he was in tears.'

'And today?'

She paused as she tried to sort out her thoughts and find the exact words. She said, 'Today I thought for the first time that he could have done it.'

He had been a mixture of emotions; anger, suspicion, resentment. The emotions she would have expected to find in the average prisoner. They hadn't been talking for more than a few minutes when he said, 'Why didn't you tell me about the psychiatrist? The one who's coming from Loxton. You lied to me.'

'That's not true, Jason, I didn't lie.'

'You didn't tell me and that's a lie by omission.'

'Has this been bothering you? It shouldn't, you know. He's just another doctor. All we're trying to do is what's best for you.'

He looked at her scornfully. 'Do you know what you're saying? He's coming from a hospital for the criminally insane. Like Broadmoor. Where they put serial killers and axe murderers and God knows who else. He's *not* just another doctor. I thought you were my friend. Honest to God I thought that if there was one person I could trust it was you.'

She felt bruised.

He rolled a cigarette and lit it with a lighter she had seen before. As he raised the cigarette to his lips she noticed several circular burns on the inside of his wrist.

'Jason, listen to me. It's only because of what you did in

the police station. I've spoken to Dr Melville and he says that kind of violent behaviour in a police station often ends in a request for a psychiatric report. But you don't have to worry about it. And I *am* your friend. In fact I've been doing everything I can for you. So has my father. I told you he'd been to see Clare and today he went to see your grandfather. I haven't deserted you and I won't desert you and if you think I haven't been honest with you then let me tell you the reason why.'

He was staring down at his huge hands in his characteristic way, but the bewilderment and grief that had been in his face when she had first seen him was now replaced by sullenness and anger.

'I would have told you, you've got to believe that, in fact I was about to when you mentioned the letter from Margaret and the fact that she wanted a divorce. I felt I just couldn't add to that. Not at that moment. Because you see, there are other things.'

'What other things?'

'Things she's accused you of.'

The heavy head came up quickly.

'You're not going to like this and it's the reason I wasn't able to find a moment to tell you. But we have to talk about it some time. I personally think they're ludicrous but I must tell you how her mind is working.'

'Go on.' His voice was little more than a whisper.

'She's got it into her head that you may have ... interfered ... in some way with Julie.'

'What do you mean interfered?'

'Sexually.'

'Jesus!'

'I told you it was unpleasant. But I also told you we had to deal with it.'

'She says I *abused* Julie?'

'She told my father she saw you in the bath with her. I'm sure it was absolutely innocent but she thinks there was something going on.'

'She never said anything to me.'

'Maybe she was too frightened to. Don't forget you'd been rough with her.'

'I don't believe this is happening.'

'Women ... mothers ... sometimes do become convinced of situations like this. There's been so much publicity, so much unhappiness—'

'Me and Julie! For Christ's sake I love Julie! This is a nightmare.' He thrust his head at her. 'You believe her!'

'Jason I—'

'I bet you do!'

'I've already said I thought the accusations were ludicrous.'

'You keep on saying accusations. I don't think I ever took Julie into the bath more than once. And I remember now. It was her bath time and she was awake and crying and Margaret was trying to light the bloody stove. I was already in the bath and I got out and I went into Julie's room and picked her up and brought her back. She loved it. We played with her plastic toys. And after a while I soaped her. She had her own baby soap. And I think she rubbed her soapy hands over my chest. And Margaret came in and all she said was had I washed her properly and I said yes. So she picked her out of the bath and sat on the loo and dried her and then took her down for her supper. There was nothing more to it than that.'

'There were other accusations.'

'This sounds like the police station all over again. They started on about me and kids and I thought they were going to accuse me of abducting those two little girls.'

It had come too quickly. She was still trying to arrange sentences in her head and here it was.

He knew by her silence.

'You're kidding. Tell me this is some sort of joke.'

'She said you were away from home both days.'

'Oh, Jesus. Listen . . . That wasn't unusual. We were . . . well, we were fighting a lot and I couldn't take it so I'd get into the car and just drive and drive. Sometimes for hours.' Abruptly he said, 'You're trying to railroad me into Loxton.'

'Who?'

'All of you.'

'That's nonsense. I didn't say I believed her. I'm telling you for your own sake. She might go to the police with her suspicions. You might have to face questions about this.'

'Where? In court?'

'From the psychiatrist.'

'Hey, wait one bloody minute. There was going to be a court case. I was going to be able to defend myself, right? Now you're hedging.'

'No, Jason, I'm not. Of course there'll be a court case. Anyway you're going up for remand again. Nothing's going to happen very suddenly. You'll be remanded again and we'll talk and—'

'Fuck you!' he said. 'I'm not talking to you or anybody.'

'Jason.'

He looked down at his hands again.

'Jason?'

But he was like a statue. He neither moved nor spoke.

'And that's how it ended?' Tom said.

'I must have tried to coax him into speaking for about ten minutes. He simply paid no attention. He was like stone. I felt dreadful. Dreadful for Jason, and dreadful that I'd screwed it up.'

'You didn't screw it up. Let me get you another drink.'

'I'd rather have white wine than brandy.'

He came back and stood in front of the fire. They were still the only patrons in the snug and it was like being in a private suite.

'What's interesting,' Tom said, 'is that you say you had this feeling that Jason had changed *before* you told him of his wife's accusations.'

'I had the feeling from the moment he came in. He just seemed different to me.'

He was silent, sipping his drink. Then he said, 'Do you think he's a suicide risk?'

'I didn't, but now I don't know. We had a kind of rapport but—'

'Don't blame yourself. Remember, he'd changed *before*

261

you saw him.' He looked at his watch. 'Damn! The shops'll be shut.'

'Food shopping?'

He nodded. 'I might be able to—'

'Look, why—'

'There's an Indian takeaway in Castle Street, I can get something there.'

She suddenly visualised him going back to the cold dark house with Beanie his only company, eating the greasy rice out of the containers.

'What I was going to say is why not come back and have some supper at my house? It won't be much, my father does the shopping, but Hilly would love to have news of Beanie. And to see you, of course.'

He looked closely at her for a moment then said, 'No, no, that wouldn't be a good idea. Why don't we have a meal in town. Let me take you to dinner.'

'It's a perfectly good idea. Anyway, they're expecting me. That's unless you're worried about Beanie?'

'No, Harry Joyce looks after her for me. I couldn't manage otherwise.'

'Well, then . . .'

'If you're sure?'

'Of course I'm sure.'

There were lights on in the house when she got there but neither her father nor Hilly was present. On the blackboard in the kitchen Henry had written: Hilly and I have gone to the fair at Petersford. Back about nine-thirty.

'Deserted,' spe said. 'No matter.' She found a bottle of wine and gave Tom a corkscrew and two glasses. She looked in the fridge. 'I'm afraid we have a somewhat limited menu. How about smoked haddock and poached eggs?'

'Sounds wonderful. I haven't had it for years. Our cook used to make it for me when I came back for the school holidays.'

'That sounds rather grand.'

'It wasn't really. My mother couldn't cook. Simple as that. Either couldn't or wouldn't. Have you ever been to the Wye near Hay?'

She slid the haddock into the pan. 'No.'

'You should go one day. It's lovely countryside.'

'Toast?'

He sat in a kitchen chair and watched her. 'This is good,' he said, holding up the wine.

'My father knows a bit about wine.'

'I like him. He's a one-off.'

'Is your father still alive?'

'Which father?'

She turned to look at him and saw the same flash of cynicism on his face she had seen before.

'I had lots of fathers. One of the reasons my mother didn't have time for cooking. She was always in bed with someone. She was an artist. A portraitist. Most of the time she went to bed with her male sitters. I assumed she wanted to discover the inner man.'

Anne decided she didn't want the evening to become too heavy and she said, 'What did you do while all this was going on?'

'Rebuilt barns. How about that for a reply? I went to a school that still believed in teaching non-examination subjects. They thought it was important we should know about woodwork and restoration. My brother and I started off on our own tithe barn which my mother wanted for a studio. When other people saw it they asked us to do up theirs. Sometimes I wish I'd stayed with it, except my brother couldn't stand what was going on at home and made a bolt for Australia.'

'My mother was a bolter, too. She bolted from Africa. Left my father and me to cope. I can't say I blame her. Living in tents and being bossed by Watch can't have been much fun. So she bolted to Scotland and the arms of a laird. Are you really saying you didn't know who your father was?'

'Nothing as dramatic as that. I knew who he was all right. He couldn't stand the strain of my mother's life either and left when we were little. I don't think it made much difference to her whether he was there or not.'

'And you? You weren't a bolter.'

'No, I stayed. I didn't much like what she was doing but I thought someone had to stay behind and look after her. She couldn't cope very well by herself. Anyway one forgave Mother. She was amusing; the sort of person who left other people to handle her affairs.'

'You speak about her in the past. Is she dead?'

'No, she's still in the same house. It's not the sort of place one would ever want to leave if one owned it. On the bank of the river; our own stretch of fishing; a great overgrown garden. And on the far side of the river the land swelling up to a line of low hills which my brother and I used to climb when we were children.'

'It sounds wonderful.'

She put the food down on the table.

'It was, until we put two and two together. Not that Mother ever tried to hide her affairs. I think she thought of herself a little like a female Augustus John. She was built for polyandry. What about Hilly?'

'What about Hilly?'

'Who was *her* father?'

She ate in silence for a minute. She did not like this turn in the conversation. She did not like talking about the past as he had talked about his.

'Paul was an architect. They were building a new wing at the hospital where I was working in casualty, and he used to be on site almost every day. I met him when they brought in one of the building workers who'd been hit by a dumper truck.

'We began to see each other, fell in love, I became pregnant and we were going to be married. Then one day they had another casualty on the building site. A crane toppled and crushed a man. We were warned about it and got things ready while they were raising the crane. Then they brought the man in and it was Paul. We worked on him for a couple of hours but there wasn't any chance at all – and really he was so badly injured I thanked God. End of story.'

Tom opened his mouth but she said, 'Don't say anything. People never know quite what to say.'

'All right, I won't. Except for one thing. You don't talk about it much, do you?'

'How would you know that?' It was said acidly.

'By the way you reacted. The way you told it.'

'You're right. I don't.'

'You should. I don't mean go round like the Ancient Mariner, but I don't think you should hide it and preserve it.'

She was suddenly angry. 'It's all I have to preserve!'

'Sorry. It's none of my business.'

'Right.'

'But you see what you're doing, don't you? You're doing a Jason.'

She got to her feet and began to clear the table. 'That's nonsense.' But she knew it wasn't nonsense.

He rose to help. 'I'll do it,' she said.

'I'm quite domesticated.'

He washed while she dried and put away. 'Is there anyone current?'

'Yes. He was good to me after Paul died. Like your mother I needed someone to help me cope. He took over.'

'Love or gratitude?'

'That's the lot,' she said, indicating the dishes. She did not reply to his question. Tension had been growing between them and they hardly spoke. She told herself it stemmed from talking about Paul's death. She'd been irrationally angry and knew it. She was glad when he excused himself and left.

There was a message on her machine from Clive but she decided to leave the return call until the following day. She got into the bath and lay back and tried to relax but the conversation went over and over in her head. He had originally said he didn't think coming to the house was a good idea. He'd been right. She was worried about him being a complication, a really genuine complication which she would have to handle.

22

'Your hands are too big, old fruit, old bean. Okay for holding a tennis racquet but—'

'Don't call me that, Billy.'

'Don't call you what?'

'What you just called me.'

'What d'you want me to call you?'

'Jason.'

'Say please.'

It was late afternoon and they were in the cell. They no longer watched tv with the other remand prisoners.

'Please.'

'That's nice. Let me show you again, *Jason*.'

He poured the tobacco onto the white cigarette paper and deftly rolled it. Then he licked it and gave it to him.

'You still got my lighter?'

'Your lighter? I thought you gave it to me.'

'Gave it to you? Come on.'

'You said—'

Billy was suddenly harsh. 'Listen, Jason, I've had that lighter for years. I'm not going to give it away, am I? It's precious. Sentimental value. You can borrow it for today but only for today. Then we'll see.' He paused, waiting for a response. 'Well? What do you say?'

'Thank you.'

'It depends on you. Understand?'

'Yes.'

Jason lit his cigarette. He was sitting on his bunk, Billy on a chair facing him.

'So?' Billy said.

'What?'

'Listen, you come in all upset and you don't say nothing. I thought you were my friend.' He moved to sit beside Jason. 'You are, aren't you?'

'Yes.'

'What do friends do?'

'Support each other.'

'And?'

'What?'

'They tell each other things. That's what they do. Things that are too heavy for them. They get them off their chests by telling them to friends. It helps, Jason, it really does.'

Abruptly Jason said, 'They're trying to push me into Loxton. They don't give a shit about me. All they want is to get rid of me.'

Billy waited. After a few moments he said, 'Go on, Jason.'

And out it came in a rush: everything Jason had never meant to say. It was like vomiting. Afterwards he was shaky and sweating, but he felt better. Billy waited, watching. He took Jason's hand and held it. Softly, he said, 'I told you so. Didn't I tell you? You got no friends except me. You know that now, don't you?'

Jason nodded.

'Say it.'

'Yeah.'

'Say, yes I know it.'

'Yes I know it.'

'Okay, Jason, I'm your friend, I'll look after you but you got to be truthful with me. You understand?'

'Yeah.'

'Well then I got to know, did you do it?'

'Do what?'

'Did you do the kids?'

Jason flung the hand away. 'You bastard, you said you were my friend, now—'

'Listen . . . listen . . . don't get so upset. We're all of us in the nick. Why? 'Cause we done bad things, okay? We've *all* done bad things. I don't give a shit what you done. But you got to get it out. It's choking you. I spoke about secrets. Remember that?'

'I remember.'

'If we keep secrets bottled up they're going to do us harm. So I'm going to make a deal with you. You tell me yours and I'm going to tell you mine. That way we'll be true friends.'

'I already know yours. You burn down barns.'

Billy laughed. 'You think that's all? I got real secrets, old mate. You don't know about the thieving. You don't know why I took Rule 43. I mean, you don't ask to be segregated because you burn down barns. No one's going to cut you up in here for doing that. No, Jason, I got lots of secrets. But so have you. And they got to come out.' He paused and took Jason's hand again. 'Who loves you, baby?'

271

Jason got up and went to the window. Billy followed and put his arm around his waist.

'Jason. Who loves you? Who's the only one who loves you?'

'You do.'

'That's right. Me. I'm your friend. So all right, your wife accuses you of doing in two kids.'

'Not only that.'

'What?'

'She says that I ... I ... my own daughter... She says...'

'Do it, Jason.'

Jason looked at the cigarette for a moment then pressed the glowing coal to his arm. A wisp of smoke rose up and there was the sudden smell of a barbecue.

'Better?'

'A bit.'

'Listen, I want to tell you something. You're like a little kid in here, you react like a kid. You can't look after yourself but – look at me, Jason – right in the eyes – you listening?'

'Yeah.'

'I'll look after you. You leave things to me. Okay?'

'Yeah.'

'Give me your hand. Come and sit down. We'll talk a bit.'

They talked – at least Jason did – for nearly four hours. He talked and talked. Most of his life spilled out: his childhood, his tennis career, the Lloyds crash, Margaret, his arrest. When it was done he felt weak and soft; and he was filled with an irrational gratitude to Billy. Not only that, but he felt like a child again; gentle, defenceless, the way he dimly remembered feeling before he became a tiger.

They sat together on his bunk and by the time he was finished the cell was thick with smoke.

'Tiger?' Billy said. 'They called you Tiger? I better watch out then, hadn't I?'

He put an arm round Jason's shoulder. 'A really big tiger. But a tiger who can't look after himself. Are you still a tiger, Jason?'

'Not any more.'

'You're more like a lamb, aren't you? And I'm more like the tiger, don't you think?'

'Yeah.'

'And they wrote all those things about you? About bad behaviour and swearing at the umpires and all that?'

'I'm not proud of it.'

Billy shook his head. 'Amazing. You must have been like another person. A tiger with a sore head.' He giggled. 'Shall I call you Tiger?'

'You sound like my father.'

'You must have really hated him.'

'I did.'

'There's one thing you didn't tell me.'

'What's that?'

'Did you do in the two little girls?'

Jason began to cry then.

The following morning after sick parade Tom called Anne

into his office and waved her to a chair. Les Foley was already seated.

'I wanted you to hear what Les has got to say.'

Les wasn't smiling now. He said, 'It's about Newman, doc. There's something going on between him and Billy Sweete.'

She frowned. 'You mean sexually?'

'I don't know about that but I wouldn't be surprised. Happens all the time in the nick. No, it's more like a ... an ...'

'Association?' Tom said.

'That's it, doc. More like an association. Emotional if you like. A kind of dependency.'

'How do you know?' she asked.

'We hear things. Info's the most valuable thing in the nick after drugs and snout. The place is always a hive of rumours, some true and some false. It's what keeps people going. Little bits of information that are arranged in big pictures. Some of the information's wrong so the big picture's wrong, but some of it's right, and I believe this is right. Came from two separate quarters. The first was a prisoner who was cleaning near their cell; second was the chap in the cell next door.'

'What's happening?' Anne asked.

'He's got to Newman, doc. My information is that Newman's been crying a lot. And they don't mix with the other remand prisoners. They keep to themselves, which is unusual. Sweete's been through it all before. Knows the ropes; knows how to play the system. But he's a right bully. I've seen his type often enough. They do it for pleasure, like a cat plays with a mouse. They like to see how far they can go in breaking someone down.'

Tom said, 'Okay, Les, thanks. When does he go up for remand again?'

'Couple of days. I'll check. I'm not sure they don't go up on the same day.' He went out.

Tom rose and began pacing. 'Have you ever heard of the Stockholm syndrome?'

'Sounds like an old spy thriller with Paul Newman.'

He smiled. 'Yes, it does rather. But it's common jargon in the prison service and in the anti-terrorist and hostage branch of the Ministry of Defence. About twenty years ago there was a bank robbery in Stockholm and a series of hostages were taken by the robbers. There was a siege. By the end of it the hostages had empathised with the robbers.'

'I think I've seen a movie like that except it was set in New York.'

'Sweete could be manipulating him in a similar way; hard, then soft. Finally the victim becomes the "friend" of the victimiser . . .'

'And Jason has no other friends, or doesn't think he has, so he's even more susceptible.'

'Right. Everyone's dropped Jason – except you of course, and by now he thinks you've changed sides or perhaps never were on his side but only pretended to be.'

'And the only person who seems to be his friend is Billy Sweete?'

'That makes sense, doesn't it? After all they're banged up together. Alone a lot of the time. Why not? Can't you see the beginnings of paranoia?'

'There's something that I've been meaning to check. Why has Sweete taken Rule 43? Arson and masturbation aren't likely to get him attacked by other prisoners are they?'

'He's got a juvenile record. Exposing himself. That sort of information gets round the nick like one of his barn fires.'

'What about splitting them up?' she said.

'If you agree, I think we should let them go up for remand. If Les is right it's the same day. Then when they get back we could bring Jason into the hospital where we can monitor him. It's a natural break in the relationship. Then perhaps he'll transfer back to you or one of us.'

'Provided we can show we're on his side.'

She rose and he turned towards her. 'Thank you for last night,' he said formally. 'I'm sorry if I spoke out of turn.'

'We all have skeletons of one kind or another. It's just that I'm not used to talking about mine.'

Hilly was on holiday and went to an afternoon playgroup when her grandfather was unavailable. And he seemed, to Anne, more and more unavailable these days. What with his own work and the investigations he was making on her behalf, she realised that she was putting an extra burden on her father by expecting him to take over Hilly and the house in her absence. But what else could she do?

She picked up Hilly after work and did a little shopping. She was opening the door of the house when the phone rang. She remembered then, with a feeling of guilt, that she had not returned Clive's call.

But the voice on the other end was not his.

'Who?' she said.

The line was poor and the voice sounded as though it was coming via outer space, which in a way it was.

The man spoke again.

'I can't hear you. Can you speak up?'

Then she caught the word 'judge'.

'I'm afraid you must have the wrong number. This is Kingstown one-oh-four-two. What number did you wa—'

'Mizannie?' the voice said.

And then she knew.

'Watch! Is that really you?'

'Yes, yes, it is I, Watch.'

'Where *are* you?'

'I am spikkin from the Holiday Inn.'

'In Maseru?'

'Yes . . . yes . . .'

The loved voice of her childhood swept over her. She smiled as she visualised his thin, prim, old-maidish face. She asked how he was.

'No good, no good. Too much expenses. Where is Judge Henry?'

'Watch, he's not here. But he'll be in any minute. Let me get him to call you. You're not sick, are you?'

'No. I am not eh-sick.'

'Can you tell me what it is then?'

'I must eh-talk to Judge Henry. My money is running out.'

'All right. Have you got a phone?'

'No. I be here tomorrow this time.'

'Yes, but what's the number?'

The line went dead and as it did so her father opened the front door.

'Watch!' he said, when she told him. 'Damn! How did he sound? Was he all right? I'll have a try now. He mightn't have left the hotel yet. I remember it. Big place overlooking the Orange River. They've got a gambling area, roulette, blackjack. I don't know what it's like now but when I was staying there the place was full of white South Africans who'd come across the border to gamble and pick up black women. In those days both were crimes in their own country.'

He got through to international directory inquiries and in a matter of minutes was talking to the receptionist at the Holiday Inn in the capital of Lesotho. Anne picked up the other phone.

'. . . Smallish, elderly man,' her father was saying. 'He's just phoned from there. He may still be in the foyer.'

'You mean Mr Watchman Molapo?'

'Yes, yes . . .'

'I think he has just gone into the gaming rooms.'

'Can you give him a message, please. Tell him Henry Vernon called. Tell him I'm home and he can reverse the charges.'

Anne was bathing Hilly when the phone rang. Her father spoke for nearly twenty minutes and was pouring himself a whisky with shaking hands when she came downstairs.

'Well?' she said.

'Poor old chap's broke. He says his sister's family has milked him dry. He's been paying for their children's education out of his savings. But I don't think he's telling the whole story. Once when I was there I found him at the blackjack tables. He'd lost almost a month's wages. I wonder . . . Anyway, I'll send him some money.' He paused. 'What he really wants is to come here.'

'What?'

'He says he's fed up with Lesotho. He says there's too much violence and too much corruption.'

'And he wants to come *here*?'

'It may not always seem like it, but this country is a paradise compared to some. And Lesotho's one of the poorest in the world.'

'Anyway, it's out of the question.'

'I know.'

'I mean what would he *do* all day? And we'd feel responsible for him the whole time.'

'That's why I'm sending him some money. But it was horrible saying no. We were together for almost forty years. I know him better than I know you or Hilly.'

Anne began to make supper. She could see that her father was upset and changed the subject. He had been up to London that day and she said, 'Tell me about Stegman.'

'I don't feel like talking about him just now and I don't feel like supper. I'm going downstairs and I'm going to have another drink. When you're ready, come down. I'll tell you then.'

23

Tennis World was off the M4 motorway near Newbury in Berkshire. Henry had discovered in his researches that this corridor along the motorway between London and Bristol was the home of hi-tech in England and when he arrived at the tennis complex he saw that it fitted aptly into its surroundings.

He stopped at the big steel gates. There was only one button to press and he pressed it. 'Hi,' said the nearest gatepost. 'My name is Sandy. How may I help you?'

With some embarrassment he identified himself to the gatepost and the voice said, 'Mr Stegman is expecting you. Please wait for your escort.'

While he waited he looked around. Ahead of him he could see a large ranch-type building with tennis courts on one side and what looked like an aircraft hangar on the other. This, he was later to discover, housed four indoor courts each with a different surface.

His escort arrived, semaphored him into a parking space, opened his car door, and said, 'Hi, I'm Denise. Please come with me.'

The way she moved reminded him of one of the big cats;

a leopard or a young lioness. She was just under six feet tall, had short blonde hair, blue eyes, and a skin that glowed with health. The muscles in her long legs rippled and flowed in the most amazing way.

They entered the split-level building through doors which Denise opened with a plastic key-card. Above the doors were the words, emblazoned in gold paint; 'World harmony through tennis'. The receptionist signed him in, gave him a visitor's tag and asked him to take a seat.

The place was all stainless steel and potted greenery. The dominant colours were purple and gold. People flowed in and out continuously. They wore tracksuits in what he considered to be unalluring colour combinations, carried nylon bags on their shoulders and bundles of racquets under their arms. Through the huge glass windows he could see a dozen all-weather courts – some concrete, some clay – all in use. There was a constant stream of announcements: soft xylophone triplets followed by calls for David or Serge or Natasha or Mel to go to court number so-and-so. It reminded him of an airport.

He sat back and examined the foyer more closely. It was dominated by a large painting of a man in a purple and gold tracksuit, who he assumed was the founder of Tennis World, Lionel Stegman. Underneath, on a wooden panel, were the words, 'Release! Reinforce! Encourage! Succeed!'

In front of Henry was a low glass table on which there was a pile of magazines and books. One book was titled *Psychological Motivations in Sport* by Lionel Stegman. Henry opened it at random. He saw a sub-heading, Implosive Therapy, and read, 'Implosive therapy (Stampfl

& Levis, 1967) is a flooding procedure that adds to the learning-based extinction model concepts derived from psychodynamic theories. The most important of these is the avoidance serial cue hierarchy . . .'

He frowned and turned a few pages. He read, 'Intervention directed toward the modification of affect-eliciting cognitions . . .'

He closed the book with a snap.

'Mr Stegman will see you now,' a voice said, and in a matter of seconds Henry was in the Presence.

Stegman's office reminded him of the interior of a modern church. The wooden ceiling soared upwards, the upholstery and curtains were mauve, and there was soft piped music. The Founder was seated at a white desk underneath a series of photographs showing young men and women receiving large silver cups and salvers on courts throughout the world. Henry assumed they were clients.

Stegman was what his portrait showed, a big man and deeply tanned, with a bony, coarse face. He was dressed in his purple and gold tracksuit, his neck was decorated with several strands of gold chain, and on his feet he wore heavy Nike tennis shoes. His hair was thick and white and Henry remembered that he was nicknamed the Silver Fox.

He waved Henry to a low chair on the opposite side of his desk – cheap psychology, Henry thought – and said, 'So you want to talk about Jason.' He had a marked South African accent.

Henry had explained the reasons for his visit in the telephone call setting up the meeting.

'You said his family had abandoned him?' Stegman picked up a small replica of a tennis racquet done in silver so fine it looked as though it had been spun, and began to fiddle with it.

'Let me put it this way,' Henry said. 'He needs a friend.'

'Jason always needed a friend. I was that friend. I was his father and his mother. I was his family. That is how we operate. I give my all and that is what I demand in return.'

He had a way of speaking as though addressing an audience.

'This is a place of commitment,' he went on. 'A place of dedication. Those who dedicate their lives to tennis are welcome; those who do not have no place here. I am a bringer forth. I bring forth tennis. I release the tennis within the individual. Release! Reinforce! Encourage! Succeed!'

He began to stride up and down the room swinging the tiny racquet as though making forehand winners from the base-line.

'Those are our four key words.'

'To bring about world harmony,' Henry said.

'World harmony through tennis. Yes. Have you seen my book?'

'I was especially interested in the cognitive aspects of implosive therapy.'

The Founder paused, frowned, and said, 'I see.'

'And in the flooding procedure that adds to the learning-based extinction model concepts.'

'You're interested in sports psychology?'

'Aren't we all part of a great sporting family? What brought *you* to sports psychology, if I may ask?'

'I come from the dark and mysterious continent. I am a child of the bush and the jungle, the mountains and the trees; an inheritor of the great skies. I grew up with the Bushmen; guardians of the holistic integral.'

'I must have misread your biographical notes,' Henry said. 'I thought you grew up in Johannesburg.'

The Founder scowled at him. 'Only partly. You won't find everything in the newspaper cuttings, you know. There is an inner life that is private, untouched ... untouchable.'

'Tell me about Jason. His behaviour on court was pretty terrible, wasn't it?'

'That depends how you define terrible. He won tournaments. He might have won many more. He might have been up there with the real giants. But—'

'But?'

'Burn out.'

'Burn out?'

'Whatever fire glowed within burned out early. Jason was a disappointment to me.'

'But wasn't he your first great success?'

'What? No, no, not at all. There were others...' He waved the racquet vaguely. Then he said with irritation, 'Are you a tennis expert, Mr ... uh ... Vernon?'

'Not really.'

'Well, I am. And let me tell you something; when Jason came to me after his father died I found a personality that was in conflict. He was a manufactured young man. He was also a manufactured player. My job was to release the man and so release the tennis.'

'And did you?'

'Top ten on the computer for two consecutive years. Semis in two grand slams. Davis cup. The Diamond Challenge. I made him—'

'What he is?'

'You know, Mr Vernon, I don't think I like you. You come to me for help but your manner is confrontational.'

'My apologies. That must be the old legal experience.'

'Yes, well . . .'

'We were talking earlier about Jason's behaviour on court.'

'*You* were talking about that. But since you ask let me say this: when his father was alive he was inhibited. I broke down those inhibitions.'

'And released whatever was inside.'

'I erased what was there so I could begin again.'

'The tabula rasa.'

'The what?'

'The clean slate.'

'I like that phrase. I may use it in my next book.' He asked Henry to spell it for him and was writing it down when he stopped. 'One moment. It sounds as though you are suggesting . . . you're not suggesting I'm to blame for what has happened, are you? Because I find that impertinent, and anyway you don't know Jason as I do. On the surface he appears a big simple guy who loves to hit balls, but underneath is another Jason and underneath that a different one again—'

'Like peeling an onion.'

'What?'

'Nothing.'

'Well, Jason knew what he was doing all the time. Those losses of temper, that bad behaviour, was all calculated. And if you think I'm going to come to Jason's assistance over this then you're mistaken. You see, it's not the first time.'

'What does that mean?'

'Ask Jason. Ask him about a beach party in Cape Town after he'd won the Diamond Challenge.'

'Why don't you tell me? Jason isn't talking any more.'

'History repeats itself, Mr Vernon, you can be sure of that.'

'Attempted rape? Assault? What?'

'She was fifteen. It cost a great deal of money. I know, because I had the dirty job of fixing things.' He pointed the little racquet at Henry. 'You won't find that in your newspaper cuttings.'

'Did they give you a diamond?' Billy said.

'Of course not.'

'Why call it that then?'

'They've got to call it something. Anyway South Africa produces diamonds and the main diamond company put up the money.'

'How much?'

'A million rand.'

'What's that in real money?'

'It varies. Divide by five.'

'Two hundred grand! Jesus! You made that much?'

'Sounds a lot, but when you've paid your coach and your agent and your physio and your manager, etc, etc, then it's not so much really.'

'Of course it is! You want some coffee?'

'No,' Jason said. 'Do you?'

'Two sugars. Don't make it sickly.'

It was evening and the coffee machine was working on the landing. When he came back, Billy said, 'Come on, I feel like a story. Tell me one.'

'What about?'

'Anything. My First Fuck, by Jason Tennisplayer.'

'Don't call me that.'

'Come on, Jason, stop being such a prick. We've got the whole night to get through.'

'I don't want to talk—'

'Not about that. Tell me . . . oh, I know . . . tell me about the bloody Diamond Challenge. Tell me how you won; how you became a champion. You don't have to tell me any secrets. Just tell me something.'

'I don't feel—'

'Jason, what are you?'

'What do you mean?'

'You know what I mean.'

'I'm your friend.'

'Right, and friends tell stories, so get on with it.'

Heat.

Table Bay like a sheet of glass. Cape Town hotter than anything he could remember as a child, hotter than the Australian Open on the rubber surface in Melbourne, hotter than New York, hotter than the Davis Cup tie in Rome.

Just outside the city they said animals were dying; dropping dead in their tracks. In the city it was people.

39 . . . 40 . . . 41 . . . 42 . . . The Mercury crept upwards.

The Diamond Stadium was under Table Mountain. There

was a wind but no air. People called it a 'berg' wind, but it came not so much from mountains as from deserts: the Kalahari, the Namib, Bushmanland. It was so dry and hot that in a couple of hours lips cracked and bled.

Margaret wouldn't leave the hotel room. She had pulled the bed near the air-conditioner and lay there with her magazine.

He must be mad, she said. Crazy to play in this.

It was how he made the money. Their money.

Well, she wouldn't come if he paid her all the money.

They argued most of the time now. He knew she resented what had become of her life, her career, but she was his talisman. She and Stegman always sat together. When he was on the point of tanking he looked up and saw her and went on and won – maybe in some way he wasn't proud of, but he won.

He begged. He told her he needed her.

She repeated what she'd said. She wasn't bloody going out in this.

It was the final.

She knew it was the fucking final. She wasn't going out. Period.

And so he had waited in the lobby of the hotel for the courtesy car and Stegman had joined him.

Where was Margaret?

When Jason told him Stegman said he'd bring her down. But when he came back he was alone and he was flushed and angry.

If she was his wife, he said, he'd get rid of her.

Jason was playing Paco Berrio in the final. The local newspapers said Jason had only been a kid when Berrio was world number one. They said it was Superbrat versus Mr Niceguy. They said Jason was the best prospect in the world. They said Jason tanked. That Berrio had said so. They said Jason had called him an old man. They said it was a grudge match.

None of this was true.

The stadium was hotter than the streets; hotter than anything Jason had ever experienced. The final started at 2 pm, the hottest part of the day.

Stegman was still angry. He sat with Jason in their private locker room. He wasn't going to tell him anything more. Not going to say another word. He'd said his say about the holistic integral. About extrinsic rewards and intrinsic motivation. About cohesion. About cognitive-behavioural interventions. He was only going to give him the four key words: Release! Reinforce! Encourage! Succeed!

And then he was going to send him on court to beat the shit out of Berrio any way he could.

Oh boy, did Jason need the any-way-he-could psychology!

The heat brought him to his knees and before he could say 'conditioned anxiety response', never mind operate his game plan, he was a set down and losing the second.

He looked up but she wasn't there.

Stegman was in his purple and gold tracksuit; his face like stone. This was *his country;* his *humiliation.*

What the hell if he lost? Jason thought. What did it matter in the final analysis of the holistic fucking integral?

Berrio was belting the ball like he was twenty. Jason couldn't hit a thing. The court seemed smaller on Berrio's side; bigger on his. It changed when they changed.

Then there was a close volley from Berrio, very, very close. But it wasn't called.

What?

The line judge had his hands to the ground. No fault.

What?

The umpire was a coloured man. A coloured man in South Africa. There was fear in his eyes. No overrule.

It was out! You know what out is? You know how to spell out? O-U-T.

No overrule. Please continue, Mr Newman.

Mister. You call me mister, you understand?

That's what I said, Mister.

You calling me a liar?

He was not calling him anything he just wanted him to continue.

Berrio coming up to the chair. Hey, man, what the hell goes on?

Apologise, says Jason Tennisplayer.

Mr Newman, I am starting the watch.

Then Jason said something. And he spat.

No one agreed on the words. Those sitting near said the word 'black' was heard. And 'bastard'. Later Jason denied this. No one was sure anyway.

But the splash of spit on the umpire's shoe could not be denied.

They called the referee.

Every player spits, Jason said. In this heat mouths grew scummy. He didn't mean to hit the umpire's nice new shiny brown shoe.

He spat. That was all.

He smiled a little boy's smile.

So sorry. He got his towel and cleaned it. Carefully.

And the tv cameras were on him and the spectators were slow-clapping in the heat and they were booing.

The referee had to make up his mind. Here was the biggest tournament in the country. If he screwed up now the sponsors would murder him; that's if the twenty-five thousand fans who'd paid a hundred rand and risked heat stroke didn't kill him first.

Christ, man – the referee is talking to himself – Christ, man, there'll be a fucking riot.

So play goes on with Jason to serve 3–4 down and never mind the cognitive aspects of anything at all. Berrio hardly got another point.

Jason beat the shit out of him.

And in the newspapers the coloured man said he had heard nothing insulting and that everything had been fine, just fine.

Billy said, 'You really spat at him? You really meant it?'

'I don't know. It was a long time ago.'

'And then?'

'Then what?'

'You won two hundred grand. What did you do?'

'Nothing much. Went to a beach party.'

'With your wife?'

'It was too hot for her.'

'And then?'

'We flew to Florida the next day.'

'Jason . . .'

'What?'

'Jason ... Jason ... You're not telling everything. You're keeping secrets from me.'

'No, I'm not.'

'Liar.'

24

'Jason. Jason, wake up!'

'What?'

Billy Sweete laughed. 'You always say What? when you wake up. It's remand day, mate. We're going out today.

'I'd forgotten,' Jason said. He got out of his bunk and began a minute inspection of his clothes. Billy watched.

'You ain't going to impress anyone, Jason. It's only a friggin' magistrate. And he's only going to remand you again. It isn't as though it's some big trial on tv where they tell you to put your best clothes on so the jury will think you're respectable and never done it. It's not – hey, wait a sec, I get it. It's the media. The press. All rushing down from London in their cars with their big telephoto lenses and tv cameras and sound trucks.'

Billy grabbed a pair of Jason's socks rolled up into a ball and held them to his lips like a hand mike.

'Crowds attended the court appearance today of Jason Randypants, the former Davis Cup tennis player and bad boy of the courts. Jason is charged with stickin' his cock into a seventeen-year-old shop assistant. She says she loved it. He says, and I quote, "It's a frame-up, your worship. I never done it." This is William J. Sweete for News at Ten outside the magistrates' court in Kingstown. Pip pip and toodle-oo.'

'Very funny.'

'I thought you'd enjoy that. Don't you get it yet? They've forgotten you, Jason. Everybody's forgotten you. You're a has-been. You're just a dot on the horizon, a piece of shit. They don't give a tinker's about you. Nobody does. Except . . . ?'

Jason began to get dressed.

'Except . . . ? Answer me, Jason.'

Jason kept silent.

'Give me back my lighter then!' The teasing tone had gone.

Jason fished the lighter out of his pocket and gave it to him.

'D'you think you can survive without me, Jason? D'you think you can get through life in Loxton?'

'I'm not going to Loxton!'

'You carry on like this and you will, old fruit. Remember, when they do your evaluation they also do me. What if they ask me about your behaviour? What am I going to tell them?'

Jason looked at him sharply.

'Yeah,' Billy said. 'Think about it.'

'I'm sorry.'

'You're always friggin' sorry. You want to act proper and then you won't need to be sorry. Now . . .' he came forward and straightened Jason's collar. 'Who loves you, baby?'

'You do.'

'And don't forget it.' He patted Jason on the cheek.

The escorting officers came for them just after nine o'clock. There was a rattle at the door and the sound of a key in the lock. The door opened . One of the officers said, 'Get your gear together. All of it.'

They were signed off the wing and taken to reception. Jason and Billy were told to take their clothes off and given dressing gowns to put on. Their clothes were searched by hand then passed back to them. Once they were dressed staff went over them with metal detectors.

'Right. Get the rest of your gear.'

This came from the bigger of the two officers. He was a man called Prosser with a reputation for standing no nonsense.

'What for?' Billy said. 'It's only remand. We're coming back.'

'Because I said so.'

'Yes sir, Mr Prosser, sir.'

They collected their gear at the reception counter. Billy put on a tweed jacket that had seen better days and wrapped a claret-coloured woollen scarf round his neck. Dressed up in his street clothes he seemed, to Jason, a different person from the one he had shared a cell with.

'Come on,' Prosser said. 'Let's get going, the taxi's in the yard.'

As they moved off, the second officer, a smaller, thinner man called Hall, grinned at Jason as though to say: Don't mind him, we're not all like that.

The car was a black London taxi and it was parked on the cobbles in the yard. Prosser looked at Jason and said, 'You're a big bloke, give me your right hand.' He fixed a handcuff to Jason's right wrist and coupled it with Billy Sweete's left.

The driver was a pale, thin young man who looked bored, as though he had done this a hundred times before; which he had. The four men got into the rear of the cab and it was then Jason realised why they used these cabs. He and Billy sat on the back seat, the two escorting officers on the fold-down seats directly opposite and facing them. The glass partition separating the driver from the rear of the cab was partially closed.

Once they were settled they waited a few moments until the visitors had been cleared from the front reception area, then the steel gates to the yard were opened, and the big doors were opened, and the taxi drove through both into the outside world.

The day was dismal with black clouds, wind and rain. The traffic was heavy coming down the hill but finally there was a gap and they moved away from the prison into the Kingstown rush hour.

The four men stared out of the windows. In the grey light the prison looked forbidding. Officer Hall said, to nobody in particular, 'The forecast never said anything about rain.'

'They never get it right,' Prosser said, sourly.

'You remember that bloke on tv who said we were definitely not going to have a hurricane and then half the country blew away?'

'Bloody civil servants,' Prosser said.

'Aren't prison officers civil servants?' Billy said.

'You being funny?' Prosser said.

''Course not. I just didn't know whether you was privatised or not.' Billy turned to Jason. 'They're privatising everything these days. Prisons. Prison officers. They're going to privatise the Queen. She's going to have a stall outside the palace selling home-made marmalade.'

Jason continued to stare out of the window. Prosser looked at Billy Sweete with unreserved contempt.

'Yeah,' Billy went on. 'It's because everything's becoming too expensive for the country to run. Now you take us, Jason. We been told to collect all our gear. But we're only going for remand to the magistrates' court. Then back to the hotel on the hill. But we got to take it to court. Check it in with the police there. Go to the courtroom. Stand up and be remanded. Go back to the police. Check our gear out. Be searched. Go back to the hotel on the hill. Check in our gear again. Etc, etc, etc. That's bureaucracy, Jason. That's why the Prison Officers' Association doesn't want no private firms muscling in. That's why they need so many blokes. Like counting lamp posts. There's no work any more so the government has this brilliant idea: they send you out to count lamp posts and then they send me out to check that you counted them right.'

'Highly amusing,' Prosser said.

'Thought you'd get a smile out of that, Mr Prosser. That's why the country's deep in the shit. It's from counting lamp posts.'

'You know everything, don't you, Sweete?'

'Not *every*thing, Mr Prosser.'

'I've seen people like you before. Know-alls. Well, you don't know everything, Sonny Jim. If you knew everything you'd know why you were taking all your gear.'

The cab was caught in traffic, the diesel engine idling with the sound of safety pins rattling in a cup.

'Yeah,' Prosser said. 'Mr Bloody Know-all. If you know everything, how is it you don't know you're being split up?'

Jason turned sharply from the window to look at Billy and saw his expression change.

'Split up, Mr Prosser?'

'You're not going back to the same cell. He's going into the hospital.' He nodded towards Jason.

'What?' Jason said. There was alarm in his tone.

'Don't worry,' Billy said. 'He's talking balls.'

'Don't be cocky. You'll see.'

There was something in the smug way Prosser said it that seemed to enrage Billy 'What the fuck do you know!'

Hall said, 'Steady the buffs.'

Prosser laughed. It was an unpleasant sound. 'Let me tell you what I know, sonny, and then you might not be so know-all about everything. Mr Farley from the hospital told us. Isn't that true?' He turned to Hall for confirmation.

Hall nodded. Then he said to Jason. 'They want you by yourself. Mr Farley said you'd gone silent.'

Jason had turned to face Sweete. 'Billy?' he said.

'He's lying. He's trying to upset you, can't you see that?'

'Why would I want to upset him?' Prosser asked. 'What's the point!'

'The point is because you're a friggin' screw; that's the point!'

Hall said, 'Come on, Sweete, none of that.'

'Oh, leave him,' Prosser said. 'He's round the bloody bend if you ask me.'

'Billy?' Jason said again.

'Don't take no notice, Jason. Can't you see he's trying to make you lose your cool.'

'Like he did in the police station,' Prosser said.

'Don't listen to him!'

Prosser said, 'I don't give a monkey's what you do. Listen or don't listen, it's all the same to me. All I'm telling you is, you're going into the hospital, and you,' he leered at Billy, 'you're going back to Loxton.'

'What?'

'Stands to reason. You were there before. You set fire to your cell here – or so they tell me. You're a bloody nutcase. We don't want nutcases. We don't want all the aggro. I bet the magistrate sends you to Loxton. Unfit to plead.'

'Balls. They can't do that.'

''Course they can. New powers under the Criminal Justice Act.'

'What's he mean?' Jason said to Billy.

'He's talking bullshit.'

Prosser sat back and folded his arms. There was a faint smile on his lips.

'He's only doing it to wind us up,' Billy said, but there was doubt in his voice.

The taxi moved forward more swiftly.

'I want a smoke,' Billy said.

The cab driver said, 'Didn't you see the notice? This is a non-smoking vehicle.'

'Piss off. It's a free country.'

'Let him have a smoke,' Hall said. The driver closed the window angrily. 'Where's the packet?'

'Just the makings. In my pocket. This side.' He indicated his right-hand side and held up his hand waiting for Hall to give him the go ahead, but the prison officer leaned forward, reached into Billy's pocket and came out with papers and tobacco.

'You going to roll it too?' Billy said.

'Not me. I used to smoke tailormades, but that was a long time ago.'

'What about you, Mr Prosser?'

'You want to ruin your health, you go ahead by yourself.'

Billy lifted his manacled hand and began to roll the cigarette. 'Jason, you want one?'

Jason shook his head.

Billy licked the paper and put the rollup in his mouth. 'Anybody got a light?'

'I thought it had a self-starter,' Prosser said.

'There's a lighter in my pocket,' Billy said, indicating his left side.

Hall leaned forward and stretched his right hand into Sweete's left-hand jacket pocket. As he did so, Billy clamped his arm down hard, trapping Hall's hand and pulling him forward so that his head was almost touching Billy's knees. Then Jason saw something the colour of blood in Billy's right hand.

Prosser said, 'What the fuck!'

Billy said, 'Anybody move and he gets it in his eye.'

Hall said, 'Dave, I can feel it. He means it.'

'You bastard,' Prosser said to Billy, 'You think you—'

Hall said, 'Shut up, Dave, I don't want to go blind.'

'That's better,' Billy said. 'And I know what your orders are. Anybody in danger from a prisoner and you don't try heroics, you just do what you're told. Isn't that so?'

'That's so,' said Hall.

'Okay, you tell the driver—'

'Listen, Sweete—' Prosser began.

'Mr Sweete. You call me Mr Sweete. And you call him Mr Newman. Okay?'

Hall said, 'For Christ's sake, do as he says!'

Prosser looked at Billy as though he'd be pleased to see him pulled apart by bulldozers.

Billy said, 'You, Prosser, you tell the driver to get out of this traffic. Tell him to take the first street he can. And you tell him that if he touches that radio I'll stick this through this bloke's eye into his brain.'

'Do it, Dave,' Hall said.

Jason watched this happen like time-lapse photography, fast yet slow. He was bewildered and mentally unanchored.

Prosser opened the sliding window. 'Take the next street to the left, driver.'

'You think I don't know the way to court?'

'We got a problem,' Prosser said. 'My mate's in danger.'

The driver turned. 'Oh Christ!'

'And don't touch that radio,' Billy said.

'I don't want any trouble,' the driver said.

'You won't get no trouble,' Billy said. 'Just do what I tell you.'

'I didn't mean that about smoking; you smoke as much as you like.'

'For Christ's sake shut up and turn out of this traffic. Now you,' he said to Hall. 'Slide down off your seat and onto the floor. And you, Prosser, you just sit upright and look at the view. There were four of us. There're three of us now.'

The taxi swung into a side street.

'What you want me to do?' the driver said. His voice was showing signs of panic.

Billy said, 'You just listen carefully. You know Fernham?'

'No.'

'Black Down?'

'Yeah.'

'Okay. Fernham's to the east of that. Take the road towards Petersford. But don't go into the town. There's a by-pass. You come off the by-pass on the Winchester road then you go up Fernham Hill. When you get to the top there's a lot of little lanes. I'll tell you from there.'

'What happens if the radio starts? They may want to know where I am.'

'It's not linked to the prison is it?'

'No. The taxi firm.'

'They often get onto you?'

'Only when they need me to pick up a punter. But today's special. They never know how long the court's going to take. So they don't usually bother.'

'If they do and you don't answer?'

'They'll think I've gone for a cup of tea.'

'Then don't answer. And listen very carefully; I grew up in these parts. I know the roads and lanes like the backs of my hands. You try and do anything and this bloke loses his eye. Okay?'

'Okay.'

Prosser said, 'You must be out of your skull.'

Billy giggled. 'You hear that Jason? That's what he said a little while ago. He said I was a nutcase. That we both were. But now I got something that's going to get some respect.'

Jason looked down and what he had thought was blood was the deep red handle of a toothbrush sharpened to a needle point.

Billy said, 'They're so bloody clever with their searches and their security – and it was here all the time.'

He pointed to the seam of his tweed jacket collar. There was a small cut in the stitching. 'Just sitting in there waiting. And not all the metal detectors in the world could find it.'

Hall said, 'My knees are hurting, can I move? Lie down?'

'No,' Sweete said. 'You keep your head where it is.'

'What're we going to do, Billy?' Jason said.

'We're going to look after ourselves, that's what we're going to do.'

'But—'

'Yeah, what *are* you going to do?' Prosser said. 'When we don't show up at court there're going to be coppers all over these roads.'

'You think so do you, Prosser?'

'Yeah.'

'Billy?' Jason said.

The driver half turned.

'You keep your face to the front,' Sweete shouted. 'And don't drive more than thirty. You understand?'

The driver nodded.

'Say it!' Billy yelled.

'I understand.'

'Billy?' Jason repeated.

'For Christ's sake stop saying "Billy" like that! You want to go to Loxton? Because that's what's going to happen. They split us up, they put you in the prison hospital, then you ain't got a chance from there. I'll look after you, don't worry.'

'What about these people? What're you going to do with them?'

305

'Kill them if I have to.'

'What?'

Hall said, 'Mr Sweete, you're hurting me.'

Prosser said, 'Listen, I didn't mean all that about the Criminal Justice Act. I was only having you on, like.'

'Well, I'm only kidding you too,' Billy smiled at Prosser. 'Don't worry I ain't going to kill you unless you don't do what I say. Okay?'

'Sure. Anything.'

'That's the spirit.'

They drove towards Petersford, the black cab making its way at a sedate speed along the road.

Hall said, 'It's not too late, Billy. Let us go now and we'll put a good word in for you. Tell 'em you treated us right.'

'I'm not Billy to you, only to Jason. You understand?'

'Right.'

Billy winked at Jason. 'You want co-operation, you got to be firm. Let that be a lesson to you, Jason.'

The taxi left the by-pass, wound up a hill, and when it came to the top, Billy told the driver to take a small road. They entered a tangle of lanes in the parish of Fernham. The rain, which had followed them all the way from Kingstown, now turned into low mist which hung over the top of what was, in reality, not so much a hill as an escarpment eight hundred feet above sea level.

'They call this place Little Switzerland,' Billy said. 'You ever been to Switzerland, Prosser?'

In spite of the chill, sweat was standing out on Prosser's face.

'No.'

'No, what?'

'No, Mr Sweete.'

Through the mist they could see isolated houses, beech woods, the occasional surprised face of a Friesian cow.

'Driver, turn right.'

A narrow lane appeared. At its entrance a sign, covered in green fungus but still legible, said, 'Unsuitable for Vehicles'.

The driver took the lane. It went up steeply and then flattened out. Now they were in a different world. Another sign said, 'Forestry Commission. Keep Out'. A muddy track disappeared into a dark coniferous forest.

'Take that,' Billy said.

'The motor'll never—'

'Take it!'

They bumped and churned slowly along a logging track until the trees seemed to close over the taxi. What light there was became dimmer and dimmer and they were surrounded only by mist and the spectral shapes of tree trunks. They were as lost to human contact as it was possible to be in the south of England in the latter part of the twentieth century.

25

Anne stood at the window of her office and watched the rain beat on the towering prison walls. It was a sight out of Dickens, and names like Newgate and the Marshalsea rose in her mind. On such a day, she thought, Magwitch had been on the run from the Hulks in the Kent marshes, Smike on the Yorkshire moors.

It was not a day to be out. She remembered toasting muffins in Tom's house, the roaring fire, and Hilly's look of wonderment as she stroked the dog.

It was that sort of day.

Tom had been pressing her to bring Hilly out again but she was unsure. There was a sense of creeping involvement which made her uneasy. It would be simple to have an affair with him, very simple, but the consequences could be dire. She had never become emotionally attached to someone she worked with, and hoped she never would.

Thinking about Tom brought back the last conversation she had had with him. Inevitably it had been about Jason and what her father had discovered. Tom had not been impressed.

'Bad behaviour on court is almost *de rigueur* these days, isn't it? I mean it doesn't show any form of psychosis. I suppose one could argue the reverse; the path to victory begins with bad behaviour.'

'Not all all. Not everyone behaves badly. But I wasn't really thinking about that, rather of what happened afterwards.'

'What you really mean is what Stegman *said* happened afterwards. We haven't any idea whether he's right or wrong. Aren't there girls called tennis groupies who would give their right arms to go to bed with a tennis star?'

'Indeed. I knew a couple.'

'So . . . you win a major tournament. You go to a beach party afterwards. You're on a high. You meet a young girl who throws herself at you.'

'Young is fifteen in this case.'

'Would you agree that some fifteen-year-olds look eighteen?'

'I suppose so.'

'And then her father finds out or she simply says she'll report him to the police for having sexual intercourse with a minor – something neither he nor Stegman would want because of the scandal and the rubbishing of his reputation. So money changes hands.'

'You're very cynical.'

'This job makes you cynical.'

Now, as she thought over their conversation she realised she had been taking the prosecution view, Tom the defence. Yet earlier he had asked her to plead devil's advocate. The role reversal worried her. Was he simply putting a male viewpoint and she a female? Or had she really lost faith in Jason?

She remembered her own life at fifteen. Then, all she

310

wanted was to appear to be eighteen. Wasn't it natural? Understandable?

That had been her father's word. That what Jason might have done – the 'might' was important – was understandable, if undesirable. But *should* she approach it in that way? What of the girl? But the girl wasn't her problem; she was the state's. Jason was hers and it looked as though she had failed him.

The phone buzzed behind her. 'Front gate, Dr Vernon. There's a Mrs Melville to see you.'

'To see me? You must mean Dr Melville. He's in London today.'

'No, she said you, doctor.'

'What does she want?'

'She hasn't said. She's a bit . . . nervy, if you know what I mean.'

She put a mac over her white coat and ran across the open space to the main gate.

'She's in the shelter, doctor,' one of the prison officers said. 'Wouldn't come in.'

The building was like a large bus shelter opposite the main gates in which visitors could wait out of the rain. Stephanie was by herself. Again she was dressed in black and white: black trousers, a white polo-neck sweater, and a black trench coat flung casually over her shoulders. In the grey light her face looked drawn, almost haggard.

'How can I help you?' Anne said.

There were deep shadows under her eyes but the eyes themselves seemed to blaze like an animal's. She was smoking a cigarette and now ground it under a stiletto-heeled pump.

'I'm afraid Tom's gone to London,' Anne went on. 'He has a meeting at the Home Office.'

Stephanie lit another cigarette. There was something unsettling about her eyes, her whole demeanour.

Suddenly she said, 'Why are you doing this?'

'Doing what?'

'Don't pretend. You know what I mean.'

The French accent was stronger than it had been the first time they had met.

'Look, is there anything I can do to—'

'Please do not patronise me!' She began to pace up and down. 'Do you think I do not know what is going on?'

'Is there something going on?'

'Between you and Tom.'

Anne gave a small laugh. 'I'm afraid you've made a mistake.'

'Don't lie to me! I know. You think you can hide behind a child? You think I don't know what goes on?'

'Mrs Melville, I really can't stand here arguing with you about something like this. There is nothing between Tom and me. Nothing at all. Whether you believe that or not is up to you but I don't want you coming here and accusing me, or Tom for that matter, of something that isn't true.'

Stephanie walked away a few paces and then turned to stare at her. 'Tom is no good for you. He can never love someone like you. This is a warning, you understand, next time things will be different.'

In the distance, behind Stephanie, Anne saw a female figure struggling up the hill. She passed the security barrier and entered the car park. It was Ida Tribe and she had a heavy shopping bag in either hand. A gust of wind blew down the hill and caught her sideways and she stumbled. Stephanie was still talking but Anne's whole attention now was fixed on Ida. The next gust was stronger and it turned her around. She clung onto the bags, stumbled, and fell.

Anne ignored Stephanie and ran to Ida.

'Oh, my goodness,' Mrs Tribe said. She had gone down full length and was trying to push herself upright.

Anne knelt beside her. 'Are you all right?'

'Oh, my goodness.'

'Don't move.'

'Doctor, is it you?'

'Yes, it's me.'

'I'm so embarrassed!'

'There's nothing to be embarrassed about.'

'My frock. It isn't up is it?'

'No, no, nothing like that.'

Anne smoothed down the skirt. 'Don't worry about your frock, are *you* all right?'

Ida Tribe felt her limbs and said, 'I think so. It was the wind. Can you give me a hand up?'

Anne helped her to her feet and watched her anxiously. She held onto her arm and took a few steps. 'Nothing broken,' she said. Anne could feel her trembling with the shock. She picked up one of the shopping bags. It was heavy.

'You shouldn't be carrying these,' she said.

'I haven't had a chance to shop in the past few days. I wanted to give Billy some things.'

'He's not here. He's gone to court.'

'They going to try him already?' There was sudden apprehension in her voice.

'No, it's just for a remand. But he could be there for hours. It depends on whether the courts are busy or not.'

She helped Ida to the shelter and only then realised that Stephanie had gone.

Ida was limping and tears were running down her cheeks. Anne said, 'We've got to get you home.'

'There's a bus in an hour or—'

'No, I don't mean by bus. I'm not having you going by bus, you're not in any fit state.'

'I'll be all right. It's passing now. It's just that I was shook up.'

'You wait here on the bench. I'll be back in a minute.'

Anne went into reception and asked if there was any transport available. There was none. She rang through to Jenks and told him she would be away for an hour or so.

'But what about your—?'

'Whatever it is I'll see to it when I get back. Anyway I've got my bleeper. You just hold the fort.'

She returned to Ida. 'Come on, Mrs Tribe, I'll run you home.'

The farm huddled against the slope of the hill. Once sheep had lambed here and cows had been milked. Fields had been ploughed and sown and reaped. Now, where corn had grown, there was only tangled grass and weeds. The barns were empty, slates were gone from the roofs, windows were broken, and doors were swinging on their hinges in the gale.

But there was activity. Two police cars, their blue roof lights flashing, their radios crackling, stood outside the main house. A knot of people, some in uniform, stood in the porch out of the wind.

'Jesus!' Jason said. 'It's the police.'

''Course it is. Didn't I say they'd come? Didn't I?'

'Yeah.'

'Didn't I get us here? Didn't I bring us back safely?'

'Yeah.'

'Okay. So I was expecting the coppers. Had to come.'

They stopped behind a hedge. Both were wet through and covered in mud.

Jason was feeling terrible. They had come several miles through fields and dense bush and he was badly out of training. But it wasn't only that. He had been feeling physically ill ever since they had got out of the taxi and Billy had gone berserk. He had held the needle-sharp shiv to Hall's eye while he had ordered Prosser to remove their handcuffs and use them on themselves. He had cuffed the two escorting officers to the grab handle of the taxi and had then tied up the driver with a pair of jump leads.

'Right,' he had said. 'It only remains for us to say a big thank you.' And he had kicked Prosser. He had aimed at the groin but Prosser had jerked backwards and the kick had landed in his stomach. For some seconds Billy lost control of himself. He had picked up a branch and smashed it into Prosser's face and when Hall had objected he had beaten him, too.

'Don't!' Jason had said, and held his arm.

'Leave go!'

'You want some, too?' he had said to the driver.

'God no. Please. Listen. I've got some cash. You want the cash? Take it.'

So Billy had taken more than thirty quid and then he had led Jason away at a fast trot.

'Bastards!' he had said as they went through the dark woods. 'Fucking screws.'

They had stopped only once to drink at a stream. 'You okay, Jason?'

Jason thought that if he opened his mouth to speak he would vomit.

'Listen, they deserved what they got. Don't worry about it.'

He looked broodingly into the river. 'I could have killed them, you know. Anyway, would you rather go to the madhouse?'

A little further on they passed the blackened ruins of a barn. Billy stopped and looked at it. 'Yeah,' he said. 'I remember that one.' He turned to Jason. 'I used to plan it like a military operation. Had maps of the whole county. I knew every barn. Come on.'

It had taken all of Jason's strength to reach the farm. Now, using the hedge as a shelter Billy moved closer to the group of men. Jason followed.

Snatches of conversation came to them on the wind.

'. . . Dangerous?' Major Gillis was saying. 'No, no, he's not dangerous. A bloody pervert, yes, and a stupid bugger but no, not dangerous . . .'

The wind blew the next sentence away.

'Oh, Mr Gillis,' Billy whispered. 'Poor Mr Gillis.'

'. . . Not to me . . . I've dealt with him before . . . I'll deal with him again . . .'

Gillis held up a blackthorn stick.

One of the police shook his head violently, '. . . Law in

your own hands . . . Anyway, there's two of them . . . give us a call, sir . . .'

'Won't come here, anyway.'

'. . . Never tell, sir. Trouble is the dogs are useless in this weather. We took them up to Fernham Hill after the forestry worker released the captives. Couldn't smell a thing and . . .'

'Fucking forestry worker!' Billy whispered. Then he giggled. 'God, he must have had a shock!'

'. . . A taxi?' Gillis was saying. 'A black cab? What the bloody hell next? Make 'em walk, the sods.'

Two policemen got back into their cars. It was cold in the wind.

'. . . Leave someone with you if you like. We've told the local police and warned the village bobby. It's not as though he's dangerous, but if . . .'

'. . . Leave him to me . . . Oh, all right, all right, I'll phone.'

The police cars started up and drove off down the farm track, their rear lights winking in the misty rain. Gillis limped back into the house and slammed the door.

'Come on,' Billy said, 'let's get out of this.'

He led Jason along the track the police cars had taken, past the ruined barns, to a little knoll a few feet above the level of the road, hidden both by barns and by a stand of hawthorn. From a distance the place looked like a farm graveyard but instead of gravestones there were, among the docks and nettles, a small concrete emplacement and what looked like the end of a large drain pipe filled with cement, which cleared the concrete by about two feet.

They climbed through the fence. Billy pointed to a heavy

steel plate the size of a large square man-hole cover secured by a heavy brass padlock.

'You just hang on one sec, Jason, old sport. You'll feel better once we get into the dry.'

He lifted a roofing slate hidden in the grass, brought out a key, opened the padlock and raised the steel cover.

'I'll go first,' he said. A black hole yawned in front of them. A steel ladder disappeared into darkness. A gust of air, dank and reeking, came up to meet them. The smell of it made Jason feel worse.

'Okay, Jason, you can start down now.'

The light, dim at first, grew stronger as Billy turned up the wicks of a couple of oil lamps. Jason descended into a small room about fifteen feet by ten. In it was a narrow steel-framed bunk on which there was a mattress and blanket, there was a pile of books along one wall opposite a notice board on which there were a dozen or more drawing pins still holding corners of yellowing paper – all that was left of notices ripped off in times past. There were some serial numbers in black paint on the thick walls, a small shaving mirror, and on the floor was a highly coloured cheap rug.

Jason felt like he was entering a catacomb.

'Home from home.' Billy lit some sticks of incense. 'You know what this place is? This is a reservoir, that's what it is.'

Jason shook his head confusedly.

'Yeah. You look at any map. Says reservoir. But it ain't a reservoir. It's a secret place and there are six hundred places like it round the country, and hardly anyone knows about them. This is a nuclear bunker, old sport. This was for the army in case Mr Gorbachev fired his missiles at us.

318

This was where they were going to check the radioactive fallout and keep in touch with other bunkers by radio. The signal corps people used to come here and exercise every two weeks or so. See that door?' Jason made out the dim lines of a door against the far wall. 'Chemical toilet. Nasty, dirty lot the army. That's where the smell's coming from so if you need to go, then go outside, okay?'

Jason listened numbly.

'Anyway,' Billy continued, 'Mr Gorbachev didn't fire no missiles. Didn't do nothing, so these became what's known as surplus to requirements, Jason, old bean, and the government said we don't want this no more, we'll sell it to you. So old man Gillis said, you dug it on my land, you fix it all up like it was before and they said we're the real army, not the friggin' territorials, so shut your face.

'They said you can have the bunker. You can use it for anything you like. But what could he use it for? With his arthritis he couldn't even climb down the ladder. But yours truly did. Oh, yes.'

Jason sat down on the bed and began to shake with cold.

'What we got to get is some dry clothing,' Billy said. 'You hungry?'

Jason shook his head.

'Well, I am. I dunno whether I got any clothes that'll fit you but I'll find something.'

'Don't leave me.'

'I'm not going to *leave* you. It's only for a few minutes.'

'I don't want to be alone here.'

'What is it? The smell?'

Jason nodded. 'That. And the cold.'

'If the two of us go out we're more likely to be seen. Now

you just be a good tennisplayer and wait here and Billy is going to look after you.'

He put his arm round Jason's shoulder. 'Who loves you, baby?'

But Jason did not reply.

Billy climbed up the ladder and disappeared. Jason looked about him. It was a terrible place, worse than the cells. His mouth was full of saliva and tasting of copper. He lay down on the bed and pulled the blanket over him.

26

Billy Sweete stood in the shelter of a barn. The drizzle had strengthened and heavy black clouds smothered the daylight. Loose windows and doors kept up a continuous banging in the wind. The two houses, Ida Tribe's cottage, and Gillis's more substantial farmhouse, leaned against the sky and the wind. There were lights on upstairs in Gillis's house. Billy thought he knew what the old man would be doing, either playing with his toy soldiers or watching the races on tv.

It was the soldiers which had first got Billy into those upstairs rooms. He was a kid then. There must have been a thousand soldiers; two armies, both equipped with tanks and armoured cars and signalling units, everything. The old man liked to fight the World War campaigns over again, especially El Alamein.

Billy had never seen anything as beautiful as those soldiers; had never lusted after anything quite as much either before or later, not any artefact, that is. Gillis had guessed. 'Don't you want some of your own?' he'd said, and Billy had nodded. Then Gillis had said, 'We'll be friends, good friends. I'll show you what really good friends are like. Secret friends. And then you can have a soldier.'

That's how it had started. Up there, in the spare bedroom.

Keeping to the shelter of the barn walls as best he could, Billy circled the houses until he came to the rear of his grandmother's cottage. It was locked and dark but he knew where she kept the key. The smell inside was the smell of his childhood, of his whole life almost as far back as he could remember; the smell of cheap coal and frying. Smells seem to have got caught up in the cottage. The windows didn't open, the heavy thatched roof kept everything in. There was a toilet down in the garden, with a septic tank that overflowed. That had reeked, too. He'd grown up with smells.

He switched on the light, a weak forty-watt bulb, and went up to his room. His mattress was rolled up, his blankets folded. His cupboards and drawers were empty, the clothes were gone. All the pictures on the walls, the ones he'd torn out of magazines, were also gone. There was no trace of himself. It was as though his grandmother had tried to erase him.

He was angry. He went down to get food. Ida's kitchen cupboards were empty. He realised that with him gone she probably kept all food at Gillis's house where she cooked. He wondered if she was living over there now. He wondered if she'd ever suspected about him and the old man.

He walked over to Gillis's house. The back door wasn't locked and he went in. The kitchen was a mess, the breakfast things had simply been pushed aside for lunch.

He went straight to the larder. On the back of the door hung a collection of his grandmother's plastic shopping bags. He took down a couple and began to stuff things into them: bread, butter, some tinned food. On one of the larder shelves was the cheese board with its glass cover. There was a piece of cheddar there and he was hungry. He fetched a kitchen knife and sliced himself a piece. He stuffed it into his mouth. There was a noise behind him and he whirled round. Gillis was standing in the middle of the kitchen.

'I never thought you'd come,' Gillis said. 'But you were always stupid.'

They stood in the gloom staring at each other for some seconds. Gillis had a heavy stick in his hand.

Billy said, 'What are you going to do?'

'Call the police, what d'you think I'm going to do? Where's the other prisoner? The one you escaped with?'

'I dunno. We split.'

Gillis was in his long brown coat which Billy had known for most of his life. The old man would have been over seventy but his hair was still dark and thick above a bony face and sunken eyes, and it was only the bend of his spine and his limp which told of his age.

'What d'you want to phone the police for?' Billy said, edging slightly closer.

'Because you're a bloody menace, that's why. A menace to society.'

'I never done anything to society, Major.'

'"Major", is it? You never called me major before. Now it's major all of a sudden. Well, it isn't going to work. Ever since you were a little boy I knew you were rotten, absolutely rotten.'

Stung, Billy said, 'Who made me rotten?'

Gillis blinked at him. 'What do you mean? D'you mean—?'

'Of course that's what I mean.'

'You're not blaming me, are you?'

'You was an adult.'

'You wanted the soldiers, didn't you? Anyway . . . we had a bit of fun that was all.'

'You call the police and I'm going to tell them about your bit of fun.'

'What? After all this time? They'd never believe you. And you try anything like that and out goes your grandmother.'

'I don't give a shit whether she goes or stays. She doesn't want me no more. She's cleaned out all my stuff anyway.'

'That's nothing to do with me.'

There was a telephone in the kitchen and Gillis began to move backwards towards it keeping his eye on Billy.

'What're you doing?' Billy said.

'What I said I was going to do; phone the police.'

'Please, Major, don't . . .'

'First Major, now please. I've never heard you say please either.'

Billy came forward, his left hand outstretched in supplication.

'Don't do it. Give me a chance. I never had a chance. We never had no money. I never had no father or a proper mother. I ain't even done anything, not to you anyway.'

Gillis raised the stick. 'You burnt down half my bloody farm, you pervert.'

'Please,' Billy said. 'Please . . .'

'Stay back!'

Gillis's hand went to the phone.

'Just give me an hour. Listen . . . I'll make a bargain. I'll tell you where the other bloke is. Then you can ring the police. They'll thank you for that. They'll be ever so pleased.'

'You said you didn't know where he was. You split up, remember?' Gillis smiled. He had lost several teeth in his lower jaw. 'You always were a bloody liar.'

'I'll go on my knees to you.'

'Get up.'

And he did, fast, and knocked the stick away and drove the knife into Gillis's chest.

'Oh my God!' Gillis said. 'What d'you think you're doing?'

Billy stabbed him in the stomach.

'Don't Billy, don't.'

'So it's "Billy" now is it!'

He stabbed him again.

'Oh, Jesus!'

'That's for all the things you done to me. And that! And that!'

Gillis fell sideways, sprawling across the table, knocking cutlery and china onto the floor. Billy was onto him like a tiger. They went down together. Billy sat on his chest and sawed at his throat. A fire spray of blood covered his face.

He was shaking when he got up. He knew – without even thinking coherently – that what he had done had changed everything; that he had taken a final step. He ran upstairs, smashed open Gillis's gun case and took out his shotgun. He loaded the gun and stuffed more cartridges into his pocket. The walls of the room were suddenly lit by beams of light as a car turned in the gravelled drive below.

In the car Anne said to Ida, 'How are you feeling now?'

'Oh, I'm fine, doctor. It was so silly. Come in and I'll make a cup of tea.'

'Thank you, but I must be getting back. I'm on duty.'

The word duty impressed Ida.

'I'll come with you to your door,' Anne said. She wanted to see Ida on her feet before leaving her.

They walked to the cottage. Ida got out her front door key. 'I'm very grateful doctor.'

'Have a quiet day if you can. Don't try to do too much.'

She went back to the car feeling a glow of virtue. She slipped into the driving seat and instantly realised she was not alone.

Billy Sweete said, 'What's up, doc?' And giggled. 'What's new, pussycat?'

She felt the shock of his presence like a physical blow.

'What are you doing here, Billy?'

It wasn't much but she spoke before she had time to think.

'What are you doing here, Billy?' He mimicked. 'What d'you think I'm doing here? I'm sitting in the back of your car and I've got a shotgun on my lap and I don't want you to turn around. Understand?'

'Yes, Billy.'

'And don't call me Billy. You call me Mr Sweete, you understand?'

'Yes, Mr Sweete.'

'Right. I'll tell you what I'm doing here. Me and your precious Jason, we escaped. That's what we're doing here. And now we're moving on and you're going to help us.'

'But how can I help you? There's noth—'

'That's for me to know and you to find out. Understand me?'

'No, I don't.'

'You don't? I thought you understood everything.'

'Billy—'

'What did I tell you?'

'Mr Sweete, you're making a mistake. I can help you but not if you go on like this.'

'All my life people have been wanting to help me. But there was always a catch. No one ever said, Billy, I'm gonna help you; I'm gonna give you this or that. They always said, I'm gonna help you if you do this, give you this if you do that. See? There's a difference. C'mon, drive.'

'Which way?'

'The way you came. And when I tell you to stop I want you to get out of the car.'

She drove away from Gillis's house, along the track. He said, 'Go up here,' and she drove up behind the barns where the car was out of sight of the houses. 'All right, get out. See that fence? Get through it.'

She climbed through the fence and saw the illuminated hole.

'Go down the ladder.'

'Billy, don't do this.'

'I told you not to call me that.'

'But you are Billy. That's what people have called you all your life. Don't do this.'

'Get down the fucking ladder!'

She looked round for something to grab, to fight with, but all she saw was the long grass and the nettles. She began to climb down into the putrid hole in the ground. Billy followed.

'Jason. Jay-son! I'm always waking you up!'

Jason was ice cold but sweating at the same time. He felt deathly sick. It was the same kind of sickness he had felt after a session with his father, when as a little child he had run to his mother and she had taken him in her arms and comforted him. The coppery taste was worse. He sat on the bed.

'We got a visitor,' Billy Sweete said.

'Jason,' Anne said. 'This isn't going to help you.'

In the lamplight she could see that his face was wet.

'Jason, what you're doing is wrong,' she said. 'You're not a criminal. You haven't even been tried yet. But you're acting like one. Come back with me and—'

'That's right, Jason. You go back with her and you'll end up in Loxton, old man. You'll end up in a loony bin taking drugs for the rest of your life and asking some screw every time you want to go to the toilet. You fancy that, Jason?'

'That's nonsense. Dr Melville and I have discussed your case. My father's even been to the house of the girl who alleges you raped her. And he's found out things which make us believe—'

'Shut up!' Billy shouted. 'You're a lying bitch. You're all the same. Bitches!'

Jason said, 'Hang on a sec, Billy.'

'Don't listen to her!' Billy said, and struck Anne across the mouth with the back of his hand. 'Bitch!'

'Wait,' Jason said.

'There's no time to wait. Things have changed, old sporty tennisplayer. We got to move.'

'But what about her?'

'We leave her here.'

'Here? In the hole?'

'Of course. Where else?'

Anne felt the blood leave her face. 'Don't leave me here!' She thought of Hilly waiting to be picked up at her playgroup. She thought of her father. 'Jason, don't let him do this!'

But Jason slowly shook his head. His mouth was filling with bile. He looked round desperately for somewhere to throw up. He grabbed the handle of the toilet door and wrenched at it.

'Jason!' Billy shouted.

The purulent air hit him like a shock wave. His stomach heaved dryly. In the light of the oil lamps the dolls looked shadowy and menacing, all wrapped in plastic as though they had come from the shops. Big for dolls though. Too big. The eyes and the hair and the teeth suspended in liquefaction . . .

Billy slammed the door shut.

'I told you not to open it, Jason old bean, old sport. And now look what you've done.'

'Billy, you . . . you . . .'

'Me . . . me . . .' he mimicked.

'Oh, Jesus. The kids.'

'You shouldn't have opened the door, Jason. Don't you remember Bluebeard's room? You never, never open the door, do you Sister Anne?'

'You bastard!' Jason shouted.

'Sticks and stones, old tiger.' He swung the gun round to cover him. 'Do you see anyone coming, Sister Anne? And you won't neither. This is a reservoir, don't forget. No one's going to look here. And you can shout as much as you like, there's eight feet of concrete all around you.'

'You're mad!' Jason said. 'Crazy!'

'Don't say that.' He released the safety catch on the gun.

'But you are! And you blamed the kids on me!'

He raised the gun to Jason's chest. 'Who loves yo—'

The bleeper in Anne's coat pocket went off. Billy half swung towards her. And Jason's powerful hands which had been so assiduously created by his father and were so fast, so very, very fast, shot out and gripped Billy by the throat and slammed him against the wall. The shotgun came up. Anne grabbed the barrel. When it fired in the confined space it almost punctured their eardrums. But the shot went up into the dark winter sky and that was the last sound Billy Sweete ever heard, for a few moments later Jason squeezed the life out of him.

27

Hilly was asleep. She lay on her back, mouth slightly open, lips turned upward in a faint smile. Anne stood at the bedroom door looking down at her. Henry had come up too and was standing at her side.

'Isn't she marvellous?' he said softly. 'You were like that once.'

'Not any more.'

He watched her with troubled eyes. 'She'll never know. Not unless you tell her.'

'Perhaps I will one day.'

They went downstairs. The past six or seven hours had been an extension of the nightmare. There had been Gillis's body and Ida Tribe's hysteria. The police. The Governor. The statement to the press. The gauntlet of tv cameras. Jason had been the least of her worries. Indeed it was he who had phoned the police from the farm while she comforted Ida. There had been no hint that he might run. No hint of further anger. On the contrary he seemed drained, leached, squeezed dry of emotion.

But the images in her mind were not those of the police or the media but of the two little bodies wrapped in plastic.

Their faces metamorphosed into Hilly's face. Two identical faces, lying dead there in the stench.

Eventually the police had finished with her and she had been allowed to leave the prison – but not before there had been talk of counselling. Finally she had lost her temper and said, 'I don't want a counsellor, I just want to go home!'

'Do you want to talk about it any more?' her father said, as they entered the living-room.

'Not really.'

'When you do, I'm here.'

'I know.'

'Meantime, may I recommend a stiff drink?'

She shook her head. 'It would go to my legs.'

'Do you want company?'

'I think I'd like to be by myself for a little while. I hope that doesn't sound ungrateful.'

'Of course not. I'll be down in the flat if you need me.'

She kissed him and watched him go down and close the door. She was uncertain of what to do. She didn't want food or alcohol. She'd had a shower and in a little while she'd have a bath. Without conscious thought she began to tidy. She tidied the living-room and then went to the kitchen and cleaned it compulsively. She washed the dishes and put in the laundry and mopped the floor and wiped the work tops. She was just starting on the oven when the phone rang.

Tom, she thought. His had been the mystery absence. He had gone up to London for the monthly meeting at the Home Office but had left Whitehall before he could be told what had happened. He had then vanished. He should have been back in Kingstown hours ago.

She was feeling aggrieved with Tom. She had wanted and needed him by her side when they asked her questions about Billy Sweete and Jason.

Had she thought of Sweete as an escape risk? If not why not?

Not in quite those words, but that had been the burden and slowly she had begun to feel that *she* had been to blame for it all.

But it wasn't Tom; it was Clive. 'I'm on the motorway near Leicester,' he said. 'I've just heard the news. Are you all right?'

'Yes, I'm fine.'

'Listen, that's it! Okay? That's the end!'

'What's the end?'

'You haven't got a contract, have you?'

'A contract?'

'I mean you're not tied up for six months or a year, are you? Even if you are we'll break it. Let the bastards sue!'

'What's this all about, Clive?'

'You're getting out.'

'Now, wait a moment.'

Her first reaction had been to hand in her resignation, not for her own sake but because of Hilly. But when Clive put it like that in his boardroom voice, the voice which he used to steamroller the opposition into doing what he wanted them to do – something inside her reacted.

'I'm not under contract and I'm not resigning. Not yet, anyway.'

'Listen.' Now she heard anger in his voice. 'Listen, I'm not having—'

'Clive, I don't want to talk about it. You're treating me

like a parent treats a child who's been in danger, a mixture of relief and anger. I know because I've spoken to Hilly like that.'

'That's exactly it. That's how you need to be treated. I told you right at the beginning that this was a stupid thing to do. You want your independence, I can understand that but—'

'Clive, listen—'

'If you married me you'd never have to work again. Separate bank accounts. Monthly allowance – a generous one. You could look after Hilly properly and you could also look after me and—'

'What d'you mean "properly"?' Her voice was like a razor.

'I don't mean that you don't look after her as well as you can but—'

There was the sudden peal of the doorbell. She jerked with fright. 'There's someone at the door. Probably the police again. I can't talk any more now.'

'I'll ring you later.'

'No, don't. I'll ring you tomorrow.'

He was starting to say something else when she put the phone down and went to the door. It wasn't the police but Tom, and he was paying off a black cab, or at least trying to. The cabbie was doubtful about taking a cheque. 'Okay, guv, but it better not bounce. I'll come looking for you.'

He drove off in a cloud of diesel. Tom ran up the steps and took Anne's hands. He held her away from him and then, abruptly pulled her close. She broke away after a moment. 'My God,' he said. 'I couldn't believe it! Are you all right?'

'Yes, yes.'

'Are you sure? Are you certain?'

She disengaged herself.

'Yes, I'm certain. Come in.' She closed the door and was suddenly shy. 'What was all that about?' she said, indicating the argument with the taxi driver.

'I had to get a cab.'

She assumed he'd had a breakdown. 'You shouldn't have bothered tonight, we could have talked about it in the morning.'

'What? Don't be silly! I wanted to see with my own eyes that you were all right. I wanted to get down as fast as I could.'

Slowly it dawned on her. 'You don't mean you took a cab from London?'

'There was no other way. Either that or walk. Haven't you heard the news?'

She shook her head. 'I've kept away from that.'

'You must have wondered what the hell I was up to, why I wasn't down hours ago! A bomb went off at Clapham Junction. The whole of the southern rail network was shut down. All the major stations.'

'Have you been to the prison?'

'No, I came straight here. The first I knew about it was when I saw a paper at Waterloo. No one seemed to know when the station would reopen so I jumped into a cab. Of course the traffic by that time was horrendous. So . . . anyway . . . tell me.'

'Let me get you a drink. Have you eaten?'

'I had a pie in the cab. But a Scotch would be

marvellous.' He flung himself into a chair. 'I felt terrible for you!'

'It's all over now.' She handed him the drink.

'Tell me,' he said.

She started with Stephanie, for that was the beginning, and she saw his face stiffen into a frown. She thought he might want to talk about her first but he said she should go on; they could come back to Stephanie. So she told him about Ida Tribe and her fall and then, in detail, what had happened. She told him in even greater detail than she had told the police, and that helped her, too.

Halfway through he rose and began to pace and when she finished he stood over her chair and put his fingers on her cheek in the way that her father sometimes did and said, 'Poor you.'

He sat and stretched out his legs. After a moment he said, 'So we're to blame, are we?'

'No one's actually said that, but they've implied it.'

'At this point everyone's rushing about looking for scapegoats. The Home Office will be catching it in the neck from the police; the prison service will be getting it from both; and we'll be the targets for everyone; we're the soft option. The point is, it's happened before in a similar kind of way. The taxis are the weak link; no radio contact with the prison. If we had our own secure vehicles with radios it wouldn't happen so easily. But it's too expensive.' He lay back and rubbed his hair. 'My God, what a horror.'

'You were right all along,' she said.

'In what way?'

'Billy Sweete was having us on. I remember when you made me play devil's advocate; you were talking about the secret part of the human mind where the thoughts are controlled and hidden from people like us. That's what he was doing.'

'Telling us *something* but not all of it. Something just bizarre enough for us to get our teeth into. There was always one door that was closed to us.'

'The door to Bluebeard's room.'

'What?'

She repeated what Sweete had said.

She offered him another drink but he shook his head. 'I must be going.' He rose and she rose with him. He hesitated, then said, 'I'm sorry about Steffie.'

'I wouldn't have told you but I thought you should be prepared. Anyway, it's not your fault.'

'Yes it is. She's been to the house since you saw her. She talks as though she's only been away for a fortnight's holiday. She said how much she'd like to redo my sitting-room.'

Anne felt a stab of jealousy. She remembered her own reaction to that room.

He went on, 'She talked as though we were having an affair and when I denied it she didn't really believe me.'

Anne found herself flushing.

'There's something wrong with her. I think I'd always suspected it but now . . . I mean, it's been six years . . .'

'Where's she living?'

'In London. She was married to a merchant banker in France but that's ended in divorce, too. I'm afraid this is something I'm going to have to live with for a while. I just don't want you bothered.'

'Don't worry about me. I can look after myself.'

He nodded. 'Of course you can.' Then he said, as much to himself as to Anne, 'There's a theory that some men marry the mirror images of their mothers. I went to some lengths not to do that, but it turned out Steffie was a bolter. She wanted an "open" marriage. In fact, in that respect she was exactly like my mother. She'd hop into bed with anyone. The trouble was I was working in a partnership and she hopped into bed with my partners. It became intolerable. That's why I joined the prison service. We'd broken up by then but we weren't divorced and there was talk of us getting back together. I knew what would happen; she'd wreck any partnership. The service gave a kind of protection against that, plus long leaves so I could get away into—'

'The far blue yonder.'

'Precisely. As far into the blue yonder as I could.'

There was a cry from upstairs and Anne said, 'That's Hilly.'

She went up. Hilly had been dreaming, and Anne held her for a moment and pulled up the blankets. In a matter of seconds Hilly's thumb was in her mouth and she was asleep again.

Anne turned away from the bed in the half light of the room. Tom was standing at the door. 'That's what I always wanted,' he said.

'What?'

'A family.'

He left soon after that. She'd offered him the sofa downstairs, offered to ring for a cab, but he'd refused both. His Land Rover was up at the prison and he said he needed a walk.

She stood on the top step of the house. He took a few paces, then turned. 'You're not going to resign, are you?' he said.

'No. Apart from anything else I owe quite a lot of money and I want to repay it as quickly as possible.'

'Can I help?'

'No. But thanks for offering.'

He raised his hand. 'Thank God you're all right.'

He paused. She looked at him. The word 'stay' formed in her mouth. It would be so easy. But she didn't speak. He nodded as though he understood, waved, and turned away, and she watched his lanky, long-striding figure go up the street towards the castle, leaning into the cold night wind.

Henry was ironing when Dr Thorpe arrived. He had covered the kitchen table with a blanket and was ironing on that. Thorpe was fascinated.

'That's how my mother used to do it,' he said. 'She loved a big table. I use an ironing board.'

Henry, who was dressed in evening trousers, a heavy sweater and fleece-lined boots, said, 'I can't stand ironing boards.'

'I quite agree.'

'The things always seem to collapse.'

'You want to do what I do. I've got one set up permanently in a cupboard. I've bolted it to the wall.'

'My daughter won't let me bolt things to walls. I'm not sure why. Anyway, let me get you a drink. I can't match your claret but I've got a decent single malt and it's past five.'

They went down to Henry's flat where the ranks of African curios still waited to be placed as decorations.

'What a splendid room,' Dr Thorpe said.

'Anne keeps on at me to tidy it.'

'But it is tidy.'

'Of course it is.'

Dr Thorpe sipped his whisky and, after a false start, said, 'You were good enough to come all the way to Bath and take an interest in Jason so I thought it only right that you should know what's happening now. I've been to see him.'

'I'm glad.'

'He's changed. There's a kind of calmness about him. I suppose a psychiatrist would say it was a catharsis, that killing that man Sweete was like killing his father, exorcising all those demons.'

'Psychiatrists will say anything,' Henry said, dryly. 'As long as you go on paying them.'

'Yes, well, I wanted you to know ... I'm going to look after him as best I can. We'll find a new lawyer and fight the case. He says he didn't try to rape the girl, that she was keener than he, and I believe him.'

'So do I and I think I can help his defence lawyer when you get one. I've done some investigating on my own and I'm satisfied Jason has an excellent chance of acquittal.'

'Are you wearing your judge's wig when you say that?'

'Yes, I am.'

'What about the killing? Self-defence?'

'Of course. And Anne is the witness. That's a formality.'

'I don't suppose you'd consider taking Jason's case, would you?'

'Me?'

'Well, you know the whole background. And you could practise in this country, couldn't you?'

'I suppose I could. But you need somebody younger; somebody with more go.'

'My goodness, I've hardly ever met anyone with more go.'

'What about his mother?' Henry changed the subject.

'Still the same. But she gets weaker every day. It's like sand running out of a glass. You know, this has all been a bit unsettling for me, if that isn't a silly word.'

'It's been a bit "unsettling" for all of us. Especially my daughter, Anne.'

'Shocking business. I really felt for her and for you when I heard what happened. Terrible thing. And the little girls. They say they found torture marks on the bodies. What sort of person does things like that? And they stuck Jason in a cell with him. Apparently they did it for Jason's own sake! Thought he was a suicide risk. Anyway, it's brought it all back and stirred things up. I thought I'd done with it, except for Elizabeth, of course'

Henry gave him another whisky.

He stared at the glass in silence for a while. 'I . . .' he bean.

'Go on.'

Thorpe shook his head. 'Why should you have to listen?'

'Because that's what my life has been . . . listening.'

'It's just that . . . Well, the trouble is that if anyone should be going on trial, it's me.'

'Oh?'

Thorpe looked round the room as though there might be a hidden tape recorder and, satisfied that there wasn't, said, 'I'll tell you something. Of course I'll deny I ever said it.'

'Then maybe you shouldn't. Don't forget that I'm an officer of the court.'

'Ah, well, there's probably nothing you could do about it, even if you wanted to. But it's been on my mind and I've never told anyone. It's about Jason's father. If the psychiatrists are right – I mean about Jason metaphorically killing his father in the guise of this man Sweete – then I'd have to tell them I already did it. I killed him. I didn't shoot him or strangle him or anything like that, but I killed him nevertheless. I could have saved him that night, but I chose not to.

'He and Elizabeth must have had a real fight, I mean a physical fight. I think what happened was that he started the fire without realising she was there, or perhaps he decided it didn't matter whether she was there. And then suddenly he saw her and they fought, wrestled perhaps. She might have hit him with something, because when I saw him he was crouched down on the floor. He'd inhaled a lot of smoke.

'He started to crawl towards the door of the bar. And after I'd pulled Elizabeth free I went back for him. He was stretched out, coughing. He looked up at me and his eyes said help me, save me, and I thought: what a bastard you've been to my daughter. And I turned away. Well, what do you say to that?' He drained the last of the whisky.

'I'm not sure what to say.'

'You were a judge; judge me.'

Henry shook his head. 'I'm not a judge any more, thank God.'

'But if you were?'

'It's a crime of omission and I'm not sure that a charge could be framed. Anyway don't brood about it. By the way, what's happened to Margaret? Does she still want a divorce?'

'As far as I know.' Thorpe finished his whisky and rose. 'Would you think about it? Taking the case, I mean.'

Henry did not reply for a moment then he said, 'You're tempting me. I'm not sure I'm cut out to be a house-mother.'

'But will you think about it?'

'There's someone I need. If I can get him to work for me again then I'll think about it.'

Thorpe stuck out his hand. 'I'll let you get on with the ironing,' he said.

Winter had come to the South Downs. The wind was from the east and powdery snow lay on the tops. On Ridge Farm the old water troughs were frozen, and dirty wool on the fences streamed in the wind. Police tapes fluttered around the front door of Major Gillis's house and around the bunker fence. The metal plate which led down to the catacomb was closed and padlocked.

The police had gone and the place was deserted except for the figure of Ida Tribe, in her long coat and head scarf, battling along the track, just as she had done all those years ago after the death of her husband Jimmy.

She'd come to the Major on a month's trial and had slept in a caravan. Even so it had been better than the flat she'd shared with Jimmy, with its rising damp and the rats and

Jimmy drunk half the time. So when the Major had offered her the job permanently and the cottage to go with it, she had thought her luck had changed.

She walked past the bunker she had always thought was a reservoir, past the old barns, to Gillis's house.

She had done her crying and she had finished her talking; she had cleared her goods and chattels from the cottage and taken them to a cousin's near Chichester. Now that the police had gone there was only one thing left to do and she had come up on this bitter morning to do it.

No one was supposed to enter the Major's house, that's what the police had told her, not until they had finished their investigations.

What investigations? Ida had wondered. The Major was dead and so was Billy and so were the two little girls and they knew who'd done it – and that was that.

The police had taken the front-door key but she had a key to the side door. She opened it now and went into the freezing house. She avoided the kitchen, for that was where she had found him, and the memories would always haunt her. Instead she climbed the stairs and went along the landing. She looked in at the spare room. The soldiers were all set up. Apparently they were valuable. Well, his nephew in Wales would benefit from those. She wondered what would happen to the farm. They'd probably sell it.

She went into his bedroom. One wall was lined with books. The Major had been a great reader; not novels, books about warfare.

He had been interested in battles.

She pulled out the books one by one and shook them. Each held a five-, ten- or twenty-pound note. Sometimes two. She stuffed the money into her plastic shopping bag. She'd never touched it when the Major was alive but why should the nephew have it now? God knows she'd earned it.

She opened two dozen books and there was money in almost every one. The Major had never trusted safes. Then she opened one on the Peninsular campaign and inside was a piece of paper, not a banknote.

It was printed in red on buff and the first words were, 'Certified copy of an entry of birth given at the General Registry Office, Somerset House, London'. Under 'name' it said 'William John Sweete. Sex: male. Name and surname of father: Edward Llewellyn Gillis. Name, surname and maiden name of mother: Ida May Tribe, née Sweete'.

She had not seen Billy's birth certificate for many years.

She remembered the fight she and the Major had had over it when he found his own name on it. What had he expected her to put under father's name: Unknown? She had wanted to keep it. No, said the Major, he'd do that. She knew why, of course; he'd never wanted to acknowledge the fact that Billy was his son.

But she'd had one abortion to please him and said never again. That hadn't stopped him wanting her. And if she hesitated it was always, 'I'll have you out of that cottage.' And then where was she to go?

The lies had been born with Billy and grown up with him. The lies had become her life. Even her own relations thought she'd been his grandmother. Well, it was too late to change now.

She read the birth certificate for the last time. Poor Billy.

She'd only really wanted it to *make* the Major take up his responsibilities. But that hadn't worked either. Billy had never stood a chance really, not with a father like that.

She took the paper to the fireplace, put a match to it and watched it burn to ashes.

Billy would have liked that.

Then, like the good housekeeper she was, she picked up the ashes and rubbed them to black specks and the draught of the flue sucked them up the chimney and out into the icy skies.